ZENN SCARLE

"Christian Schoon knows his ... Scarlett has everything a sci-fi love... exotic alien life forms to quantum entanglement, ... grounded by a stellar YA heroine. Zenn's moxie and determination make this a debut to remember. Highly recommended!"

   Phoebe North, author of Starglass

"Reading *Zenn Scarlett* is like venturing into a gargantuan alien animal in one of the in-soma pods Zenn uses to provide veterinary care: delightful, bizarre, and occasionally terrifying."

   Mike Mullin, author of Ashfall

"Many young people want to become veterinarians because they love animals. All future veterinarians will want to read *Zenn Scarlett* and her adventures with veterinary medicine on alien animals."

   Temple Grandin, author of Animals in Translation

"Mars, monsters, and mysteries: *Zenn Scarlett* is a thoughtful and thrilling science fiction adventure that's perfect for readers who think they've seen it all! It's refreshing to encounter an original young adult story that defies expectations, and the breathtaking conclusion will leave you desperate for more."

   E C Myers, author of Fair Coin

CHRISTIAN SCHOON

ZENN SCARLETT

STRANGE
CheMISIRY

STRANGE CHEMISTRY

An Angry Robot imprint
and a member of the Osprey Group

Lace Market House	4301 21st Street, Suite 220B,
54-56 High Pavement	Long Island City,
Nottingham NG1 1HW	NY 11101
UK	USA

www.strangechemistrybooks.com
Strange Chemistry #10

A Strange Chemistry paperback original 2013

Cover photograph by Steven Meyer-Rassow.
Set in Sabon and Refrigerator Deluxe by Argh! Nottingham.

Distributed in the United States by Random House, Inc., New York.

ISBN 978-1-908844-55-2
Ebook ISBN 978-1-908844-56-9

Printed in the United States of America

9 8 7 6 5 4 3 2 1

To Kathleen, my favorite life form.

BEFORE

Wind clawed at the canvas tarp covering Zenn in the cargo bed of the ancient pickup truck. The truck picked up speed, rattling and bucking down the rutted dirt road, and it took all her strength to keep the coarse cloth from being ripped out of her hands. But more speed was good. It meant her father and Otha hadn't noticed her hiding beneath the tarp... yet. The truck hit a bump; she lifted several inches into the air, then came down painfully against the rusty surface.

Never leave the cloister.

That was the first rule, the important rule. Bad things happened outside the cloister walls. Frightening things. Lurching and bouncing in the back of the speeding truck, Zenn was fairly certain she was already as frightened as it was possible to be. But breaking the first rule was only part of what made her heart leap inside her like a cornered animal. The other fearful thing floated somewhere far beyond the Martian sky above – a starship. Inside it was an Indra, one of the biggest, most astonishing creatures in the known universe. And trapped inside the Indra's body was Zenn's mother.

Zenn knew something was wrong the moment her uncle rushed into the cloister yard earlier that morning. He was breathless from running. Otha was a big man, and he seldom ran.

"Warra, it's Mai," Otha said to her father. "It's serious. You'd better come."

Predictably, her father said she would have to wait with Sister Hild at the cloister compound while he and Otha drove to Arsia City and took an orbital ferry up to the starship. Zenn had protested, had even cried a little. It didn't help. She was to be left behind. But when Hild was busy filling bowls, tubs and other containers with food for the morning feeding of the animals currently among the clinic's menagerie of patients, Zenn had quietly slipped out the side door of the refectory kitchen.

Now, breathing dust and bio-diesel fumes beneath the tarp, her uncle's words circled in her mind. How serious was "serious"? Zenn was well aware her mother dealt with many kinds of large, dangerous alien animals, including the enormous Indra. Her mother was an exoveterinarian; that was her job. This Indra was sick. And her mother had gone into its body to cure it. Then something had gone wrong. Very, very wrong.

The truck hit an especially deep hole in the road, tossing Zenn so high she was almost thrown out the back. She forced herself not to think about what would happen to her if she fell out, even if she survived the impact. People caught alone, out beyond the cloister walls or the safety of villages, were being robbed of anything they carried: money, food, supplies, even their shoes. Some were beaten when they resisted, a few had been killed, if the stories could be believed. And with every story, it seemed to be getting worse.

Never leave the cloister.

Another vicious bump and her head banged down hard. The rough fabric of the wind-whipped canvas bit painfully into the skin of her fingers, and the acrid exhaust smell was making her feel sick. Then, thankfully, the truck slowed, the wind died. They must be close to the ferry port outside Arsia.

A minute later, the truck turned sharply and skidded to a stop. Two doors creaked open and slammed shut. Zenn threw off the tarp and stood, releasing a cloud of fine, red dust. Her father and Otha were striding toward the ramshackle hut that passed for the launch pad's control tower.

"Dad!" she yelled, her voice cracking.

It's serious. You'd better come.

He couldn't go without her. That's all there was to it.

"Dad!"

Her father was angry, of course. She'd expected that. But there was no time to drive her back to the safety of the cloister, so they had to take her with them.

Just nine years old at the time, Zenn wasn't really surprised that now, thinking back on it, she recalled little about the ferry ride into orbit or their arrival at the starship. She did remember the ship was vast, bigger than anything she'd ever seen. Her next clear memory was of the piercing, almost shocking cold inside the ship's pilot room. She recalled clearly the air there was cold enough to turn her breath into spheres of ice-crystal mist that formed and disappeared like tiny, glittering ghosts.

The pilot room was a long, low, dimly lit space. The walls flickered with lighted dials and screens, and there was a strangely sweet, smoky scent in the air that seemed somehow out of place in the frigid room. Zenn saw that the scent arose from a bundle of smouldering twigs on a tiny stone altar set into an alcove on one wall. She realized this was the incense her mother had told her about; it was burned in the pilot room as part of the secretive rituals conducted by those who attended the Indra.

A large chair sprouting odd machinery and wires was mounted on some sort of swiveling base in the center of the floor, and a viewing window filled most of one wall. The window looked out into the Indra chamber. From her mother's stories of treating other Indra, Zenn understood that this was the place the animal would come when it was called to by the starship pilot, the Indra groom. Then the Indra would take the starship to its destination. Young as she was, Zenn had no inkling how this was accomplished; but she did know that since Indra ships were the only means of travel between the stars, Indra were very important creatures.

Zenn's father and Otha were talking to a tall woman dressed in a close-fitting bodysuit of a cloth that shone like metal. The patches on the shoulders of her uniform, and the shifting pattern of animated tattoos visible on her neck and face, identified the woman as the starship's Indra groom.

For a moment, Zenn stood staring at the many metal rings, tiny chains and jeweled studs the groom wore on her face and in her ears. Then movement caught her eye. She went to stand on tiptoes at the viewing window – and gasped at her first glimpse of a real, live Indra. The animal's head, big as a hay barn, was all she could see. The rest of its colossal body coiled off into the shadowy recesses of the chamber.

Of the many facts Zenn's mother imparted to her about the Indra, two stood out: the Indra's size, and how the creature got its nickname, Stonehorse.

"Indra are among the largest animals in explored space,"

her mother had said during one of these talks. She showed Zenn a v-film drawing of an Indra. To indicate its size, the creature's legless, slightly flattened serpentine body was drawn next to a starliner. "Indra grow to be over seven hundred feet," her mother continued. "See? It's almost a quarter the length of the starship."

Zenn was puzzled by this. It didn't seem possible such a big animal could be contained in the ship and still leave room for any passengers.

"How does it fit?" she'd asked.

"Good question." Her mother pointed to one end of the starship. "See how the ship bulges out at the back? That's the Indra warren. It curves around inside, like a giant seashell. The Indra lives in the curving tunnels of the warren."

"Why does it live there, in a ship?"

"In the wild, Indra live inside the caverns of asteroids. When the Indra wants to travel somewhere, it does something called tunneling. Well, Alcubierre null-spin quantum tunneling, but that's kind of hard to explain. What's important is that the Indra have evolved the ability to move very long distances through space in a very short time. When the Indra does this, when it tunnels, it carries its asteroid home in front of it. The nickel and iron metals in the asteroid act like a shield, to protect the Indra from dangerous particles in space. Long, long ago, a race of beings that no longer exists figured out a way to harness the Indra to propel starships. To make the Indra feel at home in the ships, they built the warrens to be like caves in an asteroid. In fact, in an old language called Latin, the Indra are called Lithohippus indrae. Litho means stone. And hippus means horse. That's why some people call the Indra Stonehorses."

Zenn liked that the Indra had this nickname. On the one hand, it was comical, since an Indra's body looked nothing at all like Earther horses. But on the other hand, the fact that the Indra took starships to other places was just like a horse taking a wagon somewhere.

At the moment, the Stonehorse Zenn was looking at floated in the zero gravity and airless vacuum of its chamber. The scales of its armored skin gleamed gold and red, its face covered in tendrils that waved slowly to and fro. The creature's head, she had to admit, did look vaguely like an Earther seahorse, or possibly like a sleepy, fairytale dragon. Impossible as it seemed, her mother was inside this animal. And she couldn't get out.

Behind Zenn, Warra Scarlett's voice rose. He was almost yelling at the tall woman now, and this was enough to pull Zenn's attention from the Indra. Her father never yelled. He was asking how the groom had lost contact with her mother, something about backup systems and how they were not supposed to fail.

Also in the pilot room was a short, stout, gray-haired man in an all-white uniform. Otha addressed him as captain. The captain tried to calm her father, but it didn't seem to have much effect. Her father said that her mother's assistant, Vremya, should be able to help get her mother out of the Indra. Zenn looked into the chamber again and saw that the assistant was floating high up at the back of the huge room, wearing a helmeted vac-suit as she bent over a small console tethered to the wall next to her.

The groom explained to her father that Vremya had tried to help, but for some reason she was unable to make contact with the pod carrying her mother. Then the groom waved one hand and a virtual readout screen shimmered to life in the center of the room. Zenn moved in closer to see the virt-screen better – and to be nearer to her father as the voices in the room grew more urgent and upset.

On the virt-screen, the outline of the Indra's upper body glowed as a sort of three-dimensional x-ray. Just below the point where the Indra's long body joined the seahorse head, Zenn could see a small, oval-shaped blinking light – the in-soma pod that held her mother. With every blink, the pod moved a little closer to the Indra's head.

Otha pointed to the blinking dot and said the in-soma pod wasn't working correctly; that it was carrying her mother toward the Indra's skull. He said the pod was only designed to travel in certain parts of the animal's body. Just hearing Otha's steady voice and calm, matter-of-fact explanation of the situation made Zenn feel a little better. Otha had assisted her mother during other in-soma pod insertions into Indra. He knew the animals almost as well as Mai. If anyone could help her mother now, it was her uncle.

"If the pod reaches the Indra's skull," Otha said then, "it will trigger a lethal spike in Dahlberg radiation." Zenn's father shook his head, not understanding. "It's surge of quantum particles. A by-product of the Indra's tunneling ability. It's a protective mechanism – something like an immune response." Otha gave her father a look. Zenn could tell from this look, and from Otha's tone of voice, that this was a bad thing.

Her father became even more excited and angry then, and was speaking very fast to the groom when a loud alarm blared through the room. Everyone turned to the viewing window. They saw the animal seemed to be in distress, or some sort of pain. It shook its massive head up and down, back and forth, as if to rid itself of something. Flashing emergency beacons came on, bathing the Indra in stark, intermittent bursts of illumination.

Then a blinding, blue-white surge of light exploded out from the Indra. Zenn clapped her hands over her eyes. Another flash, even brighter, was visible through her fingers. And, at that moment, a feeling unlike anything she'd ever felt flowed through her. It was a sort of dizziness; a sudden warmth, a feeling she might faint. But more than that, it was a feeling that her body was no longer her own, familiar body. The odd sensation ran through her like an electric charge, and then vanished as quickly as it had come. It was, she thought later, probably just a reaction to the fear and confusion that gripped her. It was as if some part of her knew what was happening to her mother; knew but didn't want to know.

Everyone was shouting then, and a very bright, blue-white glow streamed steadily from the Indra chamber into the pilot room. It appeared to Zenn that no one there knew what to do, and this scared her more than anything. A deep, grinding sound came from the ceiling, and a thick slab of dull gray metal began to slide down to cover the viewing window. The groom yelled for them all to move back and a second later the slab hit the floor with an impact that shook the room.

"No!" her father cried, turning to the woman. "We can't see into the chamber. We need to see."

Zenn ran at the metal slab that now stood between her and the place where she knew her mother was in unspeakable danger. Zenn pounded on the cold, hard surface of the metal, but it didn't move. She screamed – she couldn't remember if she screamed words or if she just produced some meaningless sound.

"The blast shield deployed automatically," the groom said, not looking away from the multiple virt-screens now dancing in the air around her. "It will remain in place until levels are safe again."

"Levels?" her father shouted. "What levels?" She didn't answer him.

The alarm continued to blare for a few seconds more, then cut off. The groom stood very still, staring at the virt-screens.

"No..." she said quietly to herself, as if she didn't believe what the screens showed her. "It cannot be..."

The blast shield rumbled to life and lifted back up into the ceiling. They all waited. No one moved or spoke. When the shield was halfway up, Zenn ran and ducked under it. She rushed to the viewing window, strained to see into the room beyond. The walls smoked as if swept by some terrible fire. Except for the smoky haze and flashing emergency lights, there was nothing to be seen. It was empty. Completely, horrifyingly empty.

"She is gone," the groom said, her voice low and strange. "My Stonehorse... gone."

Her father stared through the viewing window. He covered his eyes with one hand, and then looked again. Otha reached out and put a hand on her father's arm.

"Otha..." he said. "What happened?"

"I don't know, Warra," her uncle said. He looked out to where, moments ago, the Indra had been. "This shouldn't... I've never seen anything like it. I've never heard of this sort of reaction. I don't know what to say. Warra... I'm sorry."

Zenn stood at the viewing window, her breath visible, rising and dying before her, fogging the glass. Her father came to stand next to her. He lifted both hands to lay them flat against the window's surface. After a moment, he turned, reached out and brought her body in close to his. She pulled back just a little, so she could see his face, so she could see what this all meant, see what she should say, or do, or think. In the biting cold of the room, tears cut hot trails down her cheeks.

The one thing she did remember quite clearly from that day was what her father said next.

"It's alright, Zenn," he told her, looking at her but not seeing her, as if seeing something only visible to him, "... we'll be alright."

She knew her father meant what he said. He didn't mean to lie. He was just wrong. But in the years to come, it wouldn't be Warra Scarlett's fault that their life did not even approach being "alright." When things finally went from merely sad to utterly catastrophic, Zenn was quite certain of one thing. The fault... was hers.

ONE

Zenn could see herself reflected in the gigantic eyeball, as if she stood before a gently curved, full-length mirror. She didn't like what she saw. It had nothing to do with being inches away from a two-foot-wide eye – she'd seen bigger eyes. It was the odd angle of the tank-pack strapped to her back. She hadn't noticed before – she was too preoccupied with getting into position on the bridge of the whalehound's nose. But her reflection revealed the pack was sagging badly to one side. It could pull her off-balance if the animal made any sudden moves.

This I can fix, she told herself. *Just don't let anything else happen. Please, don't let that... other thing happen.*

She tugged at a harness strap to center the pack between her shoulders, but the motion startled the hound. He blinked and flinched, and she wobbled violently, arms flailing. Her foot slid on the slick fur – she was going to fall off. Her hand closed around something – an eyelash thick as a broomstick. A quick pull brought her upright again. She let go of the lash as though it were a red-hot poker and froze.

Had she spooked the animal? Tense seconds passed. But

the hound just regarded her calmly with his one good eye, huffed out a low groan and was still; waiting to see what the spindly little creature on his snout would do next.

She glanced at Otha on the pen floor thirty feet below. Apparently, he hadn't noticed her misstep. That was a first. He was intent on monitoring the whalehound's vitals and the sedation field, his attention on the virt-screens hovering before his face like oversized, translucent butterflies.

Congratulating herself on a disaster averted, Zenn risked a few extra seconds to savor the view from this novel vantage point. Stretching away below her, the hound's sleek, streamlined body reached almost to the far side of the hundred-foot holding pen. Still damp from his morning swim, the animal's thick, chocolate-brown fur released wisps of steam into the cool Martian air. Beyond the holding pen, the view encompassed most of the cloister grounds – over the clay-tiled rooftop of the infirmary building to the refectory dining hall. Looking past the open ground in the center of the cloister walk, Zenn could see all the way to the crumbling hulk of the chapel ruins. The chapel, like most of the cloister's earliest buildings, was a massive, handsome structure constructed of large sandstone blocks quarried from the canyon walls. The more recent buildings, on the other hand, reflected the changing situation on Mars. Harvesting and transporting huge chunks of stone was energy intensive. Accordingly, most of the buildings put up in the past few years were made from any materials that could be scrounged, salvaged or recycled.

Visible over the rooftops of the nearby buildings, the sheer, two-thousand-foot red rock canyon walls shouldered in on both sides of the compound. Squinting against the sunlight, Zenn could just make out the metallic glint of the bary-gens. About the size and shape of a fifty-five-gallon drum, each barometric ionic generator was mounted some three hundred feet up, anchored to the cliffs on either side of the canyon at regular intervals. The pressure-seal created by the generators shimmered like a heat mirage where the oxygen-and-water-rich air of the valley pressed up against the thin, lifeless atmosphere above it. Terraforming the entire surface of the planet had never been an option; too expensive, too lengthy and complex. Modifying only the land they needed, piece by piece, down in valleys was the obvious solution. Now, sections of the Valles Marinaris and the other half-dozen enclosed valleys strung out across the planet's midsection were the sole refuges of the remaining human colonists on Mars. Beyond these protected canyons, up amid the ultraviolet-blasted plains, towering volcanoes and ancient dried-up ocean beds of Mars, nothing grew, nothing breathed, and nothing moved but dancing dust-devils.

Here, in her home valley, the lush scent of freshly mowed switchgrass rode on the breeze that blew from the depths of the four-mile-deep canyon systems to the east. Above, a scattering of mare's-tail clouds drifted high in the ruddy-pink sky.

The hound yawned beneath her, and Zenn bent at the knees to absorb the motion, bracing herself as the jaws clapped together again with a click of massive canines. Adapted for pursuing their equally huge prey through the planet-wide oceans of Mu Arae, whalehounds reminded Zenn of immense, eight-legged otters, but with more elongated heads and jaws bristling with double rows of teeth long and sharp as sabers. It was only during Otha's rounds earlier this morning that he'd noticed the animal's reddened, weeping eye. Zenn's sleep-dazed state of mind had instantly cleared when, between bites of toasted muffin at breakfast, her uncle said she'd be allowed to handle the treatment. He said he was getting too old to go hound-climbing.

Otha's confidence in her came as a pleasant surprise. The whalehound had been purchased recently by the royal family of the Leukkan Kire – and they were paying royally to have him housed at the cloister until they came to pick him up. If anything went wrong, they could lose that money. And the cloister, Zenn knew, couldn't afford to lose any money right now. Just last week Ren Jakstra had come around again to badger Otha about the overdue mortgage payment. He wasn't nice about it.

"Are you set up there?" The buzz of her uncle's voice in her earpiece brought her back to the task at hand. "I'm boosting the seda-field to fifty percent... now," he said. The effect of the general sedation field was immediate: the hound's body drooped, and the lid of his open left eye lowered to half-mast. The right eyelid slowly crept up, allowing Zenn to see more of the infected tear-duct canal. "Alright. He's under," Otha said.

With the seda-field at half power, the hound should be just relaxed enough to let her gently rinse his eye with the solution in the tank-pack. Taking extra care to keep her movements slow and deliberate, Zenn eased the spray nozzle from the holster on her belt and took aim at the inflamed tissue in the corner of the hound's right eye.

Then, without warning, it was there. Inside her mind. Waking, stirring to life under the surface of her thoughts, making her vision dim and knees watery beneath her.

No...

The sensation rose up like a fire flaring from hidden embers, writhing, probing... searching... releasing a wave of unnatural warmth, dizziness and nausea deep inside her.

Not again.

The hound craned his huge head to one side. She saw his left eye focus, the huge, inky pupil dilating, his attention fixing on her, keen, unsettling.

Not now.

But this time, there was something new, something she hadn't noticed the other times she'd felt this, with the other animals. This time there was pain. Sharp, burning her eyes. No, not eyes. Just her right eye, as if scoured by sandpaper.

This can't be happening...

"Remember," Otha's voice sounded far away. "Gentle on the trigger."

Only half-aware of what she was doing, Zenn's finger closed around the nozzle trigger. But then, at the merest touch of her finger, the nozzle activated. Instantly, there was a seething whoosh of rapidly released pressure. Solution sprayed wildly in all directions. Her safety goggles were immediately coated with a thick froth, and the salt-sweetness of antibiotic-laced saline solution filled her mouth. She spit and gagged and tore the foam-covered goggles off. A second later, the whalehound reacted.

The first, violent shake of his head sent Zenn sailing into the air. With a spine-wrenching jolt, the safety line attached to her pack harness snapped tight, pushing the breath from her lungs. The world spun around her, a multicolored blur. She swung back toward the hound, slamming hard into his neck. Her headset and goggles were sheared off by the impact, one leg wedged awkwardly between her and the animal. Pain shot through her, so sharp she thought the leg must be broken. Then she was swinging away again, whipped out and up, past one huge, whiskered cheek, then jerking around to fly past the other. She gasped for air, and glimpsed Otha far below, scrambling to get out of the way.

The half-blinded hound lumbered backwards. Zenn bounced viciously in the harness, the straps cutting into her flesh. With a screech of bending metal, the animal plowed into the side of the infirmary at the rear of the pen, sending wall panels flying to the ground. Still shaking his head, and Zenn with it, he lurched forward again, heading directly for one of the transmit posts of the pen's energy fencing. She fought to get a grip on the safety line, the slick rope slipping through her fingers. Surely, the line couldn't take the strain. Surely, any second it would break, sending her flying like a tetherball cut free.

And then, in an instant, it was over. The hound halted his headlong rush, and stood, breathing hard. The strange sensation gripping Zenn vanished, along with the pain in her eye, as if whatever connection she and the animal had briefly shared was now severed. Beneath his dripping jaws, she swung back and forth, each arc smaller than the next. She saw Otha, working the virt-screens again. He must have dialed the seda-field up to full power.

The hound's eyelids lowered to slits, his massive frame curled in on itself and he crouched low, folding eight pillar-thick legs beneath him. The muscular tail swept side-to-side once before coming to rest on the pen floor. With a gust of exhaled breath the animal closed his eyes and was still.

Zenn hung limp, suspended from the safety line beneath the hound's jaw. Beneath her coveralls, an ice-cold trickle of liquid snaked down her back. Otha was directly underneath her, his upturned face lined with concern. Bits of debris littered the ground around him.

"Zenn! Are you hurt? Speak up, girl."

"I'm... I'm fine," she sputtered through clenched teeth, struggling for breath, her body twisting on the line, her shoulders and thighs burning where the straps dug into her.

"I'm alright."

"Are you?" Otha said, hands on his hips, watching her dangling in midair. "That would be a matter of opinion."

Zenn's face flushed hot.

A simple eyewash. And I messed it up. Well done, Zenn, you just blew test number one...

Finally, she gathered herself sufficiently to grasp the safety line and regain her footing on the soggy fur of the hound's chest. Releasing the line's hand brakes, she rappelled to the ground.

Otha reached up to steady her as she touched down, his face stern. They moved away from the hound toward the transmit post that held the fence's control panel. Her left leg felt as if it might buckle under her, but at least it wasn't broken. She made an effort to keep Otha from seeing her limp. They stopped, and it took her a moment to realize Otha was waiting for her to shut down the fence so they could exit – a reminder that this was her patient, her responsibility.

She toggled the switch and the invisible energy barrier crackled off. Still trying to clear her head after what just happened, she was about to switch the fence back on as Otha came to help her out of the tank-pack. Strands of her hair lay like damp red cobwebs across her face. Her sodden coveralls, pant legs and sleeves rolled up to fit, clung to her like a clammy second skin. She didn't want to imagine what sort of scrawny, drowned animal she must look like – a Tanduan skinkstork, according to Otha. And that's when she wasn't soaking wet.

She was tall for her age, but not tall enough in her own opinion, her body thin and wiry, her straight-as-string waist-length hair the color of Brother Hamish's homemade strawberry wine. Years of clinic chores and fieldwork had left her lean, muscled and tan, with constellations of freckles spangled across arms and face. She didn't mind the freckles especially, but she alternated between liking the look of her strong arms, and then wondering if they made her look boyish, and then wondering why she was wasting time thinking about this at all.

As she stood dripping before him, Otha gave her a hard look.

"Well, novice?"

Zenn winced at the sound of the word. Halfway through her novice year – and this is how she showed him what she could do. Wonderful. Nice job.

"I... lost my balance. I must have hit the nozzle keypad when I slipped," she said, being careful to avoid his gaze so he couldn't read the lie she was telling. "I should have locked in the setting."

"That you should," Otha said, inspecting the tank-pack nozzle to confirm her error. "And what should you have done when you slipped? That is, after you hoisted yourself back aboard the animal using his eyelid for a hand-hold?"

He'd seen. Of course he'd seen. He never misses my mistakes. And now he's going to turn it into a "teaching moment". Perfect.

"I should have checked the setting again," she said, trying not to sound irritated with him, still not meeting his gaze.

"Right. But I'll tell you what you did instead. You patted yourself on the back and took a little extra time for some daydreaming, eh? Enjoy the view?" Zenn inspected the ground at her feet. Otha was mad. With good reason. But his temper was shorter than usual lately. She assumed it was the cloister's finances, or what was left of them. That and the towners. But to have Otha talk to her like this inflicted an almost physical pain on her.

"I slipped, Otha," she repeated. "If I could try one more time..."

"You know how this works, Zenn," Otha said, cutting her off. "Results for end of term proficiency tests are final. Period. I'm required to report scores to the Level Progress certification board. And even if I was allowed to show you any favoritism, I wouldn't. That would do you no good at all in the long run. Now, you just had some bad luck on the first test. But no need to panic. Two tests left. And I'm sure you'll make up the difference on those. Won't you?"

She nodded, and briefly considered bringing up the fact that the tank pack spray nozzle seemed to have developed a sudden case of hair-trigger. But Otha, she could tell, was in no mood for excuses, valid or not.

"Checklists, novice," he said. Apparently, the lecture wasn't over yet. "We have them for a reason. What's the first item on the list when treating mega-fauna?"

"Big animals are dangerous. Small mistakes are deadly," she intoned, her face going even redder as she recited this, the most basic principle of all.

I know what went wrong, Otha.

Actually, that wasn't entirely true either. She knew she should've verified the nozzle setting, of course. And checked the trigger sensitivity. But she had no idea what had just happened with... the other thing. She certainly couldn't tell her uncle that, though. With his fiercely bearded face, graying braids and barrel-chest, facing Otha's displeasure was more like confronting a medieval Earther warlord than the director-abbot of a Ciscan cloister training clinic. She kept quiet and wrung solution out of her hair.

"You've been a little... distracted lately, eh?" Otha's sharp tone said this was the teacher speaking, not the uncle. "Maybe more than a little. Studies? End of term jitters? Or something else?"

Studies? Well, yes, for starters! she wanted to say. The heavy course load, the late-night cramming sessions, the merciless exam schedule, all on top of her usual chores and tending the clinic's animals. Prepping for her all-important end of term tests was just more of the same, only with the added stress that the results would determine if she progressed to the next level of training or... well, the alternative was too horrific to consider. She had to accumulate a passing score on the tests. The first was the whalehound eye wash, and she was fairly sure she'd failed that about as miserably as was humanly possible. But Otha was right. Two more chances. And no reason to think she wouldn't ace the next one: an in-soma pod insertion into a Tanduan swamp sloo. And while the mere thought of being confined in the body-hugging interior of the pod instantly provoked feelings of claustrophobia, Zenn felt quite confident about that particular test. She knew the in-soma procedures backward and forward. Despite her mother's fatal in-soma run on the Indra, or maybe because of it, Zenn had always been drawn to the device and its remarkable capabilities. She was actually looking forward to finally going beyond the textbook diagrams and v-film animations, and taking a pod into a living animal for the first time. So, test number two was in the bag.

Test number three, however, was much more worrisome. Legendary among exovet novice trainees, the end of term Third Test was always a mystery – at least until the day it was sprung on the unsuspecting novice. The only requirement was that it had to be roughly within the parameters of something the novice should already know at that point in the program. As director-abbot of the Ciscan cloister school, Otha was allowed to pick the procedure and the animal for the Third Test, but was not allowed to so much as hint at what the challenge entailed. This, as any exovet novice in history would freely admit, was crazy-making.

And, of course, beyond her schoolwork, there was her father. But Warra Scarlett was a different kind of problem altogether. Worst of all of this was the hard fact she couldn't bring any of it up with Otha. Being overworked and stressed was simple reality for any would-be exoveterinarian in their first year of training. And besides, none of this was the real issue. The real issue was what just took place between her and the whalehound, whatever that was.

Why now? Why is this happening to me now, of all times?

Maybe it was nothing, she told herself. Maybe it was her imagination. Maybe it would just go away. The problem was that she simply didn't have enough information to form a working hypothesis. And without the building blocks of a basic premise about what was happening between her and the animals recently, she had no hope of getting to the truth. She had to wait, gather data… or in this case, let the data happen to her, and attempt to sort it out afterwards. The facts so far simply made no kind of sense, gave her nothing to work with. This was deeply frustrating. But Zenn had been raised in a house of science. And the clean, unambiguous answers science yielded had demonstrated the superiority of this approach time and time again.

Let the world speak for itself.

She heard this from Otha on a regular basis. This was the simple key, the scalpel-sharp tool of the scientific mind. Of her mind. She would wait for the data.

"…and if the course load is too much for you, if you need a break," Otha was saying, his voice a little softer now, one large hand coming to rest on her shoulder, "you need to speak up. These animals don't just deserve your full concentration. They demand it. You know that."

"I'm fine, really," she said quickly, a sharp flutter of fear passing through her. Zenn knew she would be – knew she had to be – an exoveterinarian from the moment she learned there was such a thing. She also knew novices had been dismissed from the cloister exovet school for less serious mistakes than the one she'd just made. She couldn't tell Otha what she'd been feeling lately. She couldn't risk being washed out of the program. And after what just happened, that unthinkable disaster suddenly edged a little closer to the realm of the possible.

"I'm just tired, that's all," she lied again. "I'll do better." To avoid Otha's eyes she turned toward the sedated hound. He could have been hurt. So could she and Otha.

"Right," her uncle said. "That would be wise. When we send the royal family's hound back to them, we want to hand over a healthy animal, don't we?"

Zenn nodded.

"Good. Lesson learned." Otha waved his hand at the virt-screens still drifting around his head. But instead of turning off, the screens flickered fitfully and gave off a harsh whine. The main CPU needed new optic relays. That, however, would take spare parts, and spare parts of any kind had been in short supply on Mars for as long as Zenn could remember. The Rift with Earth made sure of that. Now stretching into its second decade, the Rift's imposition by the ruling Authority on Earth had totally shut down Earther trade with Mars, or with any of the dozen alien-inhabited planets of the Local Systems Accord. The effect on the Martian colonies had been minimal at first. The true scope of the Rift only gradually revealed itself. Now, as old machinery and technology began to wear out, break down or become obsolete, there was no chance of replacement parts or software upgrades from the original Earther suppliers.

And the increasingly troublesome "Indra problem" was only making it even harder to get supplies from the other planets of the Accord – not to mention bring new clients to the clinic. Another starship had been reported missing just last week. During the past five years alone, almost two dozen Indra-powered ships and everyone on board them had vanished without so much as a neutrino trail. So far, the losses were limited to ships plying the far frontier areas – military scouts, survey missions. Some sort of on-board mechanical failure was suspected, but at this point, the sporadic reports that filtered through to Mars made it sound as if investigators had turned up nothing conclusive.

The fact was that the only place on Mars that would have anything as exotic as optic relays for their virt-screen was New Zubrin. And the only mag-lev train still running regularly from Arsia to Zubrin was being stopped and robbed by outlaw bands of scab-landers on a weekly basis. Pushed out into the most inhospitable and barren canyons known as scab-lands, these lawless, roving gangs were made up of the men and women who'd entirely given up on adhering to the rules governing what remained of civilized life in the towns. Scab-landers took what they wanted, whenever they wanted it.

Otha frowned at the malfunctioning screens circling him and waved his hand again, more emphatically. This time the screens obeyed, winking off with a series of quiet popping sounds.

"I want to try again," Zenn said, attempting to sound more confident than she felt. She bent to rub at her aching leg, but then stopped when she thought Otha might see. She saw Otha frowning at her. "I know it won't count in the test scoring. But he needs his eye taken care of."

"We'll take a break. Get you some dry clothes and pour a mug of hot cider down you. It's best we let the animal settle a bit." Otha gave her a steady look. "And you too." The chill of fear raced through her again. She managed to give her uncle a half-hearted smile, but kept silent as they left the hound and headed for the refectory dining hall on the other side of the cloister grounds.

TWO

In the spacious kitchen adjoining the refectory hall, Zenn sat on a stool and blotted at her hair with a towel before gulping the last of the warm kipfruit juice. She now wore a dry pair of coveralls over her outfit of rough hempweave pants, low corvis-hide boots and the light blue, second-hand linen shirt Sister Hild had found for her at the Arsia City co-op.

"Right. I'm good now," she said, hopping off the stool. A spasm of pain jolted up through her leg, making her suck in a quick breath.

"You sure?" Otha raised a questioning eyebrow at her.

"Yes, I'm sure." She leaned with one hand on the stool, attempting a jaunty pose, while taking the weight off her leg. "I need to get back on the horse that threw me, don't I?" she said, repeating one of her uncle's favorite sayings. Of course, she'd never seen a horse in the flesh, let alone been thrown off one.

"You are your mother's daughter, no doubt about it," he said as they set off, Zenn walking gingerly, hanging back just slightly behind her uncle. They crossed into the refectory dining hall, past the long rows of empty tables and benches, their footsteps echoing. "You know, there was a time," Otha said, "when your mother was at the same point you're at now. I can see her plain as day, bright-eyed, all business, just starting her novitiate."

This was promising, Zenn decided. Family talk. Casual talk. Anything to distract Otha from what had happened with the hound.

"Of course, Mai was older than you," Otha said. This was a long-running issue between her and Otha. And between her and her father as well. They'd both insisted she was too young to begin her novitiate, and they'd both engaged her in several rounds of arguing over it. But Zenn knew she was ready. In the end, she wore them both down.

"Mai was nineteen during her first year, if I recall correctly," Otha continued, giving her a quick glance but not bringing up Zenn's own age again. That battle had been won, she told herself with some measure of satisfaction. For reasons Zenn never really understood, the colonists on Mars clung to a number of outdated Earther traditions – like how they measured the passage of time. With Mars' orbit lasting roughly twice as long as Earth's, a Martian year equaled about two Earth years. By that computation, in Mars years Zenn wasn't seventeen, she was eight-and-a-half. It sounded comical.

"I remember this particular incident – one of Mai's first patients was a Grosvenor's thorn-throw," her uncle said as they stepped out of the refectory and headed for the calefactory meeting hall.

The calefactory's large, main hall was where Otha or other instructors would have given presentations meant for the entire student body, back when there was a student body. Now, it served mainly for storage, with dwindling heaps of supplies stacked against the walls.

"One of the thornies got all ripped up in transit, fighting with its pen-mate. Now, as it turns out, Mai had identified them both as males…"

Otha's thorn-throw story wasn't a new one, and Zenn's mind wandered as they walked on, passing through the calefactory and exiting into the cloister walk, the covered, columned walkway that ran around the open square at the center of the compound.

Built two centuries ago according to Earther architectural plans that Otha said dated back almost two thousand years, the entire cloister compound was arranged around this open square. To the south was the huge, stone block building that housed the infirmary, its immense, double sliding doors big enough to accommodate even the largest patients. Except the vacuum-dwelling Indra, of course. Those could only be treated in orbit on board the ships they powered.

Attached to the western side of the cloister walk were the kitchen and the refectory. Just outside the kitchen's back door was the physic garden, the aromatic scent of its medicinal herbs and kitchen savories perfuming the air this time of year. Opposite the garden stood the small Chapter House, where Otha had his office and bedroom.

Above the calefactory meeting hall on the north side of the cloister walk was the dormitory, where Zenn, Sister Hild, and Brother Hamish had their rooms. Beyond that to the south were the remains of the old chapel, looming like some derelict shipwreck, its roof long ago fallen in, the tiles salvaged to maintain other roofs. The chapel's few intact Gothic window frames pointed naked at the sky like broken teeth. Deep-felt religious fervor had brought the Ciscan order to Mars long years ago, fired by visions of new beginnings and fresh converts in the canyons of the recently settled Valles Marinaris. These days, science and the treatment of alien creatures held sway within the thick mud-brick walls ringing the compound, the sandstone remnants of the fallen chapel a reminder of a distant, half-remembered past.

As Otha continued his tale, Zenn thought of her own novitiate and her serious slip-up this morning. Raised among the many creatures brought to the clinic from the dozen planets of the Local Systems Accord, she'd followed Otha and the Sister on rounds countless times, observed hundreds of procedures on scores of animals. Lately, she'd even been granted the privilege of "getting her hands wet" assisting Otha in surgery on the more straightforward cases. The truth was, she'd started her novice year with more real-world experience than most third-year students. And she'd still managed to foul up the hound's treatment.

"… and the expression on your mother's face – priceless." Her uncle laughed as they passed out of the shade of the cloister walk. "You can bet she never forgot the difference between a thorn-throw queen and a common drone after that. Mai was every bit as green as you. Greener. And when Warra heard about it – well, let's just say your father never let her forget it." He slapped one palm against his thigh at the memory. Then his gaze met Zenn's, and his mood went somber.

As they approached the infirmary's side door, Brother Hamish was just emerging from the big double doors at the front of the building. Several feet taller than Otha, Hamish was a coleopt – a large insectoid from Siren, the hothouse jungle moon circling the gas giant Rho-Cancri B-2, which in turn orbits its red dwarf sun, Rho-Cancri B. The chitin carapace that sheathed his upper body glinted in the morning sun, the light catching veins of iridescent blue-green. Draped across his shoulders, Hamish wore a vest-like garment of brownish-red metal chainmail, with a scattering of pockets. On his head was a yellowish, broad-brimmed hat woven of some grassy material. His homeworld's star was much fainter than Mars' sun, and he'd taken to wearing the hat, one of Otha's cast-offs, to shield his eyes. Two holes cut in the hat's crown allowed his long, plume like antennae to poke through.

Close behind Hamish's looming form walked Liam Tucker. The towner boy, Zenn was amused to see, was pushing a wheelbarrow piled high with an assortment of exotic manure.

Just a year older than Zenn, but much taller, with a solid, athletic build, Liam had the sunburned complexion of someone who had recently started spending a lot of time outdoors – and the generally smug manner of a boy who thought pretty highly of himself.

A new arrival, Hamish was still in his "postulant" trial period as cloister sexton, a sort of all-round attendant and go-fer. Shortly after Hamish took up residence, Liam had initiated an unlikely friendship with him. Unlikely, because, before this, Liam had shown a distinct disinterest in anything to do with the cloister and its inhabitants, human or alien. It was only recently that Liam had taken on the job of regularly picking up the food the Ciscans traded with those in town. And today, it appeared Brother Hamish had cajoled the towner into helping him with one of a sexton's main chores: mucking out the animal pens.

Zenn didn't know Liam well, but he was a towner which, of course, put him in the category of people she was inclined to either ignore or actively dislike. She also knew this was closed-minded and judgmental. But she had her reasons.

Zenn waved at them, and Hamish energetically waved back. His claw-tipped digits rattled like castanets.

"Good morning, Novice Zenn," Hamish said. Or rather, his Transvox-generated voice said. The small, egg-shaped Transvox unit, mounted on the shoulder area of his carapace, instantaneously translated Hamish's coleopt language into passable English. The Transvox software also generated a stream of inaudible, dampening frequencies that almost completely cancelled out the sound of Hamish's actual speech, which was a soft, musical hissing produced by the breathing holes in his lower abdomen. Otha had dubbed him Hamish due to the sound of his name as spoken in coleopt, which registered on human ears as a breathy "Hoo-aymeesh-eh".

"The pen of the large grass-eater mammal that was my chore to clean is now clean," Hamish told them proudly. "Clean and ship-shape."

"Good work, sexton," Otha said. "Now, I'd like you to attend to that busted door on the granary next. You'll need the small hand-jack to lever it up into place."

"A small... hand-jack?" Hamish said, his long, feather-like antennae quivering uncertainly. "I am unclear regarding the working of a small hand-jack, director-abbot."

Otha rolled his eyes at Zenn and went to explain the task to him.

"Morning, Liam," Zenn said as the towner sauntered over.

"Morning, Scarlett," he said, brushing at the longish blond hair that always seemed to be falling across his face, and, as usual, calling her by her last name.

"So," he said, lifting his gaze to look past her, "What poor unsuspecting animal are you harassing this morning?"

"The Kiran's whalehound. And he's lucky to have me looking after him," she said, skipping over the fact she'd just half-drowned the creature.

"Whalehound?" Liam leaned towards her and sniffed at Zenn's still-damp hair. "I thought I smelled wet dog." Typical Liam, Zenn thought. She gave him her "Oh, aren't you comical?" look. "So, what's the big boy's problem?" he asked.

"Obstruction in one of his tear ducts. I'll flush it out and he'll be good as new," she said, allowing herself to sound as if this was something she did every day before lunch.

"Yeah? He'll let you do that? Squirt stuff in his eye?"

"We'll use the seda-field, gentle him down," Zenn said.

"Sounds kinda dicey. I mean, they're meat-eaters, right? They eat... whales."

"No, they mainly prey on Mu Arae icthythons, which are the size of Earther whales but are really marine reptiles. The first settlers on Mu Arae just called them whales, so the animals that hunted them became whalehounds." Zenn stopped herself from going on. She realized she was just showing off.

"Right, reptiles, big as whales. Makes sense." Liam looked away, swiped at his hair. "You must think I'm a dope. Not knowing stuff like that."

"No, not at all."

Well, yes, actually. But, you're a towner. Not really your fault.

Recently, Liam had begun to show more interest in the cloister's animals. Zenn didn't mind answering his questions, but she usually had more important things to do. And, besides, it gave her some small satisfaction to instruct someone from town. Nothing wrong with a little showing off. Now and then.

"You know, I fed him once, your whalehound," Liam said. "I was with Hamish. We gave him some of those big chunks of stuff that smell like fish."

"The dried lurker flakes? Yes, he loves those."

"Yeah, it was actually pretty fun. I mean, he kinda sat down and waited for me to throw it to him. Like a big tame dog or something."

"Uh huh. They're not really aggressive, or dangerous to humans. And not related to dogs, of course. More like giant marine mustelids. Like big aquatic weasels."

"Right. Well, I'm still glad he's on the other side of the fence," he said. "Though you're probably safe. Hardly enough meat on you to make more than a crunchy little hound snack. See?" He pinched her arm to illustrate her lack of food-value.

Zenn pulled away, shook her head at him, but didn't really know how to respond to this sort of behavior from Liam. Lately, he'd been acting... what? More familiar with her. On several occasions, it seemed to Zenn that he'd deliberately sought her out for the purpose of talking with her. She couldn't be certain, but she thought he might be trying to be friends. A towner, trying to be friends. This was just odd. And, of course, she couldn't allow it. That would mean breaking the Rule. Unlike the rule she'd been given about not leaving the cloister when she was young, "the Rule" was a law of her own making. But just like the earlier rule, the Rule was meant for protection. And for years now, it had kept her safe. The Rule came about because emotional attachments had proven to be, quite simply, a luxury she wasn't willing to pay for. Expect something good from people, and they'd invariably disappoint. Rely on someone, and they'll end up leaving. Or dying. It wasn't a complicated formula. Otha, Hild, Hamish, and her father were exempt, of course. And frankly, she still had occasional doubts about Warra Scarlett.

And besides, what was the point of even considering

friendship with someone from Arsia? Towners were, as a group, irrationally suspicious of the cloister and its inhabitants, both human and alien. No, suspicious didn't express it; paranoid and hateful summed it up better. Towners feared alien creatures with such automatic, ingrained intensity that it made these people impossible to engage with in any meaningful way. Zenn had given up trying years ago. There were, she conceded, a handful of scientifically literate towners who knew better, but these few kept their opinions securely to themselves. So, could Liam Tucker be added to the list of people actually worth talking to? Zenn was skeptical, but told herself to try to keep an open mind.

"Alright then," her uncle said, coming over and rubbing his hands together. "We've all got work to do. Liam, tell your Aunt Vic I got her message. About worming the goats. We'll get that taken care of soon as we can."

"I'll tell her." He gave Zenn a parting smirk and hefted up the barrow handles. "Lead on, boss-bug." Hamish started off and Liam followed, heading for the garden.

A few moments later she and Otha were inside the cave-cool darkness of the infirmary building. He turned to her.

"Zenn, is it Warra? Is that what's been bothering you lately?" He folded his arms across his chest. "If it is, you need to stop being such a worrier."

"But it's been almost two months," Zenn said, going over to the tank-pack. "And I'm not just being a worrier."

It seemed so inconsiderate of her father, not to get in touch. She worked to keep her voice calm, level. "We should have heard something by now."

"Not necessarily. There's no rule saying your father has to contact us every time you get a little anxious."

Zenn scowled at this dismissal. In fact, she was more than

a little anxious. Worse, she didn't know why. Two months really wasn't all that long without a message. But somehow it was making her jumpy and irritable. Two things she couldn't afford to be right now.

Instead of arguing the point, she picked up the tank-pack nozzle and jabbed at the keypad, entering the sequence for low-pressure, narrow stream. She checked the setting twice, locked it into place and checked it once more.

"You mustn't blame your father for going away, after... what happened to Mai. You mustn't be angry with him for that."

Was that what was unsettling her? Still? No. Yes. Maybe. She couldn't even say for sure what she was feeling about it anymore.

Yes, her father had left. And there was no doubt about why he'd gone, at least as far as Zenn was concerned. Warra Scarlett had loved his wife, deeply, unconditionally. And she'd died. Afterward, it seemed clear to Zenn, he had simply hurt too much. Her father's entire being was like a fresh wound. He couldn't tolerate contact, couldn't make any sensible response to those around him, no matter how much they wanted to help.

When she was young, she was constantly reminded of her parents' attachment to each other, at their obvious, unmistakable joy in simply being around each other. Even then, Zenn was old enough to know these two people were more than mere husband and wife. They were best of friends; no, more than even friends. They were like a single person, with two independent personalities that somehow entered into a communication that only they shared.

The winter Solstice celebration when Zenn was seven, for instance. Warra and Mai had promised her a big surprise. For weeks ahead of time, she'd begged and whined at both of them for clues, but all Mai would tell her is that "You're getting a present you won't be able to see, but one you'll really, really like."

When the big night finally arrived, Zenn had been ushered into the calefactory meeting hall where Sister Hild had set up the scrubby little pine that served as that year's Solstice tree. As Otha and Hild looked on with knowing smiles, Warra and Mai entered the room, her father ceremoniously carrying a large, wrapped box. He set it down before her. She saw immediately there were air-holes in the wrapping.

"It's alive. What is it?"

"Open it and see," her father said.

"Or, open it and don't see," her mother added. Inside the wrapping was a carry cage. Zenn peered in through the wire door and saw... nothing.

"It's empty!" she said, on the verge of being severely disappointed. If this was a parental joke, it was a very poor one.

"Oh? Is it?" Her mother said. "Open the door."

Zenn unlatched the cage door, and watched. Still nothing. Then, a section of the floor at her feet began to go strangely out of focus. A small, oblong area began to shimmer with colors – violet and cream. And the next second, an animal appeared. The little marsupial was about the size of a housecat, with pale, violet tiger stripes set against thick, cream-colored body fur. The head was round, with a double spray of long cheek whiskers on a fox-like muzzle, topped by comically large, lynx-tufted ears. It waved its long, ringed tail and looked up at Zenn with two large, golden-amber eyes.

"A rikkaset!" Zenn squealed so loudly it made the animal fluff up its fur... and promptly disappear again.

"You scared it, honey," her mother said. "Just give her a

moment or two, and she'll unblend again."

"Come back." Zenn tried to speak to the invisible animal calmly. "Please."

"I'm afraid she can't hear you, Zenn," her mother said. "She's deaf. Has been since birth. The original owners didn't think they wanted a deaf rikkaset. So they traded her to the ferry captain who traded her to us."

Zenn waited. A few seconds later, the animal reappeared. She bent and picked it up, holding it close, but not so close she'd scare it again.

"I love it!" she said, her words muffled because she'd buried her face in the creature's soft, delicately scented fur. "I mean, her. I love her."

She looked up to see her mother and father stealing a quick kiss... and sharing a look between them that, it seemed to Zenn, almost generated a sort of physical warmth out into the room.

"What's her name?" Zenn asked.

"The captain didn't say," her mother said.

"Guess that means it's up to you," her father said.

"Katie," she said then. "Her name will be Katie." She held the rikkaset up in front of her. "Is that alright with you, Katie?"

The big, golden eyes blinked at her.

"Oh, sorry, you can't hear me." She turned to her parents again. "She's beautiful. Thank you, thank you, thank you."

"Well, she was your father's idea," her mother said, beaming at him. "He was the one who convinced me you were old enough to take care of a young rikkaset."

"Me?" her father protested. "Mai Scarlett, you wanted that animal from the moment you set eyes on her." He turned to Zenn. "She really got it for herself as much as you, you know," he said. "She has no willpower when it comes to any infant creature of whatever variety. She's totally helpless."

"Helpless? Oh yeah?" her mother said, pretending outrage and giving her father a swat across the shoulder. He retaliated by grabbing her around the waist and tickling her until they both collapsed backwards onto the couch, where they laughed and tussled briefly like a pair of teenagers.

"Well, in any case," her father said, catching his breath, "it's a fact that your mother's the one who bartered with the ferry captain for her." He hugged Mai to him again. "She's a woman of many talents, your mom. We're a lucky family to have her." And he kissed his wife again. Longer this time, despite the fact that there were three other people right there in the room watching them.

Growing up, Zenn had always shared her father's sentiment. That to have someone like her mother, someone you could love so much, and who loved you back that way, was a remarkable and fortunate thing. At least, she'd felt that way until her mother was suddenly no longer with them. At that point, it became clear that to love someone that much, to love that selflessly... that was a frightening thing. So much for luck.

Later, after her mother was gone, when she'd insisted she was old enough to start her exovet novitiate, her father had argued with her. Just like Otha, he said she was too young, it was too dangerous. But he'd already accepted the position with the colonial administration out on Enchara. They'd argued some more. And, just like Otha, she convinced him in the end, made him see what the training meant to her. The truth was, she didn't really think he'd actually do it. But he did. He left. And she had stayed to begin her novice year; stayed and watched him board a ferry that disappeared into the Martian sky as she stood and watched him go. She'd actually managed not to cry until the ship was out of sight.

Sometimes, she thought she understood what made him go, that he had no choice, that he couldn't survive both his own pain and hers. At other times, she simply lost sight of this sort of understanding; as if a heavy fog had rolled in, obscuring the landmarks that had guided her at first. Then, she failed completely to see how he could have gone. And during those times, the hurt and anger would flow in with the fog that clouded her thoughts. It was then she reminded herself of the Rule: no attachments, no friends, no letting anyone in where they could maneuver close enough to deliver the blow they were certain, at some point, to deliver.

Pretending not to notice the awkward silence that had grown between her and Otha, Zenn stooped to loop a harness strap over her shoulder and gave her uncle a look.

"Ah, right," Otha said, his cheerfulness now ever so slightly strained. "That hound's eye won't mend itself, will it? Let's see if he's forgiven you."

He helped Zenn heft the tank rig up onto her back. She winced silently as she pulled the straps tight on her bruised flesh and followed her uncle out into the sunlight. As they came to the holding pen, though, he stopped so abruptly she almost ran into him.

"Nine Hells!" her uncle swore, whirled around and ran heavily past Zenn, back toward the infirmary. "I'll get the tranq bow," he shouted as he went by. "Tell Hamish. Now, girl."

Zenn had no idea what he was so agitated about – until she turned and saw the hound's holding pen. It was vacant. That was bad enough. What she saw next was worse. Fifty yards beyond the pen, disappearing over the top of the compound's east wall, was the chocolate-brown tip of the whalehound's tail.

THREE

Zenn found Brother Hamish by himself in the garden, working manure into the soil. She was so out of breath she could hardly speak.

"Whalehound..." she croaked, bent over, hands on knees, her aching leg forgotten. "Got loose! Went over the wall!"

Hamish pivoted to face her, each of his four upper arm-claws clutching a hoe or rake.

"What are my instructions?" he said, antennae twitching forward from the top of his head like a pair of black ostrich plumes.

Instructions? He wants *instructions*?

"Um... help catch him!"

Hamish put down the tools he held before scuttling past her toward the garden gate. Despite his great bulk and solid appearance, the coleopt could move with startling speed for what was essentially an eight-foot-tall, thousand-pound beetle.

"In which direction did the mammal-hound go?"

"East. He was going east." Zenn said, following him.

"How long ago?"

"Just now."

"Is anyone damaged?"

"No, no one hurt. He just… got out of the pen." She had turned the energy fence back on before she and Otha left the hound's pen. Hadn't she?

"And the director-abbot?"

"Went for the tranq bow."

The seda-field generator could only sedate animals at close quarters. To stop the whalehound, they would need to get a full dose of powerful, fast-acting liquid tranquilizer into his blood system.

Once they'd cleared the garden gate and were well out in the courtyard, Hamish stopped. Zenn saw him lower his body, flexing his two big, hind legs and turning his great head to look down at his back. In the sunlight, his compound eyes blazed like mirror-balls.

"You should stand away, novice Zenn," he told her as he shucked off his metal vest and dropped it to the ground. "I'm out of practice. In honesty, I'm unsure if I can perform this act. Or if I should."

Zenn backed off a few steps. She watched as the chitin covering of Hamish's back split itself down the middle. She knew coleopts had wings tucked beneath their exoskeleton shell. But in the several weeks he'd been at cloister, she'd never seen Hamish's wings, let alone seen them put to use. Hamish stopped then, seeming suddenly unsure of himself.

"The Queen Spawn-Mother forbids me doing this thing here on this world, with the exception of it being a dire emergency. I must have approval." He turned his mirror-ball eyes to her. "Would you classify this event as dire and urgent?"

"Yes," Zenn practically shouted at him. "It's urgent."

"And I herewith have your approval?"

"Yes."

"You are my witness?"

"Yes. Yes. Go." She thrust both arms into the air.

"Very well…"

The two shiny, blue-black shell pieces covering his back pulled apart and moved up and out of the way, exposing the wings hidden underneath. With a crackling, dry-paper sound, the wings unfolded. They were a translucent, robin's-egg blue, veined like a dragonfly's, and extended at least ten feet on either side of his body. Bringing his four upper arms in against his thorax, and rotating his two antennae to lie flat against his broad back, Hamish squatted low and set his wings to beating, slowly, then faster, then too fast to see. The vibration created a loud, low buzz, and the airflow raised a cloud of dust from the courtyard. Then, with a single push from the hind legs, he was airborne. He hovered uncertainly for a second, dropped almost to the ground, then lifted into the air, slewed left, right, seemed to gain more control and rose five feet, ten feet, twenty. Hamish was flying. The sight was almost enough to make Zenn forget why.

Suspended beneath the blurring wings, his half-ton body now tilted through the air toward the east wall. Somehow, his straw hat remained on his head despite the wind storm his wings raised around him. Running hard, Zenn followed until she'd cleared the side of the infirmary. She reached the main gate in time to see Otha pull into sight on the Yakk. The little four-wheel-drive vehicle bounced to a stop just inside the two heavy, metal doors of the now-open gate.

"Close the gate behind me," he shouted to her over the engine's noise, then drove the Yakk out onto the dirt road that ran close by the cloister wall. Zenn started to push the doors shut.

"No. Out here. Get in," he shouted, pointing to the small, railed platform on the back of the Yakk. Momentarily confused, Zenn realized Otha wanted her to go with him. She stepped through the gate, pulled the doors shut behind her and made sure they locked into place.

When she'd climbed into the back of the vehicle, Otha twisted the hand-throttle. With a throaty roar, they were accelerating down the road, heading east. East... it dawned on Zenn with a sick, sinking feeling in her stomach. Toward town, toward people. What if the hound made it that far? He wasn't sedated now. He was awake. Excited. What would he do if the towners attacked him? She gripped the railing as the Yakk careened ahead and tried not to think of an eighty-foot carnivore loose on the streets of Arsia.

Otha swerved the Yakk off the road, and they careened across a short stretch of bumpy terrain and into the dry streambed that ran down the center of the valley. The tracks of the hound were clearly visible in the sand, and the dust raised by his passage still drifted in the air.

"Here," Otha shouted, pulling the tranq bow out of its holder on the side of the Yakk and handing it back over his shoulder. Zenn took the crossbow from him.

He can't be serious.

"Otha." She hefted the bow doubtfully. "I'm not sure I can."

"He's your patient, novice," he growled at her.

He *is* serious.

"I've never shot a moving animal," she yelled.

"Would you rather drive?" It wasn't a real question. "I didn't think so. Two-hundred cc's of avosyn, already loaded, in the bag."

There was no point in arguing. And no time. She opened Otha's duffle bag field kit on the platform next to her and found the foot-long, feather-fletched metal shaft of the tranquilizer dart. She slotted it into the barrel of the bow and, after a brief struggle, managed to pull the bowstring back far enough to engage the trigger.

"There he is!" Otha shouted. A hundred yards in front of them, the elongated shape of the galloping hound was just visible through a wall of billowing dust. They couldn't be more than a half-mile from the outskirts of town.

This is insane. What if I miss?

Otha gunned the engine and they shot forward. Flying sand stung her face, and the Yakk fishtailed back and forth alarmingly as they tried to gain on the fleeing animal.

"Look!" Zenn pointed into the air above them. "It's Hamish."

The coleopt arced high over the whalehound, then dropped down to fly alongside the Yakk.

"I could attempt to reduce the animal's speed," his Transvox voice shouted at them. "Do I have your approval for this act?"

"Sexton! Slow that damn beast down!" Otha yelled.

"I will accept that as approval."

The coleopt banked hard left and lifted up and away from them, then began flying erratically to and fro in front of the hound, all four upper arms thrashing the air. The hound's pace slackened, his attention drawn to the giant insect fluttering back and forth above his head.

"Now's your chance," Otha called back. They were close enough for Zenn to hear the animal's rapid, rhythmic breathing as he bounded along. "You'll only get one shot. Aim for the superficial gluteal, just above the femur."

Half-remembered anatomy charts ran though her mind as Zenn shouldered the stock of the bow and tried to sight down the length of the bouncing weapon. Her target, the hound's haunch, was literally big as a house. But at this speed, over this terrain? It would be sheer luck if she hit anything at all.

"Now, Zenn!" Otha shouted. She took a breath, held it in like he'd taught her, squinted against the flying sand and pulled the trigger. The dart leapt away, vanishing into the dusty air. A snort of surprise came from the hound, and he bent back to bite at his flank, the massive body dropping hard into the sand and skidding sideways, blocking the streambed and churning up a huge cloudbank of dust and sand. Otha turned the Yakk sharply, the force throwing Zenn to one side. She dropped the bow, grabbed hold of the side railing and held on with both hands.

By the time they'd come to a halt and hopped out of the Yakk, Hamish had landed in front of the whalehound. The tranquilizer had already taken effect, and the animal was stretched out flat on the ground, its sides heaving like a giant blacksmith's bellows, a foot or two of pink tongue protruding over the top of a picket-fence-sized row of teeth.

"Excellent bow-shooting accuracy, novice Zenn," Hamish said, raising one arm to point at the hound's back end. "The mammal-hound is sleeping, safe and ship-shape." The tranq dart hung from the center of the hound's haunch. To Zenn's amazement, she'd hit the muscle more or less where she'd intended.

"Here," Otha said, handing her a plastic squeeze-tube from his duffle. "Get some of this into his eyes, keep them lubricated."

No praise from Otha. Standard behavior. Zenn went to the hound's head and, reaching up as high as she could, applied the solution to one eye, then went to the hound's other side and did that eye.

"Good job distracting him when you did, Hamish," Otha said. "We're almost into town. If he'd got up out of this gully, we could've had a real disaster on our hands."

"You got that right." The voice came from behind them.

They all turned to see Ren Jakstra, Arsia Valley constable, standing on a slight rise in the riverbank. On the road behind him squatted his tan-and-black half-track truck.

"Ren," Otha said, shading his eyes to look up at him. "You got here quick."

"In the area. Saw the dust." He whipped the broad-brimmed hat from his head, whacked it against his leg to clean it off. The constable was short, compactly built, with close-cropped brown hair and a thick bird's-nest of a mustache that he had a habit of sucking on. He didn't wear a uniform; the town didn't see the point of that kind of luxury. An antique, bullet-firing revolver hung in a tooled leather holster from his hip. This, Zenn had heard him say, was all the uniform he needed.

"So, Scarlett," he said, glaring at Otha and gesturing at the hound. "You wanna tell me what the Nine Hells this thing is doing here?"

"Just taking our whalehound for a little stroll, Ren," Otha said, attempting some dry humor to diffuse what Zenn knew was not a humorous situation.

"Yeah, that's funny," Ren said, smiling a mock smile. "Might not be so funny if people got hurt though, huh? Might be more along the lines of serious trouble, wouldn't it?"

"Ren, I understand your concern," Otha said. "But this is the first time this sort of thing has happened. Nobody got hurt. And it won't happen again." Otha gave Zenn a quick, baleful glance.

"Damn straight it won't," Ren said. "You know how things are in town." He paused to make sure Otha knew what he was getting at. "People are feeling the pinch. They're looking for someone to take it out on. Well, *this*," he jutted his chin at the hound. "This could set the whole council against you. You don't want that right now."

"Like I said, Ren, won't happen again."

"Yeah, but it happened this time." Ren stuck his hands in his pockets and came down off the bank. "People in Arsia are getting by on potatoes and porridge. Maybe a little goat stew now and then. It's makin' em prickly. And they're already less than cheerful about living next to you and your creatures. They talk about the crops you dump into feeding that bunch of things you keep out there and, truth be told, it's starting to make folks a little... resentful."

"They're not things, Ren. They're animals that need our care," Otha spoke as if he'd already had this conversation with the constable, which he had. "And we've always been more than willing to trade what we have with people in town, you know that."

"Right, you trade whatever's left over. But with the way things are these days, people think feeding your animals is a waste of resources. Valuable resources." The constable regarded Otha, sucked on his mustache. "So, you give any more thought to selling? Might just be the best thing for all concerned. What with your mortgage issue."

"No, Ren. I've already said. Selling isn't an option."

"Hm." Ren wiped one hand across his damp mustache and put his hat on. "Maybe not right now. But the bank in New Zubrin only has so much patience when it comes to gettin' their money. They told me that in no uncertain terms, if you know what I mean." He hiked back up the bank then turned to look down on them. "Don't hang around out here. Won't be safe come dark. Ran into Graad Dokes in Arsia. He claims he spotted campfire smoke coming from the far end of Cerberus Gorge, thought it might be scabs."

"Graad saw scab-landers? That close to Arsia?" Otha

scoffed. "Not exactly a reliable source."

Graad Dokes was Vic LeClerc's shambling oaf of a ranch foreman. Zenn had once seen him kick a small goat halfway across a corral when it made the mistake of tripping him. And from that day on, the man had never done anything to make her change her very low opinion of him.

"Yeah, well, why take chances?" Ren said. "Strange days, ya know. Strange days…" He walked off toward his truck, calling back over his shoulder, "Now, get that thing outta here. Before somebody sees it and I spend the rest of my day calming people down."

"What did Ren mean?" Zenn asked as they watched him go. "About the town council?"

"There's a vote coming up. About the cloister's lease." Otha sounded suddenly weary. He went to place one hand on the hound's heaving flank, and then moved up to the neck to check the pulse rate.

"We have a lease?" She'd never heard of this before.

"Yes. The lease comes up for renewal every five years. Allows us to use the cloister grounds as a business, as a money-making operation. It's just a technicality. Nothing for you to worry about."

She wasn't so sure about that.

"But what would happen if the council turned against us, like Ren said?"

"That's never happened," Otha said.

"But if it did?"

Otha looked off toward town, then back at her. "Well, if they voted not to renew the lease, then we wouldn't be able to run the clinic."

"Not run the clinic? But what would happen then? To the animals?"

"Zenn, I told you. You don't have to worry about that.

The council has renewed us every time." His tone said the subject was closed. But she was angry with him. A lease? A lease that could be cancelled, just like that? And then the cloister would be gone? The animals, gone? A small spark of panic ignited inside of her, blotted out any other thoughts for a few nauseating seconds. Otha should've told her. This was information she should've had. Information that affected her as well as him.

Otha patted the hound's broad muzzle. "Now then, come on Zenn, let's get this fella back home."

Otha walked to the Yakk and unbuckled the canvas carrying case strapped to the side of the cargo deck. He slid his battered, old twelve-gauge pump shotgun out of the case and held it up.

"Hamish," he said. "You can stand guard over the hound. Can you handle one of these?"

Hamish recoiled slightly from the sight of the weapon.

"No, director-abbot," he said quickly. "I have never put such a thing in my... hands. It appears hazardous."

"Yes, that's the idea," Otha said, frowning. "Well, I can't leave you alone out here unprotected..."

"I can stay," Zenn said, stepping up. "With Hamish."

Otha's frown remained in place.

"I've shot your gun, Otha," she said. "You've seen me hit tin cans with it. And in case you didn't notice, I just hit a whalehound's haunch dead-center with the tranq-bow."

He considered her statement, looking from her to the gun he held.

"Otha, I'll be fine. And Hamish will be with me."

"Well... alright," he said after a few seconds. "I won't be long." He held the shotgun out to her and she took it, a slight thrill of apprehension flickering through her. The gun was cold in her hands, and heavier than she remembered.

"I'm sure you won't even need it. But better to be on the safe side." He dug in the pocket of the gun's carrying case and handed Zenn four shells. She racked them into the gun's chamber and double-checked to see that the safety was on. "And we won't mention this to the Sister," he said, giving Hamish a look. "Is that understood, Sexton? No need to get Hild all... needlessly concerned."

He straddled the Yakk and started the engine.

"I'll get the truck and bring a couple hay wagons and the winch." He turned a stern gaze to Zenn. "Then we'll discuss how the Leukkan Kire royal family's very expensive whalehound got loose. And why he will not be getting loose again."

After Otha had driven off, she and Hamish had just settled on a nearby boulder when the sound of falling rock came from behind them. Startled, Zenn jumped to her feet and spun around, her heart pounding, the gun suddenly even heavier in her grasp.

FOUR

"Ha!" The high-pitched laugh came from a small boy standing at the top of the bluff above them. He spoke to someone unseen. "I told ya I heard voices. Whoa! Lookit that…" The boy was dark haired, twelve or thirteen years old, with a dirt-smeared face and a brown, quilted jacket several sizes too large for him.

The boy pointed down at the whalehound, and now a second figure appeared. Another boy, this one blonde, stout and wearing stained coveralls and a tattered red stocking hat.

"Holy crim-in-oly!" Red Hat exclaimed. "What is that thing?"

"It's a whalehound," Zenn called up to them. "Nothing to be afraid of." This wasn't good. If the boys got scared and ran back to town, she'd have a mob on her hands. "It's alright. He's asleep."

"Asleep? You sure?" Dark Hair said, eyes wide.

"It looks dead. How you know it ain't dead?" Red Hat asked.

"I'm an exovet," she lied. "I… We put him to sleep. So that we can take him back to the cloister. You know, the

57

Ciscan cloister." She pointed down the valley.

"Is it safe? To come down?" Dark Hair said.

"Yeah. Can we... touch it?"

"Yes. Sure," Zenn told them. "Come on down." The fact they didn't appear terrified by the mere sight of the hound was an encouraging surprise. From prior experience, she knew that most of the younger children in Arsia had already had their minds made up for them as far as the cloister and its animals were concerned.

"Let me do the talking, alright?" she said quietly to Hamish.

"I should not speak?"

"It's just that... this could be a problem. That's all."

When she was younger, she'd sometimes go into town with Otha. On one of those outings, when she'd gone by herself to window-shop at the co-op general store, a gaggle of towner kids gathered on the street nearby, whispering, laughing together, giving her furtive looks then talking louder, making sure she overheard what they said.

"Them Ciscan weirdoes," a girl with blonde pigtails laughed. "Them and their slimy monsters."

"Yeah," an older boy hooted. "They're monster-lovers. And they've got monster-slime all over them. Like snot."

The others started chanting: "Snot monsters. Snot monsters."

It was too much.

"Yeah. We've got monsters, alright." Zenn said. That shut them up. The older boy made a face at her — and held his nose. Anger boiled up insider her. She affected what she imagined to be a mad-scientist expression and went toward them, arms out, eyes wide. "Gigantic monsters. Flesh-eating monsters. Run away, the monsters are coming."

The younger kids shrieked and bolted, while the one older

boy did his best to look unimpressed, laughing a little too loudly before he turned and walked off. She knew she shouldn't have done it, that it just gave them more to snigger about. People could be so narrow-minded and intolerant. Later, if Otha ever asked her to join him on a trip to town, she often found there was something else she'd rather do. She decided in her usual straightforward way it simply didn't make sense to waste her energy worrying about this state of affairs.

Now, she leaned the shotgun against the boulder they'd been sitting on and watched the boys make their way down the bluff.

A minute later, the boys were standing, mouths agape, at the hound's side. Dark Hair worked up the courage to reach out a hand.

"It's... soft. The fur," he said. He pulled his hand back and examined it closely.

Red Hat edged closer, touched the hound's ribcage and kept his hand there.

"I can feel it... breathing," he whispered, unmistakable awe in his voice. "And... it's warm."

"It's a mammal," Zenn said. "So it's warm-blooded. Just like you are."

"Yeah," Dark Hair marveled, touching the great, leathery pads on the hound's hind foot.

"Just like us."

"What's it eat?" Red Hat asked. "People. I'll bet it eats people, don't it?"

"No," Zenn said, trying to sound matter-of-fact. "Not at all. Whalehounds eat big reptiles that live in the oceans of Mu Arae. And the hounds are actually very beneficial creatures, because if they didn't eat these animals, there would be too many of them. Then the reptiles would eat all the fish in the sea, and the humans living on Mu Arae wouldn't have anything to eat themselves. See?"

"Yeah, right," said Dark Hair, going to the front of the hound to stare at its teeth. "But they could eat people if they wanted to, huh?"

"You got more of these out there? At your cloister place?"

"No. He's the only one," Zenn said.

"But you've got lotsa others, huh? Man-eaters, huh?"

Zenn took a deep breath.

"We don't have man-eaters," she said. "We have alien animals that need our care. Just because they're strange to you, or big, or from far away, it doesn't mean they eat people."

"That's not what my dad says," Dark Hair scoffed. "And he says that when the Authority takes over Mars, all those things will have to go."

"Yeah," Red Hat chimed in. "The Authority will make Mars just like Earth, with no aliens anywhere. My mom says it'll be good to have Mars for humans only."

At this, Hamish stepped forward, and seemed about to respond.

"He's a Rho Cancri bug, ain't he?" Dark Hair said, preventing any comment from Hamish. "He live with you and all those things?"

"He's a coleopt," Zenn corrected him. "His name is Hamish, and he's our new sexton. That's like an assistant. I'm Zenn. And you are…?"

Dark Hair gave Red Hat a look, and they both turned back to the hound.

"You're a little young to be this far from town, aren't you?" Zenn said. "What are you doing all the way out here, anyway?"

The boys exchanged another look. This one clearly guilty.

"We weren't doin' nuthin'," Red Hat said, not looking at her.

"Yeah, we're just... foolin' around."

Zenn approached Dark Hair, and looked more closely at his dirty face.

"You're Pelik Shandin's kid, aren't you?" she said. "Kellin, right?"

"Yeah..." He seemed unhappy to be identified.

"We were over at the quarry, with Kellin's dad," Red Hat said. Pelik Shandin ran the rock quarry on the western outskirts of Arsia. Zenn had been there just last month with Otha when they'd gone to load up on gravel for the pen floors.

"Does Pelik know you're out here?" Zenn asked. The boys were prevented from answering by a distant, high-pitched keening sound. It was the town's noon whistle.

"Holy crim-in-oly..." Kellin Shandin said. "Is it lunch already?"

"We gotta get back, fast," Red Hat said. "Your dad's gonna yell at us."

"You're not supposed to be wandering around, are you?" Zenn said. The boys shook their heads, concern plain on their young faces.

"My dad said we could look around the quarry," Kellin told her. "But we kinda... kept walkin'. You won't tell him we were out here, will ya?"

Zenn thought for second.

"Tell you what," she said, sensing an opportunity. "If you can keep the whalehound a secret, I won't say anything to your dad. Deal?"

They exchanged a long look. This was obviously a hard bargain. But they had no choice.

"Deal," Kellin said. "And you won't tell nobody we..."

touched that thing, will ya?"

"Hey... we won't... catch something from it, will we?" Red Hat said, suddenly nervous. He held both hands up to his face and squinted at them. "I mean, they've got diseases, right?" Zenn's heart sank at this. For a moment, it seemed as if this encounter might actually do some good. But no. It was already too late.

"No," she said. "You won't get sick. They don't carry any microbes that affect humans."

"I'm washing my hands anyway, soon as I get back," Red Hat said, holding his arms out from his body.

"Me too," Kellin agreed.

"Fine, but there's really no need," Zenn said. "Now, remember our deal. If you don't say anything, I won't."

"Yeah, alright," Kellin said.

They trotted off, now giving the slumbering hound a wide berth as they went to the bluff and climbed up and out of sight.

"I may speak now?" Hamish said, coming to stand by Zenn. He tilted his head at her. "What the young one said about the Earth-humans' Authority. Will this Authority come to Mars and abolish alien life forms here as it did on the Earth?"

"I don't really know, Hamish," she told him, the thought making her weary. She sat down on the bank of the dry streambed.

"I have never had a clear understanding of the Earth-humans and their feelings against forms of life from other worlds. Their thinking on this issue seems... extreme. Do you have an explanation?"

"I'm no expert on sol sys politics," Zenn admitted. "But it started about thirty years ago. You ever hear of the Orinoco Event?"

"I have not heard this term. We did not study Earth-human history in my hatchling group's education."

"It was a disease outbreak. A pandemic, a sort of super-influenza hybrid, worse than anything seen on Earth before. Started in the jungles of the South Amazonia Prefecture. It spread fast, and killed almost two hundred thousand people in three months. Then it subsided. No cure was ever found. The virus just seemed to dry up and disappear. Everyone thought they were safe, that the threat had passed. After eight months, though, it flared up again. This time, it spread worldwide. Killed over two billion people."

"This is a terrible toll," Hamish said. "Such a loss is hard to comprehend."

"It was hard alright. Pretty much made things fall apart on Earth."

"Things disintegrated into pieces?"

"Socially, I mean. Governments couldn't cope. Law and order broke down. Industry and farming, too. Entire countries started starving to death. People took things into their own hands. You can't blame them. Anyway, the Temporary Executive Authority was formed as a kind of global army. They took charge, and things got better. Slowly. And it wasn't easy. The Authority was pretty brutal about it. I guess they had to be. It wasn't a democracy, that's for sure. You either did things their way, or you were on your own. And people on their own didn't have much of a life during those years."

"But what of this Authority's sense regarding alien life forms? That they should not be tolerated? Other beings in the Accord of Local Systems do not behave in such a way."

"It was because of the Orinoco Event. The cause of the outbreak was never determined. But that didn't stop people from making accusations. Some people claimed the virus was a military experiment gone bad. Or that it was bioterrorism cooked up by religious fanatics. But no one had any real proof. In the end, I guess people felt they had to blame someone, anyone. So, they blamed aliens. They said off-worlders brought the virus to Earth with them. After that, all aliens were unclean, contaminated."

"With no proof whatever?" Hamish seemed genuinely shocked by this. "Are Earth-humans so uninterested in the truth of a thing?"

Zenn wanted to say "Yes, exactly." But she'd always made an effort to see the issue from the Earth's point of view. "It was too traumatic. The horror of what happened just made Earthers kind of… crazy. If they said the outbreak came from beyond Earth, they could tell themselves they weren't responsible."

"And it is the Authority on Earth that promotes this thinking?"

"Well, yes and no. The Authority was only interested in maintaining some kind of global order. Having aliens as an enemy to focus people's attention made their job easier. I don't think they really care one way or another about what caused the Orinoco Event."

"But are not the Authority's feelings toward aliens the cause of the Great Rift between Earth and Mars, as well as the other worlds of the Accord?"

"It's complicated," Zenn said. "You see, when the Authority came to power, they needed someone to be their muscle."

"I am assuming this is not bodily tissue you refer to."

"Right. I mean they needed a group who could carry out their orders when people got out of line. Someone to do their dirty work. The group that became the Authority's enforcers were the New Law faction. They're the ones who really, really hate aliens. The Authority just wants to keep power. The New Law wants Earth and the rest of the solar system permanently 'cleansed' of aliens."

"So this New Law is the source of the Earth-humans' wild and unreasonable dislike of alien life?"

"Well, it turns out it's not all that unreasonable, from a certain perspective. You see, the New Law had its origins way back before humans knew there was life anywhere but Earth. Back then, some fringe groups were making claims about alien abductions. Gruesome experiments. People being probed by alien creatures. These people were called UFOers. They were also called nuts, because no one believed their stories."

"Were their stories true?"

"Only in one or two rare cases. The point is, after Earth's 'First Contact' with an alien civilization, the UFOers crowed that they'd been right all along. They claimed they had some secret knowledge that aliens were out there all along. By the time of the Orinoco Event, the UFOers had organized into the New Law faction. And then they said aliens were not only real, but a threat to humanity. A lot of people were ready to believe them. By then, the Authority needed the New Law to help them keep control of things. So when the New Law insisted that Earth cut all contact with other worlds, the Rift was born."

"But Mars continues on, as does our cloister, despite this Rift?" asked Hamish.

"Well, there are a few big, commercial mining companies making a go of it on Mars, some ag co-ops and half a dozen private groups like the Ciscans. But the Rift has just about strangled the life out of the smaller farms and colonies still hanging on in the valleys. It's only trade with the planets of the Accord that's kept Mars alive. Just barely, but alive. And now there are rumors that the Authority might be ready to start up trade again with Mars. That's what the boys were talking about."

"But will that New Law segment not object at ending the Rift, if there are aliens on Mars?"

"Like you? And our patients at the cloister?" Zenn said. "Yes. They'd object, alright. But we don't get much real news from Earth, so we don't really know what the balance of power is like right now. We'll just have to wait and see."

A low, distant rumble could be heard then, echoing off the cliffs from the direction of the cloister.

"Sounds like Otha's on his way," Zenn said. She went to the boulder where she'd left the shotgun and picked it up. "Good thing I was armed. Those kids could've stolen our whalehound."

"But why would…" Hamish said. "Ah. You jest with me."

"Yes. Just kidding," Zenn said. But she thought then of what might have happened if adult towers, and not those boys, had discovered her and the helpless hound. She hefted the gun in her hands and decided not to pursue that line of thought.

FIVE

Early the next morning Zenn woke to the sound of voices echoing up the stairwell outside her dormitory room. She rose and draped her robe around her shoulders. Katie, curled up in her usual sleeping spot at the head of the bed, looked up and blinked at Zenn.

Zenn made sure the little rikkaset was watching her, then raised her hands and made the sign for "Good morning, Katie." The rikkaset responded with a luxurious stretch and a yawn that showed off a set of needle-sharp teeth. Then, she sat up on her haunches and, dexterously using her long-fingered, raccoon-like front paws, signed "Katie hungry. Hungry Katie eat?"

Zenn signed back "Yes. Come on," and Katie hopped down from the bed and followed her out into the hall.

Eleven other doors lined the hallway on this floor, all closed, all the rooms empty, except for Hild's and Hamish's. The ground floor held another twelve identical rooms – rooms that once housed paying students.

Hamish's door opened, and he ambled into view, ducking through the doorway before standing up to his full height. He came down the hall, adjusting his chainmail vest with two claws while grooming one of his antennae with the specially adapted claw on his upper left arm. His straw hat hung down on his back, its leather chinstrap looped around what passed for his neck. Otha had only recently convinced the coleopt to vacate the sleeping burrow he'd dug into the hillside next to the cloister's physic garden. Her uncle had made it clear to Hamish that he needed to move into the dorm, explaining it simply wasn't proper for the cloister sexton to live in a hole in the ground. Coleopts only required two to three hours of sleep at night. In order to wake up when everyone else did, Hamish had adjusted his sleep periods so that he went to bed around four in the morning. This let him synchronize his schedule with the waking hours of the cloister's human residents.

"Good morning, novice Zenn," he said, his hard hind claws scraping on the floorboards. "Hello, mammalrikkaset." He leaned down to pet Katie, but then straightened back up immediately.

"I would stroke the animal. Do I have your approval for this act?"

"Yes, of course," Zenn smiled up at him. He bent down again, but the rikkaset shied away, hiding behind Zenn's legs.

"She doesn't quite know what to make of you."

"I'm still peculiar and outlandish to her."

"Here," Zenn said, picking Katie up and setting her down again between her and the towering insect. "We'll show you what she's learned to do. She likes to show off." Zenn signed, and also spoke the words aloud so Hamish could follow: "Katie, sit."

Katie sat.

"Very impressive," Hamish said. "Good mammal."

"No, no," Zenn said. "That's not the trick. Watch."

She signed and spoke: "Katie?"

The rikkaset's golden eyes followed Zenn's hands, keen for whatever was coming. "Katieeee... blend."

The rikkaset instantly crouched low, froze in position, and stared straight ahead. Then, her violet-and-cream fur began to move. For a second or two, the fur rose and fell in ripples from head to tail, then the rikkaset's entire body seemed to blur. This slightly out-of-focus Katie-outline now took on the brownish tint of the synthwood flooring beneath her. A second after that, she disappeared.

Hamish started to say something, but Zenn wasn't finished.

"Katieee... un-blend."

A spot on the floor before them quivered, the brownish, indistinct shape of a rikkaset reappeared, turned to a vibrating swirl of violet and cream, and then Katie was there again. Her ringed tail whipped back and forth with excitement as Zenn praised her.

"Good Katie. Good girl," Zenn said. "We've been working on blending and appearing again on command. I think she's got it."

"I have heard such animals are capable of this. But I have never seen it. How is it accomplished?"

"It's her fur. It's refractive." Hamish shook his big head, not understanding. "That means each hair can re-direct light that hits it, kind of like a bunch of tiny prisms. It's a defense mechanism, rikkasets evolved it for hiding from predators. There are a couple species of lightshifters, but Smithson's rikkasets do it best."

"Yes, I can see that." Hamish leaned down again to pet Katie. This time she let him draw his grooming-claw through the fur on her back. Then she sat down at Zenn's feet. "And you have taught her hand-language. She must have an excellent brain."

Zenn laughed. "Yes, quite the brain. Rikkasets have the mental ability of an Earther chimpanzee."

Hamish continued stroking Katie, and the rikkaset trilled her pleasure at him.

"We had considerable excitement yesterday, did we not? With the mammal-hound," he said. "Is the animal alright?"

"He lost a little skin under his chin. Probably scraped it when he went down, after I darted him. Nothing serious."

"Your wielding of the tranquilizing bow was admirable. This must give you some pleasure."

"Well... actually," she said. "It might have been my fault he got out in the first place."

"Your fault?" He tilted his antennae toward her. "How is this so?"

Good question, Zenn thought.

"I don't really know," she said. "It's possible I... forgot to reactivate the energy fence." The admission irked her, intensely. It was bad enough having Otha reprimand her about the fence. And she couldn't defend herself from his accusation. In the aftermath of the weird feeling she'd had while treating the hound, she'd been disoriented, her mind fogged. The truth was, she couldn't say positively whether she'd reactivated the fence or not.

"You left the fence inactivated?" Hamish said. "Have you done such a thing before?"

"No. That's just it. I always turn fences back on. Close the gates. Make sure everything's secure. But this time... Well, I've been a little off, lately."

"Off... off of what?"

"It means: not my usual self."

"This sounds as if it makes you regretful."

"Well, let's just say I sunk my chances of getting a perfect score on my end of terms."

"Ah, your testing scores. Can this damage not be remedied?"

"Sure. If I score high enough on the next two rounds."

"And what is the next round?"

"In-soma insertion. In a swamp sloo."

"Yes. The in-soma pod device. I must say that this seems hazardous. Is it? A hazardous device?"

"Not really. Not if you know the procedures."

"But you enter this device, and then it is taken into the body of an organism many times your size. This is not a thing I would do voluntarily. Are you forced to do this?"

"No," Zenn laughed. "I can't wait, actually."

"And what happens, when you are in some vast and monumental animal's body?"

"Well, you navigate your way through the digestive system."

"This has the sound of being highly unpleasant."

"No. It's fascinating. Really. And you're doing it to help the animal. To diagnose and treat things that are wrong. Let's say your swamp sloo has a duodenal ulcer. You navigate through the stomach and into the intestinal tract. Then, you stop the pod and activate the manipulator arms to extend. If the ulcer is small, you could apply some medicine and close it up with protein stitching. If it's big, you lay on a derma-plast patch."

"And then how does one… exit?"

"You've got two options. You could lightly irritate the stomach lining and have the animal regurgitate you."

"You are vomited out?"

"Right. Or, you keep going forward through the small and large intestines and into the sloo's cloaca."

"What then?"

"You just let nature take its course and... *plop!*"

"So, the animal..."

"Yeah, you get pooped out."

"I repeat: I would not volunteer for such a journey. I will acknowledge your enthusiasm, although I fail to understand your eagerness."

"I'm eager because I've been looking forward to it forever. Plus, I know I can do it. I've screened every v-film on insoma insertions that we have in the scriptorium library. And I've re-run them till I see the control panel in my sleep. A high score will help make up for the whalehound."

Hamish was quiet for a few seconds.

"Novice Zenn, I haven't been in-cloister long, but to forget a fence-switch, to allow an animal to escape. That doesn't seem like your usual standard of behavior, if I may say so."

Until the last few weeks, Zenn would have agreed.

"Thanks," she said. "But I guess we all make mistakes." Whatever happened, she wasn't eager to dwell on it. "So, how are you settling in so far?"

"Oh, settling well. Although there is much to do. I'm learning that a cloister sexton has a multitude of demanding chores and tasks. Cleaning of pen and corral spaces, repairing items, feeding of the animals, more cleaning, running here and there."

"It's not what you expected?"

"Not entirely. Especially the chanting."

"Chanting?"

"There is no chanting. Or wearing of brown cloth robes with hoods. I was under the impression there was considerable group vocal chanting at a cloister such as this. And robes. But there is not. This was disappointing."

"Hamish," Zenn said. "Did you look at the message shard

we sent you, before you came to Mars? The information packet about the cloister?"

"I did not." He admitted this with no apparent embarrassment.

"Well, the shard would have told you all about life here, the responsibilities of a sexton, the lack of chanting, things like that."

"I understand. You are saying my knowledge of the cloister was deficient and if I had viewed the shard I might have decided cloister living was not to my liking."

"Yes, Hamish, that's what I'm saying."

"But the Queen Spawn-Mother selected me from among all my sibling hatch-mates to come to Mars as sexton. I would therefore be sent despite any prior knowledge I might or might not have, if you see my situation."

"Oh. I knew things on your world were... highly structured. But I didn't know that's how things worked."

"That is its working. But still, I cannot help but feel it's unfortunate there are not more students in attendance here. To help with the many tasks."

"I've noticed Liam helping you out," Zenn said.

"Yes, the person Liam Tucker. He is quite willing to assist me. He is very friendly, and curious, for a local human. Very curious, to know about the animals."

"That's great, though, isn't it? A towner taking an interest. Maybe there's hope for those people after all."

"Hope? Are they otherwise hopeless?"

"Well, like those two boys and the whalehound. People can be afraid of things they don't know anything about. Maybe Liam will tell others what it's like here. That the animals aren't just huge, dangerous alien things. He might tell them how... interesting they are. And that we're just trying to help them."

"He might well do this. And that might have instructive value," Hamish said, then he looked down at the line of closed doors. "Novice Zenn, do you recall the time when there were more students at the cloister school? Helping with tasks?"

"Not really," Zenn said. "The Rift with Earth had already started when I was born. So, it's basically been this way for my whole life."

His question prompted her to imagine, not for the first time, what it was like when the entire dorm had been buzzing with activity. Did students talk and joke with each other as they hustled out of their rooms every morning? Were they all good friends with each other, sharing their excitement about the animals they would work on or learn about that day? And did her mother join in the banter, when she was Zenn's age and going through her novice year?

"Were you not lonely," Hamish asked, "growing up in the absence of others in your hatchling group?"

"No, actually, I'm used to being the only... hatchling around here," she told him.

"And what of your friends in the surrounding environment? With the townfolk in Arsia indisposed toward alien animals and those of us who deal with them, do you in fact have friendships or associations with others?"

"Um, no," Zenn said. "I don't... associate all that much." The truth was, even if she was inclined to ignore the Rule about making friends, kids in Arsia City and the valley didn't stay around. They grew older and left. They moved to Zubrin, or went to find work in one of the other larger settlements.

Friends leave. Everyone... leaves.

Talking about it, thinking about it was making her feel testy.

"Besides, it would be weird to have lots of others here," she said. "All those bodies and voices, all those faces, swarming around all the time. I'm not really sure I'd like it." But even as she said it aloud, she could feel the tug of curiosity. What would it be like? Other bodies, other faces, other personalities all around, every day, day in and day out? The strange mix of emotions this train of thought provoked made the whole idea almost overwhelming. No, she decided. It was better as it was. Less confusing. Safer.

"Zenn?" It was Sister Hild, calling up from downstairs. Zenn walked to the banister and looked down. The Sister was in the entryway of the calefactory hall. Next to her, Otha was pulling on his heavy work chaps.

"So, the princess awakens," her uncle said, glancing up. "Good. You can assist. Get dressed and meet me in the courtyard. Did I hear our new sexton up there?" Zenn turned to see the big coleopt attempting to move quietly back to his room.

"He's here," Zenn said, then immediately felt guilty. "Sorry," she whispered as he came to join her on the landing.

"Yes, director-abbot," Hamish said, only half-concealing his disappointment at being discovered. "I am here."

"Did you give Griselda that dose of mineral supplement with this morning's feeding?" Griselda was a crypto-plasmodial seepdemon being treated for membrane parasites at the clinic.

"I haven't fed her yet, director-abbot. I was about to attend to it. Right after breakfast." His mouthparts quivered at the mention of food, the crescent-shaped mandibles rubbing together with a sound like sharpening knives. "Do I have your approval for…?"

"You haven't had your breakfast yet?" Otha cut him off.

"Early to wake, sooner to work, sexton Hamish." It was a saying Zenn had heard many times. She got an uncharitable amount of pleasure hearing it quoted to someone else. Hamish's antennae drooped, and he gave her what she imagined was a coleopt's version of a long-suffering look as he went by, descended the stairs, and started off for the kitchen.

"Sexton," Otha said, stopping him. "Patients eat first. Remember?"

"Yes, director-abbot," Hamish said, turning reluctantly toward the door leading to the cloister yard.

"Did we get a shard?" Zenn called to her uncle. It was the same question she asked almost every morning.

"No, Zenn," Otha said, kneeling to check the contents of his veterinary field kit. "Still no message from Warra. You'll be the first to know, I promise. Hamish?"

Hamish paused, one claw on the door latch.

"Director-abbot?"

"We'll be at the south gate in a few minutes."

"Oh…?" Hamish dipped his antennae at Otha, waiting.

Otha sighed. "Be there to let us out and close the gate behind us. Alright?"

"I see. Of course, director-abbot." He placed his hat on his head and adjusted it so his antenna could protrude, then he ducked out the door.

Sister Hild came up the stairs and shooed Zenn back into her room. Startled at the Sister's approach, Katie blended and was gone.

SIX

"It's the Bodine place. Again," Hild said, taking a pair of coveralls out of the closet and handing them to Zenn. Beneath wind-burnished skin, the old woman's cheeks blushed red from the chill morning air outside, her long, gray hair gathered in a tidy bun on top of her head. No doubt she'd already been up doing chores for hours. She wasn't a strong-looking woman. Quite the opposite; slightly-built and smaller than Zenn with a delicate, bird-like manner about her. But she had more energy than Zenn and Otha put together, and she was the cloister's resident tech expert, repairing balky computers and aging medical equipment with apparently effortless speed and efficiency.

"Gil's new sandhog is in a bad way," the Sister said, "And he can't afford to lose this one."

"What's wrong with it?" Zenn said, pulling on the coveralls. She knew Gil Bodine had bartered away a full first cutting of high quality gensoy for the new sandhog boar. He'd already lost two sows, and he'd be more than a little upset if this hog expired on him.

"Something gastro-intestinal, from the sound of it."

"A sandhog with indigestion? There's a shock," Zenn

said. Burrowing into the ground, devouring soil by the gaping mouthful and excreting it back out again, a big, grub-like sandhog could convert an acre of sterile Martian sand and rock to fertile, crop-growing humus in a matter of weeks. At least it could back on Sigmund's Parch, its home world. "Otha says Parcher hogs need to get used to Martian soil gradually before you turn them out full time. You think Gil put this one to work too soon?"

"Could well be. Patience isn't Gil's strong suit," Hild said. "If he'd taken more care with penning in those first two sows, maybe they wouldn't have disappeared on him."

"At least they were spayed females," Zenn said, contemplating the unpleasant prospect of a sandhog population boom. Hogs were useful animals, but they were also large and belligerent when riled up. "You'd think he'd be a little more careful."

"Gil just has a lot on his plate," the Sister said. "A farm that size? It's too much for one man to handle."

"I think he's had some help lately. Liam said he'd been out there a few times."

"Liam…" Hild said. She gave Zenn a look. "Ah yes, Liam Tucker."

"And Hamish has him helping out with chores around here, too," Zenn said. The old woman continued to give Zenn a look she couldn't decipher. "What?"

"Oh, well," Hild said. "Just that Liam seems to be in evidence at the cloister more than usual lately. He seems to be acting more… friendly."

Zenn had no idea what Hild was saying. Then it dawned on her.

"With me?" She had to smile at this. Yes, Liam was interacting more with her. But not in the way the Sister was implying. "I don't think so, Sister. Liam's a towner. There

are plenty of towner girls for him to be friendly with."
Alright, she conceded to herself, maybe not plenty of girls,
but at least three or four who came immediately to mind.
The Sister's cryptic expression stayed put.

"Zenn," Hild sat on the bed. Zenn could feel one of the
Sister's "little talks" coming on. "Liam Tucker has a bit of a
reputation. I don't know if you're aware of it."

"A reputation?" Zenn said. "For what? For joyriding in
Benji Kao's flatbed truck? It was a stupid stunt, I'll grant
you. But Benji got his truck back, didn't he?"

"I'm referring more to Liam's general attitude. Toward
responsibility. Toward others. It's not just that he gets into
trouble. Lots of boys his age do."

"Then what is it?"

"Liam and his family have had to contend with some…
difficult times," Hild said. "He's grown up in a very different
world from us out here. A harder world. I just mean he's a
boy who has a certain kind of attitude about life."

"So?" Zenn said, a small kernel of righteous annoyance
forming within her. "Who doesn't have an attitude about
life?"

And if Liam had attitude issues, Zenn told herself, there
wasn't any mystery about it. After his father's death in some
sort of farming accident years ago, his mother took up with
Deg Bradden, a prospector from Syrtis Forge. Liam and Deg
never got along, and things came to a head when Constable
Jakstra was called out one night to break up a fight between
the two of them. Shortly after that, Deg moved back to the
mining camp at Syrtis and Liam's mom went with him. Liam
stayed. He was related to Vic LeClerc, so he moved out to
live on her ranch. Since then, he'd had other run-ins with
the constable, but nothing all that terrible far as Zenn knew;
fistfights with other boys, "borrowing" Benji's old truck, kid

stuff. Maybe that was her main impression of Liam. Street-smart but not school-smart, self-centered in a boyish way.

"In Liam's case," the Sister said, "I'm afraid the attitude is one that tells him to act first and think later. And he's at an age that... well, you're old enough that I don't need to explain hormonal surges. And the quantity of available peer group females in Arsia doesn't enter into the equation. If you're the girl he's talking to at the moment, you're the girl he's going to 'be friendly' with."

"Oh, thanks a lot!" Zenn half-laughed at Hild's retort. But it was only half a laugh. "So the only reason he comes to find me and talk is that he's enslaved by out-of-control hormones? I'll have you know he's taken an interest in the clinic's patients. He's curious. He asks questions about them and he appreciates the things I tell him. Are there hormones for that kind of behavior? I guess we haven't gotten to that chapter in the textbook yet."

"It's just this," Hild said, reaching out to take Zenn's hands in hers. "You need to use a little common sense around boys like Liam. That's all." She patted Zenn's hands and released them, giving her an indulgent smile.

Zenn didn't return the smile, but bent to scruff Katie between her tufted ears.

"I think I'm old enough to know I need to use common sense, Sister."

"Hm," she said, her clear, blue, old-woman's eyes fixing on Zenn's. "Well, the truth is, I'm surprised Vic can spare Liam." She rose from the bed and started straightening the covers. "First he's here doing Hamish's work for him. Now he's going all the way out to Gil Bodine's? Seems like the boy would have plenty to keep him busy at the LeClerc place. All those goats."

"He said Vic is thinning out her herd. Not enough decent

grazing land," Zenn said, knowing that Hild was just trying
to direct the conversation to some subject other than the
chemical changes in Liam's adolescent bloodstream. "I guess
that gives him the free time to help Gil. And Hamish. And
that's encouraging, isn't it? That he's willing to spend his
time at the cloister, work around the animals, ask about
them. Not many towners would make that kind of effort."

Hild didn't argue with this, and Zenn felt like she'd scored
a point for Liam. Even though he was a towner, at least he
seemed open to the idea that the cloister's animals might be
something other than a toxic menace.

"So," the Sister said, going to stand by the door. "You'll
be careful out at Gil's, won't you? No wandering off?"

Hild had likely heard the same rumors as Zenn. That the
scab-landers stalking the more remote areas were getting
bolder every month. Liam had even told her when scabs
robbed the Zubrin train or held up other travelers, they
weren't just stealing cargo or food. They were taking people
– and selling them to off-world slavers. Zenn found this
hard to believe. But not impossible.

"I'll be perfectly safe with Otha," Zenn said, though the
prospect of venturing far beyond the cloister walls always
filled her with a quick rush of apprehension and excitement.
In fact, she'd never been out of sight of the walls without
an adult by her side. "And if Gil has a sick animal, it's our
duty to go out there and help, isn't it?"

"Of course. But I still don't like it," Hild said. "Gil is one
of the good ones, though. At least he sees the benefit in off-
world creatures, that they have their place just like we do.
Not like others I could mention."

The unmentionables, Zenn assumed, included most of the
population of Arsia City. "Sister," Zenn said to Hild, her
gaze drawn to the window and the compound's buildings

and grounds. "What if the Rift really is ending? If contact between Earth and Mars starts up again, what will happen to the cloister?"

"I suppose we'd have Earther students enrolling again, wouldn't we?"

"But what if the stories about the Authority on Earth are true? If they got control here on Mars, with how they feel about aliens?"

"I think the Authority is changing, Zenn," Hild said. "It sounds to me like they've decided Earth can't just go it alone any more. They tried that, it didn't work out for them. They're starting to see the value of working with the planets of the Accord again." She paused, folding Zenn's robe and setting it on the dresser. "The New Law faction, they're another story. They've got some strange ideas. About human superiority. About Earther purity. About hanging on to the past, no matter what it costs. And even if the Rift does end," the Sister's voice lifted, affecting a lighter tone, "the VIPs on Earth and Mars will have more on their minds than our little cloister. And you have a patient waiting, child. Now go on with you."

Hild waved her hands at Zenn to urge her out of the room, but suddenly the bedspread seemed to come alive, making Hild take a quick step back. Katie materialized, her fur fluffed out defensively. She leaped off the bed and positioned herself between Zenn and the Sister.

"Katie," Hild exclaimed. "I hate when she pops out of nowhere like that."

"She's just looking out for me. Aren't you, Katie-Kate?"

"Well, it's alarming," Hild said, but she was smiling in spite of herself. "Now then, you stay close to Otha out at Gil's."

"I will."

At her feet, Katie sat up and signed: "Katie hungry still.

Hungry now to eat."

"Oh, right. Um…" Zenn looked from Katie to Hild.

"Yes, I'll feed the little imp. You go."

"Thanks. There's a bag of dried grasshoppers in the bread box."

"Next to my fresh-baked rolls?" Hild said, not pleased. But Zenn was already in motion. Grabbing her work gloves from the desk, she hurried into the hall and bounded down the steps, taking them two at a time.

SEVEN

Outside, Zenn jogged across the cloister's outer courtyard to where Otha waited in his cherished Mistuchev. The worn, old pickup truck had been wired up, welded together, and jerry-rigged so many times it looked less like a truck than a prehistoric beast with a bad case of mange. Slung over one shoulder, Zenn carried the battered leather backpack that used to serve as Otha's field kit. Now it was Zenn's, and it was one of her most prized possessions. Searching through the supply shed, she'd stocked the kit with an array of the clinic's second-hand equipment, unused bandages, older medicines and anything else she thought a reasonably equipped exovet should have while out on a call.

"I don't think we need your little assistant on this job," Otha said dryly, pointing behind Zenn. She turned to see Katie skittering across the drive, tail held high.

"No, Katie," Zenn signed and spoke, trying to make her voice sound firm even though Katie couldn't hear her. The little rikkaset was acutely perceptive; so much so that Zenn had been working on lip-reading with her lately. She was picking it up quickly. "You stay here with Hild. Stay." Katie sat down, but just barely. "Good girl."

Zenn pulled open the passenger side door.

"That rear tire still holding air?" Otha nodded his head toward the back of the truck. Zenn dropped her pack on the ground and walked around to check.

"Looks good to me," she said, coming back to the front, tossing her pack behind the seat and climbing in. She slammed the door three times before it finally latched and settled back as they pulled ahead.

Hamish was waiting for them at the gate. He'd already opened the two big, metal doors that guarded the compound's east entrance.

"Do I have your approval for now shutting tight these gates?" Hamish called as they drove past him. Otha stopped the truck.

"Yes, sexton, you may close the gates now." Her uncle spoke as if addressing a young child.

"Hamish," Zenn said, "You don't always have to ask for approval, you know. Not for every little thing. Sometimes, it's a good idea just to think for yourself, right? Take the initiative."

"Very well. If this is your wish," he said. But from the way he said it, Zenn didn't think he really thought much of the idea. Zenn wondered again about Hamish's species, and the rigid coleopt social order on Siren. Did anyone there do anything without getting clearance from the Queen Spawn-Mother herself? They drove on and Hamish dutifully shut the gates behind them.

"Gil should've learned the lesson those first two hogs tried to teach him," Otha muttered as they accelerated down the road. He shifted gears irritably, not really awake yet, sipping bitter chicory coffee from his chipped mug. "Breakfast," he said, nodding at the small wicker basket on the seat between them.

Zenn opened the basket and helped herself to one of the still-warm amaranth griddlecakes as the truck topped a low ridge and the terrain opened up ahead of them. She looked out across the patchwork of irrigated fields, barren ground and decaying farmsteads where settlers had given up and left. Bathed in the ruddy light of the rising sun, the few fields still being cropped glowed an improbable shade of green between the battlements of red rock.

Farther along the valley she could see the farmhouses and outbuildings of the neighboring families who still stubbornly clung to their land. The Swansons, with their vast lichen barn. The permafrost well operated by widower Carl Dawkins and his five sons. The Zetian place, where she was just able to see the tiny, stooped figures of Cai-Lun and Wu working their way along the tidy rows of kipfruit saplings. And farthest away, just visible at the mouth of Huxlee's Canyon, the eroded hillsides of the LeClerc spread, most of the land's scant vegetation long ago gnawed to ground-level by the ranch's ravenous goats.

Centered in the middle distance beyond them, the lights of Arsia City were blinking off one by one as the morning brightened. A handful of campfires flickered amid the squalid shantytown that had grown up around Arsia's outskirts. This sad collection of converted shipping containers and makeshift shacks was where the poor and homeless in this end of the canyon sought shelter from the steadily worsening situation on Mars. It had been several weeks since Zenn had accompanied Otha on a trip into Arsia to barter for supplies. But even from this distance, she could see that since that last visit a dozen new shelters had been hastily thrown together on the north edge of town. Zenn thought of the families driven off their failing farms and into the crowded jumble of shanties. They'd shed their role as brave, independent settlers taming a wild frontier. Now, they would assume the unfamiliar, new role of refugee, the dreams gone, the future uncertain.

The sun had cleared the horizon, and Zenn folded down the visor to shade her eyes. She tried to imagine the Martian landscape before the bary-gens stretched their protective membranes of invisible, charged molecules across the valleys, before the first colonists arrived – a time of no green fields, no farmsteads or villages. Just dry rock and sand and an atmosphere so paltry it didn't deserve the name.

"It must have looked so… harsh at first," she said. "You know, before settlers came."

"More than harsh. Downright lethal. At least here in the deep end of the Valleys there was some kind of atmospheric pressure. Enough to keep water from boiling off into the sky anyway."

"But at first the people had help, right, from Earth?"

"Not like now, you mean?" Otha snorted a soft laugh at the thought. "Sure they did. I'll tell you this, though: the Rift was a blessing in disguise. Well, half a blessing. Made us self-reliant. Made us dig down and get serious about what it meant to be a Ciscan. What it meant to be Martian." Otha sipped at his coffee, and then wedged the mug on the dash so it wouldn't spill. "I remember the day we finally heard the news. Word got passed down from Zubrin – the last radio link with Earth had gone dead. Nothing but static. I told your father, 'This is what we're meant for, Warra. This is what the Ciscan Order was designed to do: survive.'"

He paused, eyes on the road ahead. "Of course, it was a double-edged sword. It was before your time. Before the Rift, the scriptorium was full, teeming with novices and acolytes. We had three sextons then. You wouldn't have recognized the place."

Zenn could see it in his face: he was back in the glory days, when the cloister training program was in full flower, the clinic school filled with eager would-be exovets from all across the Accord. After the Rift, even the cloister's reputation as one of the premiere training clinics of the Accord couldn't prevent the disastrous decline in enrollments. There was one advantage, though. With Earth closed to all off-worlders, the cloister on Mars became the only facility in nearby space for the treatment and boarding of alien animals. That had kept clients coming, money flowing. Not a lot, but enough. Now, though, with more Indra ships going missing, and fewer coming to Mars, even that meager source of cloister income no longer seemed secure. "Pretty quiet these days, eh?" Otha said, giving her a wry grin. "I suppose you're the sole beneficiary now."

"Yes, I think you've mentioned that once or twice," Zenn said. "And I do get lots of one-on-one attention from the instructors. Both of you. That part's great. But even with Hamish's help, it just seems like there's never enough time to do everything."

"Oh, is the life of a novice so pitiful and cruel?" Otha gave her a look of simulated concern. "It's enough to make a rikkaset howl at both moons."

Zenn wasn't at all sure Otha really knew how much she did around the cloister. She was about to remind him when he turned the truck into the Bodine drive.

Gil must have heard them coming. He was standing at the heavy, sheet-metal security gate that guarded the entrance to his farmyard compound. He was a wide-load of a man, dressed in bib overalls and wearing a sweat-stained seed cap. Though a few years younger than Otha, Gil's open, friendly face had been prematurely aged to a sun-and-wind cured surface, brown and creased as the stony land he farmed.

Otha drove into the yard, and Gil swung the gate shut behind them.

"He was in here!" Gil shouted at them, pointing toward the pole barn at the far side of the yard.

"Was?" Otha said as they got out of the truck. "I see. And where is our big boy now?"

EIGHT

Gil motioned for them to follow him toward the barn. Inside, Zenn's eyes slowly adapted to the chilly, animal-scented darkness. Ahead of them, Gil had stopped. He was staring into a penned area surrounded by a fence of heavy, salvaged synthwood boards. The only thing visible in the pen was a large mound of earth and a gaping hole in the metal floor panels.

"Found him missing this morning," Gil said. "He chewed clean through my floor! Look'it this." He went to a breaker box on the wall of the barn. "Power to the floor panels was cut." Gil poked at several frayed wires sticking out from the box. "Something musta ate through the wires. Just my luck."

Otha inclined his head toward Zenn, giving her a "told you so" look.

"Uh huh... well, what's the matter with your hog, Gil, when he's at home?"

Gil sat heavily on a bale of bedding straw, tugged his cap off and wiped at his balding head with a grimy bandana.

"Off his feed, moanin' and bellowin'. Bad belly, I guess. All bloated up, colicky like. I got no idea what was wrong with him. The two sows didn't act nothing like this."

"But they got out, too, Gil. Maybe your fences need a little beefing up."

"Yeah, Ren said the same thing when he came by yesterday."

"So, what's your feed mix been?"

"Silica and heavy H, just like the others," Gil answered. Sand and modified water. Not Zenn's idea of gourmet dining, but standard fare for these dirt-eaters. "That Tucker boy did the feedings the last few days. But I showed him how to mix it up. It weren't rocket science or nuthin'."

"You should have sent for me last night, Gil," Otha said, laying his duffle bag field kit on top of a water barrel and zipping it open.

"Otha, you wouldna been any happier being out here at two in the morning than ya are now," Gil responded. Correctly, Zenn thought. Following Otha's lead, she set her own pack down on a bale of straw, the very act of having a field kit making her feel very official.

"Let's see if we can tell which way he went. Novice, you have an episcope in your kit?"

"Yes, I do," she said, smiling, feeling useful. It was a good thing she'd brought her pack, after all.

She opened her kit and reached in – felt something furry and moving and jerked her hand back out. A second later, a pair of lynx-tufted ears rose up out of the pack. Katie trilled at her.

"You little vermin," Otha said, scowling at the rikkaset. "I think you and Katie need to work on your discipline."

"Sorry," Zenn said, picking the little animal up. "Bad Katie." The rikkaset trilled louder and nuzzled against Zenn's arm.

Returning to her pack, Zenn found the episcope and

sheepishly handed it over. Otha inserted the ear-buds and placed the receiver on the ground near the pen. He twirled the volume dial. Apparently hearing nothing, he thumped the receiver against the palm of his hand and listened again.

"No sign of him nearby, if this thing can be trusted," Otha said, frowning at the episcope. "Where do you graze him?"

"East dune-pasture, mostly. I was hoping to get a crop of sorghum planted out there this year. That's what I bought the dang animal for, to get those acres turned fertile and put into production. But if he spends all his time running off instead of eating my dirt, it's never gonna get done."

"How long has he been off his feed?"

"Don't know exact. A day... day and a half?" Gil eyed the empty pen. "This is my last hog, mark my words. I'll switch back to enzymes to convert my fields, cost be danged."

"Might be a good thing, too," Otha muttered to Zenn under his breath. He took the portable seda-field generator from his kit, folded out the small transmit dish and pulled its tripod legs from underneath. He set the unit on the ground and handed the remote to Zenn. She set Katie down at her feet.

"I doubt we'll need this," Otha indicated the dish, "but hogs can be unpredictable. So, just in case he's in the area... set the level to intermediate, weight at twelve-hundred pounds – no, better make it fifteen hundred, to be safe. And if you do have to use it, keep the beam tight. You want to sedate the animal, not me, alright?"

"I think I can tell one from the other," Zenn said, shaking her head at him. She'd never been trusted with using the seda-field dish in the field before. This was good. Especially after what had happened with the hound.

Otha opened the gate and entered the pen. Stooping near

the mangled metal floor panel where the sandhog exited, he scooped up a handful of dirt and sniffed it, but turned his head quickly and threw down the soil.

"Whew! That's fresh."

On the ground next to Zenn, Katie's ears twitched. Then, she lowered her body and vanished from sight. That's odd, Zenn thought, wondering what triggered the rikkaset's camouflage mode.

Otha turned to proffer the handful of soil for Gil to smell. Gil declined the offer.

"It's as if that hog was just…"

But before Otha finished his sentence, the ground in the pen trembled, swelled under his feet, then erupted in a shower of dirt and straw as the sandhog burst up out of the floor. Thrown into the air, Otha landed hard at the far side of the pen.

The hog thrust himself up out of the hole and reared to his full, twelve-foot height, a mass of rippling muscle and hairless, pink-beige skin. With no time to stand, Otha kicked his legs frantically to push himself away. Roaring, the sandhog whirled to follow him, the huge maw gaping above mole-like claws the size of backhoe buckets.

Otha half-rose to his feet, fell again, his shoulder banging against the fence. There was no chance he could climb out before the furious animal was on him. Gil rushed up to the pen, waving his arm and yelling to distract the animal, but it ignored him. Instead, the sandhog dropped forward, its body toppling like an unstable building. Otha twisted away reflexively, body tensed for the impact, arms thrown up across his face.

NINE

"*No...*" Zenn opened her mouth to scream, but produced only an anguished, fearful whisper, her hands stretched before her as if to stop the looming disaster by force of will. To her astonishment, it seemed to work. The sandhog stopped its strike in mid-air, body tilted forward, jaws straining wide. A string of drool oozed from the animal's mouth to drape itself on Otha's still-upraised arms.

No, she thought, but strangely felt no need to speak the word. The sandhog settled back on its thick, armor-plated tail. The only sound was the animal's ragged breathing as it swayed slightly, holding itself upright in the middle of the pen. It swung its head to where Zenn stood outside the pen behind Otha. It was only now she noticed it: the familiar warming sensation and dizziness, pulsing through her head and body, strong enough now to make her feel queasy, to make her knees threaten to buckle. She struggled to focus, and saw that the sandhog's tiny, almost-useless eyes fixed on hers. Yes. She was certain of it. The hog wasn't just looking at her, it was looking into her eyes. It wasn't simply scanning another creature; it was seeing her – her mind, her intentions. It was the same look she'd seen in the whalehound's eye. The hog blinked at her, confused.

As if waking from a dream, Zenn remembered the seda-field. She knelt to where the unit sat at her feet and punched the activation pad and the small dish hummed to life.

In the pen the sandhog wavered on its tail, and then slowly slumped over onto its side as the sedation took hold. The strange feeling gripping her evaporated, leaving her body trembling, the barn's dank smell in her nostrils, the air cool on her face.

Otha was already moving. A few seconds later, he was out of the pen. He slammed the gate behind him, shoved the latch into place and leaned against the planks, breathing deep and fast.

Half an hour later, she, Otha and Gil sat on the steps of the second-hand military Quonset hut that Gil had refurbished into a semblance of a farmhouse, drinking the chicory coffee he'd brought out. After using Gil's skiploader to move the animal to a reinforced grain silo, Otha's exam produced a diagnosis of intestinal blockage. He quickly dissolved the concretion with a sonic purge, leaving the animal understandably annoyed, but otherwise no worse for wear.

"Something's off with that feed mix, Gil," Otha said, sipping his coffee. "That beast was plugged up tight as a bad drain."

"Almost plugged up with our local vetrin'ry, too," Gil said. But his words were accompanied by a nervous laugh and furtive glance at Zenn. "That was something, Otha," he said. "That hog just stopping like that."

Had Gil seen what happened? Had Otha?

Stroking Katie, dozing now in her lap, Zenn watched Otha for his reaction, but he appeared not to hear, his mind somewhere else.

"Just kinda froze in his tracks," Gil said, giving his nervous chuckle again. "Sorta like... he was hyp-natized."

Zenn sipped the bittersweet chicory, and the cup shook in her hands. She looked at Otha to see if he'd noticed. He hadn't, and she lowered her hands to her lap to steady them.

"Well, one thing's sure," Otha said to Gil, "You need to tell the co-op to be more careful with their feed ratios. Silica poisoning could've been bad news."

"Well, it weren't the co-op. Traded for the feed with Vic LeClerc. Graad dropped it by. But it don't matter anyways." He raised both hands in a gesture of surrender. "I'm done. That hog's gettin' shipped right back to the Parcher vermin I bought him from. He claimed the thing was pen-trained. I can't afford this sorta downtime with an animal that won't stay put. Not to mention watchin' him almost chew you in half. Nope. Done and done."

"Can't say I blame you," Otha said. "Sandhogs can be more trouble than they're worth. Might be pricey, though, sending him back."

"Otha, what you take me for? Got a guarantee. Six months, full satisfaction or money back, shipping included. The *Helen of Troy* is due in here soon. I'll haul him over to the port at Pavonis and be shed of him."

"The *Helen of Troy*?" Zenn said. "She does the Enchara run, doesn't she?"

"Yup. She's puttin' in here on her way out to Sigmund's Parch, then goes on to Enchara. Well, assuming she doesn't get jacked and vanish into the ether." He guffawed heartily, but Otha gave him a cool stare in response. The disappearing Indra starships were no joking matter to her uncle.

"Lucky thing the *Helen* is making a stop here," Gil went on. "Otherwise, I'd be saddled with that hog for who knows how long. Say, isn't Warra doing some sorta lawyering out on Enchara?"

"Yes," Zenn said. "He's with colony administration there."

"I thought so. Well, say hello for me next time you send a shard his way."

"We'll do that," Otha said, not meeting Zenn's worried glance. "Just let me know if that boar doesn't get his appetite back, alright?" He stood, lifted up his kit bag and shook hands with Gil.

"Thanks for comin' out, Otha," Gil said. "I'll uh... I'll settle up with you for this soon as my next crop is in. I mean, if that's good for you."

"It's tight all over, Gil," Otha told him. "You pay me when you're able. Come on, Zenn," he said to her, starting toward the truck. "Sister will wonder what's become of us."

Driving out of the farmyard, Otha stared at the road ahead. "I have to tell you, Zenn Scarlett – what went on with that animal..." He chewed his cheek that way he did when something bothered him.

He saw! He saw what happened with the sandhog.

"It's happened before," she said quickly. She turned on the seat to face him, eager to finally be able to discuss it with her uncle. "At least, I think it has."

"What has?" He gave her a quizzical look.

"I don't know. That's the problem..."

"Zenn? Speak plain, girl."

"The sandhog. Stopping its attack. You saw it... didn't you?"

"What I saw was a prime sandhog boar nearly killed by bad feed. It's a disgrace. Never would've happened ten years ago. It's attitudes toward anything off-world, that's what it is. Damnable, irresponsible behavior. What were you saying? About the hog? The seda-field did its job. And you did your job. Right?" Her stomach clenched. She was wrong. He didn't understand, he hadn't seen.

But Zenn had already made her decision. She'd been keeping so much inside lately. Not anymore. She still didn't have a sensible hypothesis about what it was, but she couldn't keep it from her uncle any longer. Not after what happened with the hog. And maybe he could help her see something she was missing. Yes, it was time to tell him.

"Otha, something weird happened back there," Zenn said. "It's like, all of a sudden, the sandhog and I shared some kind of... communication. No, that's not it." She shifted in her seat, impatient with herself for not knowing how to describe it – and not a little afraid of what Otha would think if she did. "More like a connection."

"A connection?" Otha's eyes narrowed. She was beginning to think she should have kept her mouth shut. "Like a... mental connection? With the hog? Zenn..."

"When it stopped. When it didn't strike. It knew I wanted it to stop. I don't know how. But it was like it looked at me and understood."

"Understood what? What you were thinking?"

"I know it's crazy..."

"Zenn," Otha said, "You've been working hard lately. Pushing yourself. I know what a novice contends with. The long hours, no sleep. And now Warra. I know you're worried about him. But we've talked about that, what your father went through." He paused, his jaw tight, his gaze fixed on the road ahead. "Your mother's death took a lot out of him. And out of you, young as you were."

"No, this isn't about that." Her voice took on an edge of anger, at him, at herself for not making herself clear. Of course she was worried about her father. But this was something else, something happening inside of her. "It's what I've been feeling around the animals lately. It's like, sometimes, they notice that I'm there, in some different way. It's like, maybe they sense I'm trying to help."

"And you think you've... felt this before, with other animals?"

"I felt the same thing, about a month ago, with Katie. Somebody left the cover off the well pit. She fell in and couldn't get out. I was in the side garden, tying up hopps vines. I heard her yowling. Soon as I lifted her up out of the pit, I had this... peculiar feeling. Like being dizzy, or weak all of the sudden. And then she just went quiet, flipped over and gave me this look, like... I know, I know how this sounds. But it was like she was looking into my eyes and sensing that she was safe then, that I would help. I felt so close to her. Close in a different way than ever before."

"Well, now, Zenn, let's think about this. You've always had a way with the animals. Ever since you were little. And Katie isn't just another pet. She's a bright little creature."

"But this was different, Otha. Then it happened again, with the hooshrike." It was two weeks ago. She'd been prepping the big, bat-like fruitivore for surgery when it happened. "Hild had asked me to shave his abdomen, for the gastric resection op. He knew something was up. When I turned on the clippers, the sound scared him."

"No surprise there," Otha snorted. "Those clippers are older than I am. The noise makes me jump sometimes."

"He spooked and reared up. One of his primary wings went through the cage bars and got stuck. He was thrashing around something fierce. I had to get him free before he hurt himself."

"He's bigger than you, girl, and strong. You should've come for me."

"There wasn't time. He was panicking. I was about to make a grab for him when it happened again. The feeling. Only this time I got really... wobbly, and all at once he stopped struggling. He just drooped there, perfectly still. He let me pull his wing free, he never resisted or fought me. It was like he knew I was there to help him."

"Yes, but Zenn... this feeling you say you get. Why didn't you speak up before?"

"I couldn't be sure before. But it happened again when I was doing the whalehound's eye, for just a second. And today, with the sandhog. Each time, I feel it more, like the connection is getting stronger. Otha, I know how this sounds. But something is happening between me and these animals."

Otha was silent, and Zenn couldn't read his face. Did he think she was imagining it? Having a breakdown? Did he think she was just a scatter-brained little girl? He looked at her again, sharply, for a long while, as if trying to see something beneath her words.

"Zenn, what you're feeling, no, what you think you're feeling around the animals isn't that unusual. You spend your days, all your time, treating these patients, becoming... involved. You don't see anyone else, beside Hild and me and Hamish. You don't have a chance to interact with other kids your age and..."

Zenn tried to interrupt. She'd heard this before, from both Otha and the Sister. Her uncle held up a hand to silence her.

"And what happens then is projection. You know the term?"

"Yes, Otha, but..."

"You're projecting, Zenn. You've got a ... need in your life, a necessary psychological need that isn't being met in the way that it's met for most kids your age. So you see things in the animals, you feel things that you think are coming from them, but they're not. They're coming from inside of you. Do you see how that works?"

"Otha. I understand about that, I know what you mean, but you're wrong. This is something real. Not something I'm manufacturing because I'm lonely, or cut-off or... crazy."

"Of course you're not crazy, Zenn. That's not what I'm saying. I'm saying this is a natural reaction to your situation. To our situation at the cloister. You've lived behind our walls your whole life. If anyone's at fault here, it's me. I should've seen what this was doing to you."

"Otha, I'm telling you that's not it!"

"Oh? What, then?" he said, exasperated. "What is it? You tell me."

"It's..." She was frustrated too, now, and it made her even less able to say anything convincing to her uncle about what was happening to her. "It's like the animals... allow me in. They let me in... somehow."

"Yes. Somehow," Otha shook his head. "Zenn, I'm not sure you're hearing me. You know the science about this sort of thing. And you know what I'm telling you is true. You need to take a step back. Will you do that? Take a step back, look at the facts?"

She could tell him yes, that she'd do that. But she wouldn't do it. And she wasn't going to tell him she would. She was already looking at the facts. But she was failing miserably in describing those facts to him. She turned away, watched the rock and scrub growth passing by, angry with him, angry with herself.

They drove in silence for a short time.

"We need to tell Warra about this," he said then, surprising her.

"Dad?" Zenn turned quickly to face him, no longer angry, but concerned. "Why?"

"Because it affects him too. Your life. How you're doing."

"Do you have to? Tell him? I know I've been… a little unfocused lately." That was an understatement, and almost an admission Otha was right about her mental state. She didn't care. "But… he's got other things on his mind. You've said so. Why bother him?"

And why give her father a reason to think he'd been right all along? That she wasn't ready; that she was too young to stay behind on Mars and start her exovet training.

"Girl, he worries about you. Despite what you think. Gil said the *Helen of Troy* was going to Enchara. I'll send off a shard." Carried aboard the Indra ship, a message recorded onto the holographic crystal data-shard would take at least a week to reach Enchara. It would then take more weeks for a reply to be sent on the next Indra ship headed back to Mars. The delay always maddened Zenn. While the Indra had evolved the ability to traverse interstellar distances almost instantaneously, communication signals like radio and TV transmissions were still limited to travelling no faster than the speed of light. So communication shards had to be physically transported via Indra ship from star system to star system like any other cargo.

"Otha, I know there's no such thing as telepathy," Zenn said, deciding to try a different tack. She knew her uncle's disdain for anything remotely mystical. She had to convince him she wasn't going off the deep end or, worse, allow him to make her father think that. "I know things like that have never stood up to real testing." And it was true. Claims of telepathy had never been shown to be more than pseudo-science, bad experimental controls, or just plain old wishful thinking.

The dimension-jumping Indra, of course, were a special case. It was known they could establish an elementary form of long-distance communication with others of their kind using the principle of quantum entanglement. It was a concept Zenn had never entirely sorted out in her head. But according to Otha, it involved two particles that were created in a way that makes them act like a single particle, even after they were separated. So, whatever happened to one of these particles instantly happened to the other one, regardless of where it was – in the next room, or on the other side of the universe.

Zenn knew this unique Indra ability wasn't some sort of magical ESP. It was straightforward, documented biophysics, directly linked to the Indras' billions of years of evolution. Indra brains were "entangled" in a way that let them ignore the distances between them when it came to communicating. But believing that a human could telepathically exchange thoughts with another being, on the other hand, was akin to believing in demons and unicorns.

"I know I'm not talking to animals," she went on, careful to keep her voice calm, analytical. "But it just seems as if sometimes I'm... extra-sensitive, or the animals are. What could cause that?"

There. That's a reasonable question. I'm asking for his input. He should respond to that.

"I can't say, girl," he said, running one hand over his scalp as if trying to dislodge a troublesome thought. "We'll... run it by Warra, see what your father says."

So much for the reasonable approach.

She thought hard to come up with some good reason not to tell Warra she was having trouble. She could think of nothing useful.

"But what I can say right now," Otha said, his tone brisk

again, "is that you need to focus on the week ahead. Your first in-soma run is no place for scattered thoughts. You need to be sharp for this test. Especially after what happened with the hound."

Did he understand what she was trying to tell him? Was he just dismissing everything she'd said? The truth was she didn't understand it herself. In any case, she'd told him and there was no turning back now. She couldn't press the point. Not with a man like Otha. She'd simply have to assemble her evidence, and lay it out logically for him when the time was right.

And Otha was clearly correct about the coming week, and what lay at its end. Anything less than a near-perfect score on the in-soma test was simply not an option. Calling it "a busy week" didn't do the prospect justice. But, she told herself for the hundredth time, she was ready. At least, as ready as she'd ever be for this particular procedure.

The first time she'd laid down in an in-soma pod and closed the door, she realized with a small shiver of anxiety that there was no room to move your arms or legs. The feeling as the cushioning surfaces pushed in on her body from all sides was like being wrapped tight in a high-tech coffin. But that wasn't what concerned her most about the device. What kept her up at night was the memory of one of her mother's early in-soma runs.

TEN

The insertion of the in-soma pod carrying her mother into the body of the female ultratheer had gone smoothly enough. Looking something like a short-legged, shaggy hippopotamus blown up to the size of a three-story building, ultratheers were huge but gentle herbivores from the lowland plains of the planet Taraque-Sine in the Gliesian system. The problem for Mai Scarlett started in the creature's second stomach; the pod was being impacted by the animal's grinding stones – boulders that helped break down the tough bog-ash trees it favored. The stomach muscles spasmed and two big stones caught the pod between them. In-soma pods are tough, but they do have their limits; a small rupture in the hull opened up. Finally, Otha had to fully sedate the patient and perform emergency abdominal surgery to get her mother out. Amazingly, the ultratheer survived with only a large scar.

It was Zenn's memory of the aftermath of this event that truly haunted her – the sight of her mother's foot as Otha carried her into the clinic ready room, the flesh raised into steaming blisters where the creature's stomach acid had burned away her boot.

Amid the confusion of it all, Zenn's mother had called Zenn over to the exam table where she lay and, through clenched teeth, reassured her daughter that she would be fine.

"But it hurt you," Zenn had said, feeling both fearful and angry. "It could have killed you."

"Zenn, this wasn't the animal's fault," her mother said firmly. Wincing against the pain, she reached out to take Zenn's hands in hers. Her mother's jet-black hair, usually hanging straight to her shoulders, was fanned out across the pillow under her head. Even now, Zenn remembered the scent of her hair that day, like apricot blossoms with a faint tang of antiseptic. "It's part of Mommy's job, honey," her mother said, her dark, almond-shaped eyes fixing on Zenn's. "We take risks sometimes to help animals get better. Understand?"

Her father had entered the ready room. He came to stand beside his wife.

"Mai? Are you alright? Otha said there was a problem, with the ultratheer." His gaze went to the aqua-plast cuff Otha was applying to her mother's lower leg. "How bad?"

"Not bad," she said, smiling up at him. But Zenn could tell she was hurting, and that she didn't want her father, or her, to know.

"Ah, well," her father laid one hand softly on her mother's head. "I'll assume the animal learned its lesson..." He winked at Zenn, trying, she thought, to look unconcerned. "You don't mess with Dr Mai Scarlett."

"Otha," Her mother propped herself up on one elbow to address her uncle, who had finished with the cuff and was now looking for something in a cupboard on the wall. "How's that abdominal incision look? You must've had your hands full getting that big girl closed up all by yourself."

"Hild gave me a hand," he said. "We managed. And the animal will be fine, just a little tender for a week or two."

Her mother lay back down, breathed out a long sigh and closed her eyes.

"Mom," Zenn said, "Weren't you afraid? Inside her stomach?"

She spoke without turning to face Zenn, her eyes still shut.

"Yes, honey, it's always a little scary to do in-soma work, to go into an animal." She looked up at Zenn. "But sometimes that's the only way we can help them. The important thing is to remember that these animals are depending on us. When they're very sick, they can't get better by themselves. And when I became an exovet, I took an oath. I promised to do whatever I could to help them. And sometimes, that means being a little afraid now and then. But you know what?" Her mother's dark eyes stared into Zenn's. "Sometimes, feeling afraid is how you know that you're doing something good and necessary. In fact, sometimes Zenn, doing the right thing is the scariest thing of all."

"And your mother should know," her father said. "But sometimes it's scarier for us on the outside than for her on the inside, huh kid?" He tousled Zenn's hair. "At least she could see what was going on in there."

"Dad!" Zenn ducked away from his hand, scowling. "It practically ate her. And you're just making jokes."

"You're right, you're right," he said, but she couldn't tell if he was taking her seriously or not. "Sometimes grownups do that... make jokes to make ourselves not be so scared about something. The important thing is..." he took her mother's hand and held it tight in both of his hands, "... your mom's alright, and we're here with her."

Afterwards, as far as Zenn knew, all of her mother's in-soma insertions went flawlessly. Except, of course, the last one.

As the truck rattled down the canyon road that led from Gil's back to the cloister, Zenn again consoled herself that she'd done all she could to prep for the upcoming test. And the news of her successfully completing her first in-soma run was one message she'd be eager to put on a ship headed to Enchara and Warra Scarlett.

She rubbed at her eyes, held her hands out in front of her – they still trembled. She quickly grabbed Katie, sat the rikkaset on her lap and kept her hands on the animal for the rest of the ride home.

They were about to turn into the cloister drive when another vehicle came around the curve just down the road, a plume of dust swirling up behind it. It was Ren Jakstra's half-track. Almost as dinged, bolted-together and beat up as Otha's truck, Ren's vehicle had regular tires in the front and tank-like treads in the back. Recently, Ren had cut off the front half of the roof to make it a convertible of sorts. It pulled up next to them and an arm waved from the driver's side to flag them down.

"Otha, glad I caught you," the constable said, pushing his dirty goggles up on his forehead. Clean pink circles of skin outlined his eyes where the goggles had sat, the rest of his face powdered with a coating of red road dust.

"This about the mortgage?" Otha said. "I told the bank in Zubrin I'd get back to them next week, see what we can work out."

"This ain't about the mortgage."

"Then what can I do for you, Ren?"

"Afraid it ain't me you can do for," Ren said. "It's the council. They want you there for the vote next week. Want to hear your side of things."

Otha groaned softly, squinting his eyes shut.

"Ren, why do they want me to waste a day doing that? You know the renewal is just a formality."

"Not this time," Ren told him. "Folks are tired of the situation. You may not have the votes you need."

"Why? What've you heard?"

"Just that this time, there might be a majority who think maybe you're sitting on some of the best land in this valley. Land that could be put to the common good, instead of... you know..."

"Instead of what? Instead of taking care of animals that don't have anyone else to turn to? Instead of doing what the Ciscan Order has done for over a century on Mars? And let's say they don't vote to renew, then what?"

"Then you lose your lease, Otha," Ren said flatly. "After that, you know how it works: once I serve notice, you got thirty days to appeal. If your appeal fails, your place will be declared illegal. Then the lawyers up in Zubrin get their teeth into it, and... well, who knows how that works out in the end?"

"Now what damn good would that do anybody, Ren?" Otha thumped his big hands on the steering wheel. "They come shut us down, sell off the clinic equipment and property and then what? What about the animals? Sick animals? What's the Arsia City council gonna do with them? They gonna house and feed and tend them while they wait for the owners to come get them? I'd like to see that."

"Hey," Ren held up one hand to silence Otha. "Your creatures would be the least of their concerns. Look, I don't say it's right. But they'd have to do whatever was most... expeditious."

"Put them all down, you mean?" Otha said, his voice dropping to a growl, shoulder muscles going tense.

Zenn jerked forward in her seat to look past Otha at Ren. "They'd kill them?" she said, incredulous. "Otha, could they do that?"

Otha glanced at her, eyes narrowed. He was grinding his teeth now, breathing hard through his nose. "No. They couldn't," he told her. "No one's going to do that." He turned back to Ren. "And I gotta say... seems to me this whole thing with the council coming up just now, it smells bad. I mean, now that people have abused their own land, poisoned the soil with chemicals and enzymes, depleted their wells? Well, it's quite a coincidence the lease on our land all the sudden might not get renewed, eh? Very coincidental."

Ren shrugged again, sucked at his dusty mustache and spit. "Wouldn't know about that. But I do know people are hurting. And mad. Mad as I've seen 'em. So, you show up at the council, or you don't. It's your call. I'm just doin' my job here."

"Yeah, I'll think about it."

Ren pulled his goggles back down over his eyes and put the truck into gear. "Like I say. Show up or don't. Your call." The half-track rumbled backwards into the cloister drive, came out again and drove away.

Otha watched the constable's truck clatter off down the road.

"I'm no good with this stuff," he said, eyes down, the heat gone from his voice. "Warra always handled the council meetings, mortgage details, the damn taxes. Your father was the main reason we stayed afloat these past few years. I mean, before he left." He gave her a quick look, then turned away and stared out through the dust-streaked windshield.

"Maybe that's what we should ask dad about, when we send the shard," she said tentatively.

Instead of the part about me talking to animals and

generally messing things up...

"Yes, maybe." He patted her leg. "We'll get it sorted out. Nothing to worry about." But for the first time, Zenn could hear the doubt in her uncle's voice, and for the first time, felt a new kind of fear rise inside her; fear that maybe this was more than even Otha could handle. And it had to be handled. The alternative didn't bear thinking about. She thought of her father instead, but that really didn't offer any encouragement either.

If he was here, this wouldn't be happening. Fine. We'll fix it ourselves. Somehow.

Otha nodded at the closed gates ahead of them, and Zenn started to get out to go and pull the bell rope to alert those inside that they were back. Just then, the gate doors creaked open. It was Hamish. He rattled one claw at them in greeting.

Zenn sat back again, the unthinkable thought burning in her mind: the clinic closed, the pens and enclosures empty. The only home she'd ever known, lost. Where would they go? And the animals, her animals...

Otha drove into the cloister yard and killed the engine. Holding Katie, she got out of the truck and headed in. Echoing off the high cliff walls on either side of the compound, the distant calls of the clinic's creatures ebbed and flowed through the afternoon air.

ELEVEN

It was midmorning the next day when Otha informed Zenn their supply of dried rhina grub was running low. The grub was the larval stage of the giant Tanduan rhina moth. When dried, the concentrated aroma and flavor made it irresistible to swamp sloos. As such, it was an integral part of Zenn's upcoming in-soma pod insertion test.

So it was just past noon when Zenn again found herself in Otha's venerable pickup. But this time, she was at the wheel, concentrating hard, attempting to avoid the fragments of old, shattered pavement that littered the road from the cloister into Arsia City.

In the passenger seat next to her, Liam Tucker lounged, offering occasional irritating comments regarding her driving skills, while in the cargo bed behind them Hamish crouched on top of half a dozen crates of freshly shucked gen-soy beans. She was to barter the gen-soy for rhina grub at Wilson Ndinga's grocery store.

While truck-driving wasn't part of the test, making sure that the pod and the other elements of the in-soma run were ready was her responsibility. So, in a way, the trip to town was part of the whole process. Plus, Zenn had gotten the impression from Otha it was high time for her to take over the periodic supply runs into Arsia. Despite her general aversion to towners, this was fine with her; she liked driving the truck. And, after a few practice drives in the open field between the infirmary and the southwest compound wall, she was now at the point where she no longer ground the gears each time she shifted.

Wilson Ndinga's little store on Arsia's main street carried a hodge-podge of off-world herbs and a few other hard-to-get foodstuffs along with his standard fare, and Otha had arranged with him to occasionally obtain exotic animal feed for the cloister. Wilson knew Otha would pay – or, would promise to pay – especially well for the grub, so Wilson had a standing order with orbital ferry pilots to bring some back to Mars whenever a starship returned from a visit to the Tandua system.

After her initial attack of nerves at having Liam along for the ride, Zenn was finally beginning to relax and enjoy herself at the wheel. The feeling of speed and freedom, even on a dirt road never intended for fast travel, was exhilarating. It made her wonder about what lay at the far reaches of the road, what it would be like to just keep driving and driving, over the next hill, around the next curve in the canyon wall. Her momentary lapse in focus was broken by a vicious jolt when they hit a good-sized chunk of pavement.

"Nice aim, Scarlett," Liam said, bracing himself with one leg against the dashboard. "You hit that one dead-on."

"You think you could do better?" she shot back.

"Whoa," he raised his hands defensively. "Just trying to be helpful."

"Right," she told him, swerving hard to avoid the next fragment. "Well, I can do without the help, thanks."

Hamish's presence on the drive into town made sense: he could lift the gen-soy crates with one arm; that would come in handy when they unloaded. Liam, Zenn assumed, had just attached himself to the trip to avoid being put to work back at the cloister.

As they neared the first sorry-looking huts of the shantytown ringing Arsia, Zenn down-shifted and they slowed. The scent of campfires wafted through the truck's open windows. An old man with a blanket draped around his shoulders huddled beneath a tarp he'd stretched from the top of a large shipping container to form a sort of lean-to. He didn't look up as they passed. Ahead, there was what appeared to be an entire family walking in a group at the side of the road, two adults and four children, the adults in their mid-thirties, the children young. The man pushed a wheelbarrow piled high with what looked like all their worldly possessions. As Zenn pulled up alongside them, the woman moved to herd her children away from the road, and Zenn saw her face.

"That's Sindri Govinda," she whispered to Liam. He leaned forward to see. Zenn called out, "Sindri?"

The woman stopped when she saw who it was. The rest of the family stopped too, and Zenn braked to a halt. The woman wore a tired, empty expression, and said nothing, but just stood as the smallest child, a girl, came and put her arms around her mother's waist. The whole family was dressed in multiple layers of clothing, and they all shared the same coffee complexions, black hair and dark eyes.

"What are you... Are you alright?" Zenn asked.

"We're moving into town," Sindri said, speaking as if describing the death of a loved one. "We couldn't stay at the farm." She lifted one arm to indicate the wheelbarrow. "This is all we had time to save."

"The bary-gens go off-line out at your place?" Liam asked.

"Yes," Sindri said. "The generators. They all failed at once. Not just our place. The whole canyon. We were lucky to get the kids and escape before the entire valley decompressed. Now…" She raised her gaze to survey the grim prospect of the shantytown, but she had no further words. Her husband came up behind her.

"Zenn, Liam," the man greeted them, put his hands on the shoulders of his wife and child. Dangling from his belt on a leather thong was a wooden club. Zenn wondered if that was their only protection during the family's long trek into town.

"Hello, Dharm," Zenn said. "I'm so sorry. About the farm. Do you have a place to go? In town?"

"Brin Daws offered us his spare room," Dharm Govinda said. "We'll be fine. We just need… We'll get settled in at Brin's and take things from there." It was clear he was trying to sound more optimistic than he felt. "One day at a time, right?"

"Well, please let us know if we can help," Zenn said. But she knew there was really nothing they could do for the Govindas. Or for the dozens of other families who'd been forced into town over the past year. There were empty rooms in the dorm at the cloister, of course, and they'd made it clear to everyone the Ciscans were willing to take people in. But for those from outside the cloister, even life in the shantytown was apparently preferable to living alongside the Ciscan's alien animals.

"No, no, that's alright," Dharm said, looking away. "Like I say. We'll be fine." He motioned to his family and took up the wheelbarrow handles, and the little group set out again. Zenn put the truck into gear and drove on.

"Nine Hells," Liam muttered. "If they're right, all of Tartarus just bit the dust."

"Can that be true? All of Tartarus Canyon?" Zenn didn't want to believe this. "If they lost pressure out there, what about the McCalls? The Stoyanovas? All those families?"

There were seven or eight farmsteads strung along the depths of Tartarus Canyon. If all of the barymetric generators protecting the valley really had failed, Arsia's shantytown would be seeing a serious influx of new residents.

Zenn adjusted the rearview mirror to look back at the bedraggled family.

"At least Sindri and Dharm have somewhere to... Oh!" She stomped hard on the brakes, throwing Liam hard against the dash. The truck screeched to a halt a few feet from a group of men bent over something in the road.

"Nine Hells, Scarlett," Liam growled at her, recovering himself and rubbing his forehead.

"Well, what are they doing in the middle of road?" Zenn asked.

The half-dozen towner men were attempting to raise up a frame of some sort off the surface of the roadway. It was as wide as the road, maybe ten feet tall. The framework was constructed of lengths of rusty pipe, forming a rectangular opening with old chain link fencing stretched across it. Strands of barbed wire ran along the top.

"They're putting up a gate," Liam said. "Unless you run them all down, that is."

"A gate? To block the road?" she frowned at him.

"You don't get out much, do ya, Scarlett?" Liam smirked at her. "It's the gate for this north checkpoint. They've put them on all four roads entering town."

She saw now that on both sides of the road a makeshift

wall ran in either direction. It was cobbled together from more chain link, old sections of vehicles, miscellaneous junk and heaped-up dirt.

"Checkpoints? You mean, like roadblocks? What for?"

"To keep people out of town who shouldn't be there," Liam said.

"People from the valleys? The ones who lost their farms?"

"Yeah, fraid so," Liam said. "It's cause the shantytown's getting so big. The council voted last month to start controlling who comes in. Thus, checkpoints and the wall."

"But why would they do that? What do they think people are going to do? Rob them?"

"Already happened. Somebody broke the back door lock on Gangsted's grainary, stole a truckload of amaranth. Everybody knows it was refugees who did it. Ren just hasn't caught em yet."

Zenn had to stop the truck to wait for the men to tip the gate upright. When they'd done this, she saw they'd attached metal wheels to the base of the piping. Struggling to keep the heavy structure from falling over again, they rolled it off to one side of the road and leaned it against what appeared to be a small guard shack, built of corrugated scrap metal with bars welded over its windows.

At the sight of the truck, one of the men broke free from the group and came over.

"Hey. You're the Scarlett, girl ain't ya?" It was Emrik Lund. "Thought I recognized Otha's truck." Emrik was tall, thin and scarecrowish, with a fringe of short, brown hair circling the bald dome of his head. He wore baggy, home-made hempweave pants and an old sweatsuit top with a black scarf tucked into the collar. The soles of his boots were held on with lengths of twine.

"Yes. I'm Zenn."

"Say… Zenn… do me a favor?" He squinted down at her. "Tell Otha he still owes me for the stone work I did on that foundation out to your place. It's been a couple months now. Pel Shandin's after me for payment on the stone. I need credits or goods in kind."

Zenn felt her face go instantly red. She should be used to this sort of thing by now, of course. The cloister was behind on any number of bills. But it still got to her. For some reason, having Liam looking on made it even worse.

"I'll remind him, Mr Lund. I'm sure he'll get back to you right away."

"Uh huh," Emrik said. "I gotta tell ya I've heard that before. Look, it's none of my business, but you folks owe money all over town." He leaned with both hands on the door of the truck and peered in at her. "We've all got bills of our own, ya know?"

"I know, Mr Lund," Zenn told him. "Look, we're expecting a big client to pay us soon."

His look said he'd also heard this before. "We're taking care of a Kiran whalehound. The royals always pay on time."

"Well, if they do, I'd like my name at the top of the list. But Pel tells me there's a chance the cloister's lease could get voted down next session." Did everyone in town know about their lease? She felt her checks going even redder. "It'd be good if Otha could settle up with me before that happens."

"I heard about the vote, Mr Lund. And I know that some people on the council are concerned about our animals, but…"

"Some people?" He raised his eyebrows at this.

"But," she continued, "our animals, our patients have never bothered anybody. There's no reason to make us close the clinic, to make us stop our work."

"Oh, there are reasons," he said. "Like the Authority and the Rift, for starters. You think the Earthers will ever do business with Mars as long as aliens keep bringin' their creatures down here? Sick creatures? Off-wa monsters with who knows what kinda diseases right outside our town?" Saying this, he glared at Hamish in the cargo bed of the truck, then shook his finger at him. "I mean, lookit this thing you got in the back there. Nine Hells! You're paradin' that six-legged whatzit around big as life and expect folks not to get bent outta shape? You Ciscans need to wake up and see what's what, missy. And you need to tell Otha to get back to me, pronto."

"Hey," Liam leaned across in front of Zenn to confront Emrik. "You'll get paid, Lund. Scarlett here just told you they've got credits coming from the Kirans."

Well said, Zenn thought at this unexpected show of support. Maybe having the towner boy along wasn't so annoying after all.

"Yeah, well," Emrik stood up and leaned away from the truck window. "Talk is cheap, Tucker. Now, if you people got business in town, go on through so we can finish up this gate. We gotta get it secure by sundown."

Zenn put the truck into gear, and pulled ahead onto Arsia's main street. It looked even shabbier than usual. Lined with one- and two-story buildings of stone, synthwood and the odd canvas tent, Zenn saw immediately that three or four more storefront windows had recently been boarded up. Garbage collection had also apparently become a casualty of the times, and teetering piles of trash had sprung up here and there on the curbside. Outside the derelict building that once housed the town's only dentist, a scrawny, yellow mongrel dog pulled at a scrap of something potentially edible in the debris blocking the entranceway.

"Don't let Lund's bad-mouthing get you down, Scarlett," Liam said, slouching back in his seat as they drove slowly down the street. "It's not like everybody in town hates you."

Zenn knew Liam meant this to be encouraging, but she also knew that what Emrik Lund had said about the cloister's rising debt level, and the towners' sentiments in general, was true.

When she stopped the truck in front of the cinderblock hut that housed Ndinga's store, Wilson immediately bustled out to meet them, rubbing his hands together. He was a small, energetic man in his sixties, wearing a colorful kaftan sort of garment that reached to the ground.

"Ah, mistress Scarlett. I know what you're here for," he said in his lilting Earther accent, his wide smile revealing several gold-alloy teeth. "The rhina grub, isn't it then?" He went to the back of the truck and looked in. "And what have you brought to tempt old Wilson today?"

TWELVE

Two days later, Zenn was returning from early-morning chores when she overheard Hild talking to someone in the calefactory entrance hall. Katie had accompanied her that morning, and Zenn scooped her up into her arms, opened the door leading into the hall, and was surprised to see Vic LeClerc. The woman held a mug of hot tea in her hand, and wore an old-fashioned cowboy hat atop her white-blonde hair. She was tall, attractive in a severe sort of way, and a bit younger than Otha. She was also one of the valley's wealthiest landowners, with a family history dating back to the earliest days of the colony. The LeClercs raised the only remaining source of fresh milk and meat in the area – a voracious herd of scruffy but adaptable little goats. So, instead of calling herself a farmer, Vic insisted she was a livestock rancher, the ever-present cowboy hat worn as proof. Vic LeClerc was also president of the Arsia town council.

"Zenn, you're just in time," Hild said. "Vic's herd needs worming. She asked us if you could take care of it. I said you'd be glad to."

"The Sister told me you're familiar with the procedure,"

Vic said, giving Zenn an appraising look. Katie stretched out to try and sniff Vic's arm, prompting the woman to pull back, eyebrows arched.

"Can you come with me now?" Vic said, setting her mug down on the windowsill.

"Yes, sure," Zenn said, the thrill of leaving the cloister's confines making her feel just a little more awake than she'd felt moments before. "I just need to get the meds."

"Otha left the pre-mix here for you," Hild said, pointing out the large tub of homemade worming powder sitting on the floor.

"The Sister says she's got a loaf of fresh bread for us," Vic said. "You can take the medicine out to the truck and I'll be there in a minute."

Zenn put Katie down, picked up the tub of powder and carried it out into the cloister drive.

Oh no. Not him...

Leaning against the fender of Vic's aging but well-maintained six-wheel utility truck was Graad Dokes. The heavyset ranch foreman wore bulky, insulated canvas pants and knee-high rubberoid boots. His fleshy jaw was dark with his usual unshaven stubble, and a fat ring of tarnished silver hung from one ear. He looked up at Zenn from under the brim of his leather hat and spit a gob of black tobacco juice into the dust.

"So Otha's sending in the B-team, huh?" he said, continuing to lean back against the truck.

"He's in surgery all morning," Zenn said, her mood quickly souring at the prospect of riding out to the LeClerc ranch in Graad's company.

"You comin' out on your own then? For the goats? Just you?" Graad said.

"Just me."

"Well, well. They're lettin' you out of Fort Freak all on your own. Aren't we a big girl?"

Zenn said nothing to this.

Why encourage him?

"First time outside the walls all on your lonesome?" he asked.

As a matter of fact, it was. But she wouldn't give Graad the satisfaction of knowing he was right.

"Guess we'll just have to live with it," he went on. "I mean, having the B-team. That being you." He nodded at her, grinning at his own presumed cleverness, and spit again.

"It's just worming," Zenn said, then immediately regretted taking the bait.

"Not just worming to us, girlie," he said, the grin vanishing. He jabbed a stubby finger at her. "Those goats are money, kid, and don't you forget…"

A shrill animal shriek sounded close behind him.

With a spastic jerk of his body, Graad propelled himself away from the truck, arms flailing wildly at the air. "What the…?" He spun around to see Katie materialize on the hood of the truck where he'd been leaning. He raised a hand to swat her away.

"You stinkin' overgrown rat…"

"Don't!" Zenn screamed. He stopped his swing, dropped his arm. "She didn't mean anything. Katie, come." Zenn signed, and Katie hopped to the ground, ran to Zenn and leaped up into her arms.

"It ain't natural…" he growled, red-faced. "That thing comin' outta nowhere… Nine Hells. Damn near gave me a heart attack."

"It's just her usual behavior," Zenn said, stroking the agitated rikkaset. "It's completely natural."

"And talkin'. Damn alien off-wa thing like that, talkin' to

humans in sign-lingo. That natural, too? I don't think so, girlie."

"She's intelligent. If she's smart enough to talk to us, why shouldn't she?" Zenn said, feeling proud of herself for sticking up for Katie.

"Intelligent, huh? Well, you better hope so. I mean, it better be in-tell-i-gent enough to keep away from some of the freaks and monsters you got out here..."

"You don't need to worry about Katie," Zenn said.

"Because it'd be a shame if it, you know, wandered into the wrong cage some dark night." His lips curled up into the slightest of smiles. "Wandered in and... snap!" He mimed breaking a twig between his hands. "...there go those smart little paws."

Was he... threatening Katie? Zenn felt her low-key anger mounting to fury.

He leaned down, hands on knees to bring his eyes level with hers. "Wouldn't be talkin' any smart-ass sign-lingo then, would it, girlie? No. I don't think so."

Before she could say something she would almost certainly regret, Vic appeared at the calefactory door. She cradled a loaf of bread wrapped in a clean dish towel.

"All set out here? Good," she said, oblivious to the charged atmosphere. She walked to the other side of the truck and opened the door. "Let's go. We need to get the novice out to the ranch."

Still fuming, Zenn put Katie down and shooed her back through the calefactory door.

"And you stay. Stay, Katie." Zenn spoke the words and signed emphatically. Katie sat down in the doorway and became suddenly very interested in licking a spot on her foreleg, pointedly ignoring Zenn. Keeping one eye on the rikkaset, Zenn went back out, snatched up the tub of meds and got into the back seat behind Vic and Graad. She slammed the door shut hard as she could, and that helped drain off some of her wrath. But just as Graad started the engine, Hamish appeared at the doorway, and then ambled out into the drive.

"Novice Zenn." he called to her. "Please delay your leaving a moment."

"What is it, Hamish?"

He stooped down at the truck window.

"The director-abbot instructs me to accompany you."

Graad pushed his hat up on his forehead. "What? We've gotta lug this off-wa cockroach with us? Nine Hells. What for?"

"The director-abbot tells me attending this activity will increase my knowledge of the procedure involved. He thus instructed me to..."

"Oh, very well," Vic said, sounding suddenly impatient. "If you must, then... just get in the back."

Zenn knew full well Otha had other reasons for sending Hamish along. Hamish was babysitting. Hyper-vigilant as usual, Otha still wanted Zenn to have a chaperone outside the cloister walls. And almost as irritating: her sense of relief at having Hamish come along.

"Well?" Vic said, glaring at Hamish, who hadn't moved.

"Novice Zenn, do I have your permission for this?"

"Yes you do, Hamish. Hop in."

Hamish did as he was told, climbing into the cargo bed. The truck's back end dipped with the addition of his weight. Graad glanced sideways at Vic.

"Boss?" Graad said. "Ya know, our... visitor, out at the ranch?"

"We'll just have to conduct our business another time," Vic said, her voice sharp. "Get going."

Now Vic now sounded more than impatient. She was mad. Because of Hamish? It wasn't his fault he was here. Otha had sent him out, after all. Why was the woman so put out?

With a final grunt of disgust from the foreman, they pulled out onto the road and headed east.

THIRTEEN

The ride to the LeClerc ranch was mercifully silent except for Vic's occasional curt comments about the dead and dying farms they passed and how their owners were "...just too foolish or idle to keep their places running." When they pulled into the circular drive in front of the rambling, synthwood ranch house, there was a tri-shaw taxi parked in the yard. The taxi's puller, a black-haired, raggedly dressed boy who looked too small for the job, sat on the house steps. He jumped up at their approach, and went to stand by his cart.

As Graad brought the truck to a stop, the ranch house door opened and a short, stocky figure emerged and shuffled down the steps toward them. It was a skirni. He was about a foot shorter than Zenn, with the squat, muscular build of his species. His face presented a squashed-in, bulldog muzzle of hairless, black-and-brown blotched flesh, and the under-slung jaw sprouted two or three peg-like teeth that protruded upward. The eyes were black and bulging, the ears small and round, perched low on his head. "You want me to deal with that little..." Graad scowled, and seemed to be searching for a word to describe the alien. "...with our visitor?"

"Park the truck. I'll talk to him," Vic said.

When they'd all exited and Graad had driven off, the skirni came up to them. He seemed distinctly upset about something.

"This is not as we agreed." He gestured at them with both hands, his voice a guttural rasp. His gaze landed on Hamish. "Not as agreed."

The skirni's customary garb consisted of layers of colorful robes and scarves and what appeared to be an entire store-full of jewelry and gemstones on his fingers and around his neck. It was a look that always reminded Zenn of blink-novs she'd read about certain nomadic Earther tribes. And, also like those wandering tribes, the skirni race was homeless, with a penchant for fortune-telling and crafty bargaining. Zenn waited, expecting Vic to introduce them.

"I'm afraid the situation is unavoidable," Vic said to the skirni, ignoring her and Hamish. "You should return to Arsia, and we'll... make other arrangements." She raised a hand, indicating the tri-shaw. A look of angry confusion momentarily crossed the skirni's face. He glanced up at Zenn, his probing, black-bead stare so intense it made her take an involuntary step back.

"Other arrangements," he growled. He turned with jangle of clinking jewelry and waddled toward the tri-shaw, walking with the assistance of a thick, hairless tail that poked out from under his robes, giving him a rolling, rhythmic sort of gait. "Arrangements, yes. After my time is wasted."

"Well," Zenn said quietly to Hamish. "That was strange."

"Oh?"

"A skirni? An 'off-wa', paying a visit to Vic LeClerc? Not exactly an everyday occurrence, that's all."

They waited as the skirni climbed into the back of the tri-shaw and the young puller slipped on his harness and picked up the two hand-shafts. Vic and the skirni exchanged a few more words, then the alien shouted at the boy to go and the cart creaked out onto the road and moved off toward town.

Minutes later, inside the LeClercs' vast stone-block milking barn, Zenn stood surrounded by an unsettling swarm of several dozen goats. Unsettling because every animal there - the kids, the does, from smallest to largest – was identical. Produced by cloning from a single, original Nubian Dwarf species that arrived with one of the first Earther ships to reach Mars, each cookie-cutter clone had the same pattern of chestnut-and-white markings, the same floppy ears and compact body shape, and the same plaintive bleat. Herded into the barn for their treatment, the goats milled around, hopping onto and jumping down off every available surface. Up in the barn's rafters, three furtive cats peered down suspiciously, tails twitching. When Hamish entered the barn to stand near the doorway, the cats silently vanished.

"So, he's your... friend? The skirni?" Zenn said to Vic, fishing for information.

"Not a friend. Business associate," was all Vic had to say on the subject. "Now, I'm assuming this is Otha's usual mix?" She pointed at the tub Zenn held.

"Yes. He blends it the same every year," Zenn told her. "One part mustard seed to two parts sorghum and kipfruit rind, in a diatomaceous earth matrix. It's the diatomaceous earth that kills the worms, disrupts their digestion. We have a natural deposit of it on the cloister grounds."

"Do you?" Vic said, her interest piqued.

"Yes, left over from when Mars still had oceans and algae. Otha says we should mine the stuff and sell it."

Vic said nothing to this, and Zenn realized after a few

seconds that the woman was looking at her as if she herself was some otherworldly animal come into the barn.

"So, Zenn," she said. "You seem like such a bright young lady. And capable. It seems a pity. You, all alone, the only child, out there at the Ciscan compound. I'm surprised Otha doesn't allow you out. On your own, I mean. A girl your age should really be going into town, meeting boys, making friends."

The idea struck Zenn as peculiar, and less than agreeable. It's not like she'd fit in with the kids of Arsia. Not now. It wasn't like she'd never made an effort. When she was younger, of course, before she'd formulated the Rule, several of the more adventurous girls from town had come out to visit. To "play," actually. But their concept of fun was lost on Zenn, even at ten years old. The towner girls wanted to engage in activities like make-believe tea parties and giving cute names to the dolls and stuffed animals they'd brought with them. Zenn wanted to show them her real animals, explain where the creatures came from, show them how to feed a seep-demon and watch the food being digested in its transparent intestinal tract. It only took a few visits before the towner girls stopped coming.

"I don't really have a lot of free time," Zenn said "My studies and chores at the cloister keep me pretty occupied."

But Vic's mention of town brought back Ren's words about the looming vote. "I know that some people don't like living near us. They want us to sell the land. Sell out and leave." Zenn chose her words carefully. The LeClercs were one of the cloister's few regular customers on Mars, and almost the only one that paid its bills on time. Otha would be furious if Zenn did anything to spoil that. "But the animals need the clinic, they wouldn't have anywhere to go. That's why Otha won't sell."

"And he's right," Vic said, turning away from the window, all her attention returning to Zenn again. "At least about not selling. No. The land would just be divided up and auctioned off to towners and all the other lazy no-goods in this valley. People who don't know the first thing about making their land produce." The woman's eyes flashed, her voice hard. "They'd ruin anything they got their hands on. Just like they've ruined the rest of the land in this valley."

Vic seemed to catch herself then, seemed to realize she was just talking to a novice, after all. Zenn could see it in her face, but that only made her more determined to talk about what had been bothering her.

"So, you're on the council, right? The city council?"

"Yes," Vic said. "I am."

"The council vote? About the lease? Ren Jakstra says there's a chance it could turn out bad for us."

"Ren thinks that, does he? And told you?" She sounded surprised that Zenn knew anything about the subject, let alone had an opinion about it. "Well now, novice, council matters are a complicated business. But," she smiled faintly, "It's nothing for you to worry about."

Zenn was getting fed up with hearing about all the things she shouldn't worry about.

"But what about the animals? What would happen to them?" Not to mention what would happen to her and Otha and the others.

"Ah, the animals..." Vic said. "A young girl, like you. Surrounded by all those..." She gave Hamish a sideways glance "...alien things."

"They're not things," Zenn said before she could catch herself. "I mean, they're living, feeling animals. It's our job to help them." She had a thought: "Like we help you with your goats."

"Well," Vic smiled again – but not with her eyes. "That's entirely different, isn't it? Our goats came here with us from Earth. And they're a benefit to everyone in the valley, aren't they? They supply milk, cheese, meat, leather. But you can't be blamed for the way you feel, I suppose. It's how you were raised." The woman looked off through the barn's nearest window. "You know, novice," Vic said, her voice softening just a little. "It used to be different here, in the valley. Farms flourishing. The village prospering." The woman continued to stare out the window for a long moment more, then brought her gaze back to Zenn. "But that was long ago, before the people used up the land. Before the Rift made it so they couldn't repair the damage they'd done." She fluttered a hand in the direction of the outside world, an unmistakable twinge of distaste briefly shadowing her face.

She turned to the milling, jumping goats. "Now then, you've got work to do, with all my little darlings." Zenn noticed when Vic gestured at the animals that she wore new goatskin gloves on her hands – soft, supple kid-skin gloves.

"You let me know when you've finished, and I'll have one of the hired hands drive you home." As she walked past Hamish, she pointed at the coleopt, but looked back at Zenn. "And don't let this creature of yours go creeping around the ranch."

When Vic has closed the barn door behind her, Hamish approached Zenn.

"This human – Vic does not relish my presence on her property," Hamish said. "I have also perceived a similar sentiment from the human town dwellers. I understand that Earth-humans have a difficulty with non-terrestrial life forms, due to this Orinoco illness you described. I am wondering: do Mars-humans equate myself with such an illness?"

"I'm afraid it's a case of guilt by association," Zenn said. Hamish cocked his head at her.

"I am to be guilty? Based on not even the slimmest connection to reasoning? Mars-humans behave in such a manner?"

"Oh yes. They do. In fact sometimes I think they're proud of it."

"This is not an efficient way to conduct oneself in the world, if I may say so. Why do they allow their minds to operate in this faulty fashion?"

"Good question," she said. "I guess they see all aliens kind of like these goats. You know, identical clones. They lump all aliens into the same category. It's easier than having to think about each one as an individual. Then, they tell themselves it's alright to judge you by the way you look, instead of getting to know you. Instead of paying attention to who you really are."

"But your mind does not function in this eccentric fashion. Nor does the director-abbot's or Sister Hild's. Do your brain-circuits connect differently?"

"Well, no." Zenn smiled at him. "It's more like what the brains are exposed to, when a person is growing up. But when you put it that way, maybe on some level the circuits are wired up differently."

"Whatever the circuitry," Hamish said, turning to look at the goats, "I am glad you do not view me as some goat-clone-coleopt. I thank you."

"You're welcome, Hamish." Zenn smiled up at him. "Now…" She bent to pick up the tub of worming powder. "We better get to work."

As she said this, several dozen expectant, perfectly matching faces gave Zenn and Hamish their curious, fearless looks, while several dozen identical throats filled the goat-scented barn with their one-note bleat.

FOURTEEN

When Zenn was sure each goat had eaten a sufficient amount of the medicated grain mixture, she and Hamish stepped out of dark barn into the bright afternoon. The process had taken longer than she'd expected. Most of the young kids were less interested in a snack than in playing with each other and scampering sideways through the barn until they bounced off a wall or another goat. Irritated to find the sun was already directly overhead, she started off at a trot toward the farmhouse, Hamish scuttling along behind. Liam was just coming out of the front door, followed by Graad Dokes.

"Scarlett," Liam said, coming down the steps. He raised a hand in greeting, but he wasn't wearing his usual confident smile. "Vic said you were here. Working on the goats?"

"Worming," she said, nodding back at the barn. "All done. Vic said someone would drive me back to the cloister."

"You an' your bug-freak goin' back to tend your off-wa monsters, are ya?" Graad said, ignoring the fact that Hamish was standing right there, listening. Graad pulled a rag from his pocket and blew his nose in it. "Well, better her than us, huh, kid?" He slapped at Liam's shoulder, pushing him off balance.

"We don't think they're monsters," Zenn said, tired of continually making this particular correction to those like Graad. She also had to make an effort not to add "you moron". "They're just different, that's all."

"Different. I'll say," Graad chortled. "Different enough to take your head off if you're not careful. Not to mention all the acres they squander. A waste of good grazing land, shameful waste."

"It's not wasted, Graad." Zenn said, knowing he was just provoking her, but unable to keep quiet.

"Sure it is." Graad grinned maliciously at her. "Tell her, kid." He shoved Liam again, but Liam just shrugged and looked away. Graad's eyes darted from Liam to Zenn, then back to Liam.

"Oh. I forgot. Mr Tucker here is growin' a soft spot for monsters and freaks, aren't ya kid? Liam's spendin' so much time out at the freak-church I'm thinkin' of callin' him Friar Tuck. Gonna be a certified expert in freakology soon, eh, Friar? But just keep this in mind," Graad leaned close to Liam. "Before the Ciscans touched down, the LeClercs owned all the land in this valley, far as you can see." He thrust one of his thick hands up in a sweeping arc. On the distant horizon, part of the cloister's chapel ruins could be glimpsed at the far end of the valley, jutting up like giant, black rib bones picked clean. "Before her kind moved in," he hooked a thumb at Zenn. "Before they started bringing their off-wa cockroaches and talkin' rats and devil knows what all to Mars. This dried-up rock of a planet was foul enough without their monsters with their plagues and who-knows-what. But at least when the LeClercs had the land, they put it to use for people. Human people. Not alien freaks." Graad's hand came to rest on Liam's shoulder, and it looked to Zenn as if he was squeezing, hard. Liam pretended not to notice. "You will remember that, won't ya, Friar Tuck?"

Liam seemed about to say something back at him, then turned to her instead, pulling away from the foreman's grip.

"You know, Scarlett, why don't I give you two a ride home? Now." Without waiting for an answer, he walked past her toward the shed where Vic garaged her vehicles. She motioned to Hamish and they followed.

"Yeah, don't let me keep ya," Graad called after them. "You and the Friar here will be wantin' to get back to pet your monsters. Don't worry 'bout us humans. We'll just eat the damn red dirt. Plenty of that on this godforsaken rock. You be sure and leave some for us, won't ya?"

"Ignore him," Liam said as they walked away.

"I intend to. You too, Hamish."

"I will attempt to do this," Hamish said. "This person Graad Dokes seems like a very angry human man, if I may say."

"He just... likes to bluster, you know?" Liam said as they came to the garage. "Shoots his mouth off. He doesn't really want to be here anyway. On Mars. He takes it out on anybody within earshot." They entered the garage, where Vic had three trucks and an old tractor parked.

"What's he got against Mars?" Zenn asked.

"He was in the last batch of colonists from Earth. Bartered five years' labor for a berth on one of the final flights. Being indentured, they call it. I think he had a pretty bad time working for the guy who'd bought his passage. Anyway, that kinda poisoned him on the whole idea of Mars. When he gets drunk, only thing he talks about it how he's stuck here and can't get home again cause of the Rift."

They stopped next to the six-wheeler and Liam reached

out with one hand and banged several times on the side of the truck. Zenn gave him a puzzled look.

"Barn cats," he said. "They sleep under there. Don't have the sense to get outta the way."

An orange-red cat the size of a small dog emerged from under the truck, stretched languidly and walked over to rub his head against Liam's legs. He bent to scratch it behind the ears, provoking the loudest purr Zenn had ever heard.

"And who's this?" she asked.

"He's Zeus. King of the ranch. He keeps an eye on things for me around here. Don't ya, big guy?"

Zenn bent to give him a pat.

"Looks like he's had to fight for his crown," she said, noting the battle scars on the cat's head and the missing chunk from one ear.

"Yeah, but the challengers get the idea after the first time," Liam said. "And after that it's peace and quiet cause everybody knows not to mess with him. Alright, buddy," Liam shooed him away with the wave of his hand. "Look out now, we're gonna drive outta here."

Zeus ran to the garage door and out into the yard.

Liam pulled open the driver's door and Zenn went around to climb in on the other side. Hamish took up his position in the truck bed.

"You know," Zenn said. "Graad is really annoying, whatever the reason. Why does your aunt put up with him?"

"Sometimes I wonder," Liam scowled, stepped on the starter, and the engine coughed to life.

"You and Graad don't really get along, huh?"

"Get along? I hate the bastard," Liam said, jamming the truck into gear.

The vehemence of Liam's response startled Zenn.

"Why's that?" she asked.

"Because, alright?" He gave her a look, and then stared out at the road.

Oops... touchy subject.

"So," she said, breaking the silence after they'd driven out onto the road. "The skirni back there? Vic said he was here on business?"

"Yeah, I don't really know much about it. Something to do with swapping tanned goat leather for a shipment of drip-irrigator equipment. If I know skirnis, the irrigation stuff is stolen and Vic's gonna be sorry she got involved. But hey, it's her ranch."

"Well, that's a new twist," Zenn said, "Vic LeClerc making deals with an off-worlder."

"Business is business, far as Vic's concerned. He's kind of a funny little guy, though. Asks lots of questions. Wants to know all about the ranch, about Arsia, about the cloister and the whole valley. I just never thought of off-worlders like that. Being so curious and all."

"Well, it's probably good for you to meet him. Broaden your horizons."

"Yeah, maybe... but I'd rather not talk about my aunt and her off-wa buddy," he said, his cocky smile returning. "So instead, why don't you tell me what poor, helpless animal's gonna be your next victim?"

"You mean which patient will be fortunate enough to have me looking after them?"

"Right. Sure. That's what I meant to say."

"When we get back I'll check on the Kiran's whalehound. See how his infected tear duct is doing."

"Yeah, the hound," Liam said, giving her a look of what seemed to be genuine concern. "I... um.... heard about what happened. Close call, huh?"

"It was. But we got him back safe, no one hurt."

The subject drew Zenn's thoughts back to the deeply unsettling sensation she'd shared with the hound just before his escape. And then with Gil's sandhog. The whole situation had been nagging at her for days; it was starting to interfere with her studies, becoming a real distraction. Otha hadn't understood. Hadn't been willing to try.

"Liam." She turned in the seat to face him. He glanced toward her, then back to the road.

"Yeah?"

Should she tell him? What would he think? Would it break the Rule? Would opening up about this mean she was "being friendly"? And was that the same as trying to make friends? No, she decided. She just needed to talk about something that was bothering her. Rule not broken.

"Lately, it's just that I've been having these... feelings around some of our animals."

"Feelings?" Liam gave her a mystified look.

"Yes. It's kind of hard to explain..."

After she'd laid out the situation as well as she could, Liam was quiet. They drove on. He still said nothing, brow furrowed.

Great. I've just lived up to every story the towner kids make up about the Ciscan weirdoes out at the cloister. Well done, Zenn.

"Well, Nine Hells, Scarlett," he said at last. "That's... really..."

Here it comes. She sank down in her seat.

"... amazing. You actually feel what the animal is feeling? How's that possible?"

She had to look closely at his face to make sure he wasn't mocking her. But no, he was serious. He believed her. She sat up straight again.

"That's just it," she said. "I don't do it. I don't do anything at all. It just happens by itself. One minute everything is normal, just me and one of the patients. The next minute, everything is... different. It's like there's a bridge, a mental bridge between us, a link or something."

"Well, it's sounds kind of great. To see into a mons... an animal's thoughts, ya know?"

"Actually, it's not so great. It's more like really confusing and it sort of makes me sick. But yeah, I have to admit it's... like nothing else I've ever felt."

"Sounds that way." He gave her a quick glance. "Say... you... um... don't ever do that with people, do you? You know. Get in their heads."

She had to grin at his obvious discomfort.

"No, Liam," she said, having mercy on him. "At least, not so far."

"Oh. Good. Let's... keep it that way."

FIFTEEN

"I thank you for assisting me in this task, novice Zenn. I know you're occupied with your studies," Hamish said as they entered the tool shed Otha had converted to house Griselda's tank. "Your assistance is very much appreciated."

"It's alright," she said, but she could hear the shortness in her voice. She told herself to be civil. It wasn't Hamish's fault she was feeling overwhelmed and distracted. After spending longer than she'd wanted worming the goats, she was behind schedule for the day, and still fuming about Graad. Not to mention everything else that seemed to be happening all at once lately. The only bright spot was her conversation with Liam in the truck. He had no insights to offer, of course; she didn't expect that. It had just felt good to say out loud what she'd been going through. At least he didn't think she was insane. And that was encouraging.

Griselda sensed them coming into the shed, and rose up into the water from the bottom of her aquarium, a clear ballisti-plast structure that reached from floor to ceiling against the back wall. Katie ran past Zenn, bounding up to the tank and staring, fascinated, following the creature's every move as it undulated before her. About the size of a large sofa, the seepdemon could alter the form of her gelatinous, amoeba-like body at will, allowing her to flatten out like a carpet, roll up into a ball or stretch herself out thin as wire to fit through the tiniest openings. The seepdemon's body was currently more or less the shape of a large, transparent pillow packed with various multi-colored organs, connective tissue and vacuoles floating in cytoplasm. She had no eyes, as such, but instead had tiny, photosensitive cells scattered across the surface of her see-through skin.

"Hi, Zelda," Zenn said, tapping the wall of the tank, "We're just here to change your tank filters."

"She doesn't comprehend you, does she?"

"No. But you never know what they pick up on. A tone of voice. Body language. Never hurts to be friendly."

"A sensible policy."

"So, you shut off the oxygenation pump here." Zenn threw a switch on the wall, and the hum-and-bubbling of the pump died away. "Then, you unlock this door down here, pull the filter out and replace it with a clean one." She stooped and pulled the dirty filter out, threw it in the bin in the corner, took a clean filter from the shelf and inserted it into the receptacle.

"Alright," she said standing up. "That's the basic Griselda routine. Any questions?"

Hamish thought for moment, antennae quivering.

"No. I believe I understand how to proceed. Thank you again." Zenn turned to leave. "Novice Scarlett?" Hamish pointed to the filter door on the aquarium. "Should we close that opening before we go?"

Zenn turned. She'd left the door to the filter compartment open, and Griselda had already noticed. A long, spaghetti-thin filament of seepdemon pseudopod was rising up out of the open door, where Katie sat, batting playfully at the thread of tissue waving in the air. A minute more and Griselda would have pushed her entire body out onto the floor.

"Katie. Get away from there," Zenn scolded, running to the filter door. "What is the matter with me?" She nudged Katie aside and pushed the filament back in, then shut the door and locked it. She shouldn't have allowed Katie to come. This time, it had just been easier to let her follow than to make her stay. And while Griselda wasn't really dangerous, Zenn still felt angry with herself for letting her guard down. Crouched on the floor next to the tank, she closed her eyes. To her great surprise, she felt like crying. She drew a ragged breath.

"Novice Zenn? Is something the matter?"

"No... I don't know." She stood, staring at Griselda fluttering in her tank. "Something weird is going on, Hamish."

"I do not know of this weirdness. Do you wish to speak about it?"

You know what? I do.

"First the whalehound got out, right?" Zenn crossed her arms, looked at the ground, frowned. Yes, it was time to lay this out. Maybe that would help her organize her jumbled thoughts. "I did not leave that fence off. I'm sure. Almost."

Hamish's head turned to look down at the door Zenn had just forgotten to lock.

"I know, I know." she said defensively. "But I'm sure I activated that fence."

"Are you saying the energy-fence malfunctioned?"

"No, I checked that. The switch was off when we got back."

"So, someone must have turned it off in some physical manner. Who, would you say?"

Zenn looked up at Hamish.

"That's the question, isn't it? And then Gil's sandhog dug through his pen floor, after the wires in the fuse box were chewed. Or cut and made to look chewed."

"You are proposing a deliberate act by someone in both events? Based on what reasoning?"

"There's a vote coming up in the town council, Hamish." Zenn said, thinking out loud. "People in town don't like our animals. They think they're dangerous, right? If our lease gets cancelled, they'd get rid of us and our animals."

"Some of the animals are. Dangerous. Are they not?"

"Yes, obviously," Zenn said, thinking that wasn't the point. "But not if we do our job and keep everything locked down and secure." The thought hit Zenn with an almost physical force. Maybe that was precisely the point. "Not if we don't do our job." She raised her hands to Hamish, as if to show him something. "What if that's it? What if someone is trying to make us look bad. Like the cloister can't control its animals. If the animals were a threat, then the council would have a reason to shut us down!"

"It is a possibility. But who would do such a thing?"

"I've haven't really figured this all out," Zenn said. "But one person comes to mind."

Hamish waited, antennae vibrating.

"Graad Dokes," she said.

"The human-foreman at the LeClerc property? It seems plain he does dislike off-world life forms. In addition, he is referred to by our Liam Tucker person as 'one foul-tempered mud-hopper'. I believe the phrase is non-complimentary."

"Yes, Graad has a temper, alright."

"But to accuse this Graad Dokes? This seems to be, what is the wording... jumping onto a conclusion."

"Maybe. Maybe not. I'm still collecting facts... but look,

here's what we have: the whalehound gets loose, I dart him, and Ren Jakstra says he ran into Graad in Arsia City that very morning. Coincidence he was in the area?"

"Perhaps he had other business in the…"

"Hold on. Then, Gil's sandhog. Guess who just happened to be out at the Bodine place before power to the fence got cut? Gil said Graad dropped off some feed. And we both just heard Graad saying all kinds of stuff about our animals and how keeping them alive was a waste of grazing land."

"We did. But this theorizing would demand that Graad Dokes gained unseen entry to the cloister grounds. Could he achieve this?"

"Alright. That's a weak link. But he knows the cloister layout well enough."

"And there is this," Hamish said. "I am going here and there all the day and much of the night throughout the grounds. My sensing apparatus are quite acute. The director-abbot has requested that I keep myself attentive for any animal having distress during the night hours. I believe I would have noticed a large, odiferous human going to and fro within the compound walls, even if he attempted to go undetected."

"Wait. Odiferous? Graad stinks?"

"I can smell most life types. Mammal forms in particular. It is your metabolism and porous epidermal skin. Graad Dokes smells of addictive tobacco resin, mammal-goats and fresh dung. You smell of unwashed cloth material and carbonized onion-vegetable."

Zenn made a face.

"I do not!"

"It is a true statement."

"I smell like… cooked onions?" She shook off the comment. "Look, I'll admit there are holes in my theory. But

Graad has a major motive. He hates aliens, no exceptions.
It wouldn't surprise me if he actually wanted the hound to
make it into town. Think of what would've happened then."

"Would he? Intend that kind of…mayhem?"

"Maybe. Yes, sure. The worse the better, as far as turning
the council against us and our animals. And Gil's sandhog
getting loose was just one more dangerous alien creature for
people to get upset about. Graad could've cut those wires,
easy."

"I suppose there is some limited probability to your
scenario." Hamish groomed one antenna nervously with his
claw. "Should we go to the director-abbot? Tell him of your
suspicion?"

Zenn considered.

"No," she said after a few seconds. "Otha already thinks
I'm having trouble with my training because of what's been
happening with…" She stopped. "Well, like I said before,
I've just been a little off lately. Besides, Otha will want hard
evidence. We need to show him proof."

"We?" Hamish now groomed both antennae nervously.
"Novice Zenn, I have a reservation to lodge."

"Alright. Let's hear it."

"You said you have been 'off' as of late. And just now…
" He raised one claw, pointing to the aquarium. "You failed
to secure the door on the filter. Might your being 'off' also
affect your perceptions of foreman Graad Dokes'
involvement in these events? Humans, I have noticed,
sometimes impose patterns where no patterns, in fact, exist.
I am afraid this is in your nature."

Zenn knew Hamish had a point. What was happening
between her and the animals was interfering with her
concentration, making her miss things she shouldn't, do
things she'd never done before.

"Alright," she told him. She knelt, and scooped Katie up in her arms. "I admit I don't have all the facts. It is possible I'm wrong about Graad. There, happy?"

"Now you are displaying an open mind. I am content."

But as she shut the door to the shed and they headed for the refectory to see what Hild was making for supper, Zenn told herself that, at the very least, there *seemed* to be a pattern taking shape – and Graad Dokes fit into it. Nicely.

SIXTEEN

"He must've been sleeping under the truck," Liam repeated for the third time as he and Zenn hurried toward the infirmary, the unconscious animal wrapped in a towel and cradled in Liam's arms. "He shoulda got outta the way. Stupid cat."

"Alright," Zenn said, trying to think, trying to visualize the steps from the chapters on small animal trauma. "Tell me what happened."

"Graad drove the truck out of the shed, accidentally hit him. At least, he said it was an accident... I didn't see it happen." He addressed the cat, softly, "Damn you, Zeus. Stupid damn cat."

"Was he conscious when you found him? Alert?"

"Yeah, but he wasn't moving. And he was crying. Then he got quiet, like now. You can fix him, right?"

"Liam, we'll need to examine him first, to see how bad the injuries are."

"Yeah, but you've fixed cats before... Otha... Otha has fixed cats."

Zenn flicked on the light in the ready room as they entered. She told Liam to put the cat on the smallest exam table, where the attached readout screen would register and record his weight, pulse-rate and body temp.

Zeus came to as Liam set him down, green eyes going wide. He emitted a long, low moan. Liam winced at the sound. And then it struck her, the feeling sweeping through her, fiery sheets of pain climbing like flame up her back, her legs going weak, almost dropping her to the floor. A sense of abject fear then broke over her mind like a cresting wave, her vision grew faint, and the room around her was... gone. Instead, she now saw a baffling rush of images: bright lights, dim shadows, light again, coming rapid-fire, too fast to make any sense. Then the images slowed, cleared; she could see again. But she wasn't seeing the ready room where she'd been a second ago. She was... in a dark space, there were big shapes around her. The underside of a vehicle above, fat truck wheels glimpsed beyond. The smell of oil and gas. She was in a garage, looking up from low on the ground. A sound roared in her ears, deafening, terrifying, she was pinned by a wheel, crushed. The pain surged up again, nearly making her black out with shock and fear. She was... seeing out of the cat's eyes, Zeus' eyes. Impossible... unmistakable... She was reliving the cat's experience, reliving the memory of when he'd been injured.

"Scarlett?" Liam's voice cut through the pain and terror, pulled her back. She opened her eyes to see he held her by one elbow. "You alright?"

She tried to breathe, steadying herself.

So that's what it feels like when you've been run over by a truck.

"I'm fine," she said. "I'm alright."

"You sure?"

"Yes," she turned back to the cat, away from the boy's worried look. "It's what I told you about. What happens between me and the animals. I just linked up."

"What? With Zeus?"

"Yeah... but we can't worry about that now. I'm... back. I'm fine now. He needs help."

She saw the bloodstain on the towel swaddling the cat had spread, pooling on the metal tabletop. She pulled her gaze away from the sight, but not before Liam noticed the blood.

"Nine Hells," he swore. "It's worse. It's getting worse, isn't it? Where's Otha? Is he coming?"

"He'll be here soon."

Zeus thrashed weakly, trying to escape from the towel, but unable to rise to his feet. Liam held him gently in place on the exam table. The animal cried out again, a pitiful gasp of a meow.

"He's hurting," Liam said. "Can't you do something?"

"We should really wait for Otha." Liam jerked his gaze up to her. "But I'll take a look."

Zeus moaned again as Zenn gently folded back the towel. Her jaw went tight at the sight. Liam looked away. The cat's entire rear quarter was badly mangled, a sickening pudding of flesh, blood and bone. She pushed up the cat's lips; the gums were pale and growing paler from blood loss. Pupils fixed and dilated. Breathing shallow, fast. Another yowl.

"It's alright, boy," Liam said, his voice going uncharacteristically quiet as he returned his gaze to the cat. "It's alright, Zeus. We'll get you fixed up. We'll fix it. Can't you... give him a shot?"

Of course, she could give Zeus pain medication. But she wasn't supposed to. She wasn't qualified. Not yet.

Otha will be mad.

But she knew what to do, she should do it.

He'll be really mad. Too bad.

"Hold him there," she said. "Keep him as still as you can. I'll give him something."

Zenn pulled the infusion tube up from its compartment on the exam table, found a suitable vein on Zeus' front leg, placed the line over it and pressed it into place.

"He's shocky," she said. "We need to get fluids into him, too, get him stabilized."

She dialed a knob on the table and started a slow push of electrolytes and quad-steroids through the line.

"Good. Now, we'll start some medicine for the pain."

She pulled open the drawer holding the pneuma-ject syringes, and trying hard not to fumble, found a vial of Amalan. She drew a dose up into the syringe.

Zeus moaned, struggled. Liam held him, but looked away from the broken body, closing his eyes. Zenn placed the pneuma-ject on the matted fur covering the muscles at the cat's shoulder, mentally double-checked the weight-to-dosage ratio, decided it was correct, and pressed the plunger.

"This will help," she said. "He'll feel a lot better now."

Before she'd finished speaking, the drug worked its molecular spell, the animal's stiffly arched neck relaxed, his breathing slowed and deepened, the fear and pain drained from his eyes, which narrowed as the big head drooped.

"Nine Hells," Liam swore quietly, stroked the half-conscious animal. "Thanks. For that."

"Liam, this is a bad injury, really bad." She waited for him to look up.

"But Otha…"

"We can see what Otha says. But… I'm telling you it's bad."

She'd seen towner cats brought to the clinic with similar injuries. It never turned out well. And this one was even worse than the others. Liam looked away from her, breathed hard for a second or two and looked back.

"So," she searched for something to say to distract the boy. "What's Zeus' story? Where'd you get him?"

"He... my mom." Liam put a strained smile on his face. "My mom gave him to me when he was just... just a little guy." He cupped his hands. "About this big..."

Zenn was sure Liam was on the verge of tears when the door to the room swung open. Otha strode over to the exam table, pulled back the towel and squinted down at the cat.

"Vehicle?" he asked Zenn.

"Truck. Out at Vic's place."

"How long ago?" Otha turned to Liam.

"An hour? Maybe more."

Otha gently lifted one blood-matted hind leg, probed at the animal's belly, ran a hand across the spine. He touched a button on the exam table, and a small virt-screen appeared in the air, showing a 3-D image of the cat's skeletal structure and major internal organs.

"Liam, this is serious," Otha said after a moment. He steadied his gaze at the boy. "Maybe too serious to repair."

"Yeah, Zenn said it was bad. But..." Liam gestured at the shelves of medicines and supplies lining the ready room walls, at the machines and devices surrounding them. "All this stuff? All this stuff and you can't fix him?" Liam's eyes blazed at Otha, pleading, accusing.

"There are limits, Liam. These injuries are extensive." He pointed to the images on the v-screen. "Shattered hip bones here, here and here. Fractured spinal vertebrae here and over here. Ruptured bladder, lacerated small intestine, severed arteries. This kidney is badly bruised."

"So, there's no way to... nothing you can do for him?" Liam's voice stuttered. He stared down at the cat. "There's nothing?"

"Otha," Zenn said quietly, not quite sure it was a novice's place to say anything, but unable to keep her thoughts to herself. "What about the Mag-Genis?"

Her uncle cocked a bushy eyebrow at her.

"What? What is it?" Liam said, looking from her to Otha. "Can it help Zeus?"

"If it worked it might," Otha said. "But Zenn knows as well as I do that that unit hasn't been fully operational for month. Firmware's out of date. Software's gone buggy."

"But what is it? What does it do?" Liam said again.

"It's a bone and tissue generator," Zenn said. "It uses a magnetic field to create a series of energy scaffolds inside an animal, then it manipulates cells to grow bones and organs and blood vessels around the scaffolds."

"But it's broken?"

"The software that runs it is bad," Otha said. "The process of building tissues, bones, is massively complex. Without the software, it's basically useless."

"Actually, I talked to Hild about that, just last week," Zenn told him. "I had an idea."

"Oh?" Her uncle raised both bushy eyebrows this time. "And?"

"What if a person supplied the guidance input? You know, assisted the base structuring program with point-to-point coordinates?"

"Well, I suppose…" He rubbed at his beard. "Theoretically, it might work."

"It might?" Liam said. "Then you have to do it."

"In theory, I said. But it isn't practical. Overseeing the unit's operations would mean hands-on monitoring and detailed adjustments every few minutes for… a long time, Zenn."

"Thirty-six hours," she told him. "Hild helped me work it out."

"Oh she did?"

"Well, we used a rikkaset's physiology to model the process, but a rikkaset's close enough to a cat to give me a time-frame, right?"

"Sure, their internal organs and skeletal structure is close enough. That's not the question," Otha said. "The question is, can a human being stay continuously focused and alert for that stretch of time and still get the inputs right? I can't see it working, Zenn."

"Otha," Liam said. "Can't she try? Can't you let her at least try?"

Otha chewed at his cheek, then pointed a finger at Zenn.

"If you tried this… *if*, I said… you know Hild and I have the ultratheer litter to deliver, right? That'll be two days running, maybe two and a-half. We won't be able to help. You'd be on your own."

"I know. I can do it," she said.

"And once you start the tissue scaffolding, you understand you can't stop and start over." She nodded her head that she knew this. "If you miss a single artery splice, a single synapse calibration or bone density level, the matrix will dissolve and the animal will need to be put down. Immediately."

"I know, Otha. But it's worth trying, isn't it?"

Liam fixed his gaze on Otha.

"It might be," Otha said. "But Liam, this is not a proven procedure. Right? The outcome is not certain. In fact, it could very likely be a bad outcome."

"Yes, yes I understand." Liam stroked the cat's head, then looked up at Zenn and Otha. "Thank you. Thank you for trying. Thank you for letting her try."

SEVENTEEN

Twenty minutes later, Zenn had positioned the sedated Zeus in the sling-like cradle of straps and fluid-filled cushions that occupied the center of the Mag-Genis unit. The machine's dozen articulated emitter arms were arrayed around the cat, making him look like a furry orange-and-white fly about to be wrapped up in the web of an approaching metal spider.

Zenn was seated on a rolling stool in front of the unit. Three virt-screens floated in the air above her. Two displayed different angles and magnifications of the cat's internal structures, the third screen showed a variety of system controls and progress bars. Within arm's reach on two surgical instrument trays, she'd placed the Mag-Genis user's manual and a stack of v-films detailing feline anatomy.

After Otha had gone to join Hild at the ultratheer's birthing pen, Liam said he would stay and help in any way he could. But there was little he could do. Zeus' fate was solely in Zenn's hands now.

Her finger hovered over the machine's primary system start-button.

"Alright, this will start the process," she told Liam, who peered over her shoulder. "Once I push this, there's no going back. Ready?"

"I'm ready if you are. And if Zeus is."

"Oh, we'll assume he's ready," Zenn said, and she pushed the button.

The spindly arms of the machine clattered to life, each one moving into its initial position. On the hovering v-screens, a series of colored areas lit up on the images of Zeus' body.

"What's happening? What are those?" Liam asked, leaning in to see better.

"That shows the parts of Zeus the machine is working on," she said, pointing. "Like here, the red, blinking line is the main vein to the thigh muscles of his left leg. That's what is being rebuilt. Now, I just have to direct the magnetic beam... down here..." She moved a slider on the control screen. "...like that. There."

"Oh. I get it. You have to tell it where to go."

"Right. At every juncture..." Zenn directed one of the emitter arms to move a few millimeters. "...I need to keep the process keyed in on the right area, in the right order, at the right time."

"Otha said you couldn't stop once you started, though, right?"

"The Mag-Genis has to harvest cells from Zeus' body. It will use those cells to rebuild him," she said. "To do that, it makes a sort of... liquidy soup out of his damaged internal organs and other tissues. Then it injects microscopic amounts of magnetite into the cells. So now, every cell has a little extra iron in it. That lets the machine use its magnetic fields to move the cells into place – that's the energy scaffold. Zeus is on life-support while this happens, but if you stopped the rebuilding process, that soup of cells would disintegrate. We wouldn't be able to get them back."

She poked a finger at the control screen. "Alright. We just started the rebuild of his left tibia – the bone between the knee and ankle." Liam leaned in even closer, crowding her where she sat. She spoke without looking up at him. "You might as well find someplace comfortable, Liam. We're going to be here for a while."

"Yeah, sorry," he said. He sat down on the padded bench by the wall. "How long did you say it'll take?"

"About a day and a-half."

Liam whistled softly.

"Yeah," she said, moving another emitter arm to its next position. "You can say that again…"

Six hours later, Zenn was stiff and aching from sitting, and she needed a break. Really needed a break.

"Liam?"

He hopped up from the bench.

"What?" he said, coming over quickly. "Something wrong?"

"No. We're doing fine. But I've got to leave for just a second." She nodded her head toward the bathroom door at the back of the room. "I'll be right back."

"Oh. Sure."

"I need you to watch this little meter." Liam came up behind her and she pointed to the control screen. "If this level goes into the red zone, slide this indicator to zero. See?"

"Uh, yeah, I see. You sure… I can do this?"

"This part's easy. You can do it. Red zone, slider to zero. Yes?" Before he could disagree, she was out of the chair and trotting across the room.

A minute later, she was back.

"Did it hit red?"

"No," he told her, sounding relieved as he rose from the chair. "It moved a little, but that's all."

"Great," she said, sitting down again. "We're right on schedule. And only," she checked the countdown clock on the control screen. "...thirty-one hours forty minutes to go."

Ten hours after she'd started the operation, Hamish appeared in the doorway, asking if she needed anything.

"You could feed Katie for me," she told him, not looking away from the screens. "There's kibble for her in the kitchen, in the small tub just inside the pantry door."

"I will see to it," he said. "How is the rebuilding of the mammal-feline proceeding?"

"Slow, but sure," she said. "I'm doing the main neuron group that controls tail movement right now. Oh, that reminds me – Liam, you won't mind if Zeus wakes up with a bobbed tail, will you?"

"Bobbed?"

"A shortened tail. We'll save a good hour's worth of work if we don't redo the whole thing."

"Oh. No problem. He's pretty laid back. I don't think he'll mind a new look."

At twelve hours, both of Zenn's legs had fallen asleep. She tried to stand in place as she manipulated the control screen, but it was too difficult to hold her hand steady to make the fine-control movements on the v-screen. She couldn't afford a mistake, so she sat again. Liam was pacing around the room behind her, stopping occasionally to read the label on a bottle of medication or examine some piece of equipment.

"Hm," he said, reading a v-film he'd picked up from the counter. "Says here hooshrikes have one claw that's like a hollow needle. I never knew that. They dangerous?"

"No, not to humans," Zenn said, shaking her head to clear it, struggling a little to stay on task. "The claw doesn't inject venom. It's for pheromones."

"And that would be... what?"

"It's a hormone. Like a mild drug. Moths use pheromones to attract mates. The female hooshrikes do the same sort of thing. But they inject it into the male. When they're mating."

"So it's... what?" Liam laughed. "An aphrodisiac?"

"More like something that strengthens the bond between the pair."

"Sounds like chemical warfare to me."

"Well, it's an amazing adaptation," she said. A great yawn escaped from her as she inched an emitter arm into its next position. "Our hooshrike here at the clinic is a male. And he's one handsome guy. If I were a female hooshrike, I'd definitely wanna get my claws into him."

"Remind me never to go on a date with you," Liam said. She could hear the smirk in his voice, but his remark left a conspicuous silence in its wake.

"And speaking of that," he went on after a few moments. "You ever been? On a date?"

It was a simple question. But Zenn felt heat rising to her face, which made her mad at herself, which made her face hotter.

"No. My days are pretty full, you know?"

"Yeah, yeah. Things to do, animals to mess with. I know. But..." he leaned against the wall in front of her, crossed his arms and watched her work. "Haven't you ever wanted to go out? I mean, on your own? Only times I've seen you Arsia you're with Otha or the Sister. That's gotta cramp your style."

"My... style?"

"You know. When it comes to meeting people. Like guys,

for instance. Even in a small place like Arsia I bet there's some guy... some guy you wondered about."

"No," she said quickly, uneasy with this line of questioning. "Like I said. I keep busy. More important things to be obsessed with." This wasn't entirely true. Not since her talk with Hild the other day. Despite her best efforts to ignore Hild's off-hand remark about Liam being "more friendly lately," the thought had embedded itself in her mind, like a tiny virus. She'd denied the virus any sort of nourishing attention. But it hadn't died off as she'd hoped it would, and still clung to its own, secret life in its own special area of her mind. A part that she had to admit she'd allowed herself to visit more than once in the past few days. In fact, just last night, drifting off to sleep, Liam had, for some unknowable reason, come to mind. But this, she told herself, was simply because the virus-thought that Hild had planted was novel; it was a new specimen that deserved some level of curiosity, surely, merely based on its newness.

"So let's say some guy wondered about you," Liam said, not letting the subject drop. "You know, say some guy from Arsia took an interest. Like... a great guy like me, for instance. Would they let you out of your cage here? Let you see this guy? Go on a real, live date?"

Zenn bent lower at the control console, forcing her attention where it needed to go.

Was this some kind of... boy-code? Was Liam Tucker interested? In her? Was he asking her on a date? It sounded like it. But the fact was, she had no previous experience with the subject, and found this profound ignorance on her part almost laughable.

She shouldn't be surprised, really. Ever since Hild's remark, she might've known the tiny thought-virus meant that this was going to come up in one way or another. But

Zenn had given this whole subject some in-depth consideration quite a while ago. The Rule was put in place for her own good. She needed to keep it in force.

Friends were a bad idea. So don't make friends. It was a simple equation, and the answer always computed the same way. Allowing yourself to trust, love or depend on any new people simply carried too much downside. They too would leave, or make fun of you, or make it clear they had priorities that came before you. The equation was harsh, she knew. There were probably psychological impacts for her to consider. But that didn't change the equation. Attachments to others came with a built-in pain-generating mechanism. And the pain generated was exactly proportional to the strength of the attachment. No, there would be no liking. No attaching. No... dating.

"The cloister is not a cage," she said finally, not looking up at Liam. "It's where I choose to be."

"Well, I've seen goats that choose to stay in the barn, 'cause they're too scared to go outside. What're you scared of?"

"Who said I'm scared?" she said, unable to keep the defensive note out of her voice. But the truth was: she'd considered this possibility. Perhaps she was frightened, and the Rule was merely constructed as a defense. So? Defense against pain was entirely reasonable.

I'm tired. Exhausted, actually. And this is stupid, anyway. I cannot think about this now.

"Look," she said, the fatigue she'd been successfully fending off now descending on her like a heavy, wet blanket. "I'll... leave the barn when I'm ready. Now, can we just..."

"Alright, alright. Subject closed."

She moved a slider, and a new artery began to take shape in Zeus' thigh.

"So," Liam said then, going to pick up the v-film about the hooshrike again, "You really get to know all the animals here at the cloister, don't you? I mean, it's like they're not just animals. To you, they all have personalities."

"They do. Absolutely. Just like Zeus."

"Yeah, but that's different," Liam said. "He's a cat, a person's cat, from Earther stock. He's not... you know... an alien."

"Oh, I don't know," Zenn said. "To Hamish, Zeus is just as alien as a rikkaset or a hooshrike. Or a goat."

"Don't let Vic hear you say that," Liam said. "Her goats are like family to that woman."

Zenn thought of Vic's kid-skin gloves, but didn't make the obvious remark about certain species of arachnid eating their young.

"They've really stripped her land bare, though haven't they?" Zenn said instead. "She ever think about maybe shifting them to new pastures, buy some fresh land?"

"She says there isn't any to be had. At least no fertile land she'd be willing to pay for. She left some papers out on her desk once and I took a look. Did you know her family...?" He stopped, as if his thought process suddenly veered off in another direction.

"Her family what...?"

"Nothing. It's just... boring family history stuff. Just..." He laughed. "Don't call Vic's goats aliens in front of her, that's all."

"But they are. To Hamish, they're aliens. And so are you and I."

"Well, sure. But Hamish's just a big insect. Of course he'd feel that way."

"But that's the point," Zenn said, adjusting the emitter arm reconstructing Zeus' right hip joint. "The native life forms on Mars all died out long before humans came. We're all aliens here. That's why it drives me crazy when Graad and the others complain about the cloister's patients. Calling them monsters. Calling them alien 'things' and saying they don't belong. They belong here as much as we do. A sick whalehound or a pregnant ultratheer or an abandoned yote. They all deserve a place where they can be safe. And to be treated with dignity and respect." She jabbed a finger at Zeus. "Just like this little alien here."

"Whoa." Liam held both hands up in surrender. "Fine. Zeus is an alien and so am I. Don't blow a gasket."

"Sorry... But you see what I mean, don't you? Human beings get this idea in their heads that they're the special ones – the only ones who get to say who's normal and who's... just a thing. Think about if the shoe was on the other foot. And someone decides you're the thing."

Liam was quiet then. No snappy comeback.

"People around here can be a little narrow-minded. I grant you that."

"A little narrow-minded?" Zenn laughed.

"Alright. A lot. But maybe they have their reasons."

"What reasons? Like ignorance? Intolerance?"

"Like alien animals can get you killed," he said, a hard, new edge in his voice. "How's that for a reason?"

Zenn was caught off guard, and it took her a moment to realize their talk had taken a sudden and serious turn.

"Killed?" she said. "Our animals have never killed anyone."

"Maybe yours haven't. You don't own all the alien things on Mars, though, do you?"

"Liam..." She saw what he was getting at. And it made her heave a frustrated sigh. "There's never been a documented case of an alien life form killing anyone on

Mars. I've heard those rumors. Everybody has. They're just stories."

She heard him start to pace, moving to and fro in front of the Mag-Genis.

"Are they?" His voice now dripped with... what? Scorn? Rage? "Well, I've got a story for you, Scarlett. It's about my pa. It's about how he didn't get pulled into the blades of a combine out at our farm. That's not what got him. That was just what we told people, my mom and me."

"Liam, I'm so sorry." She made herself keep her eyes on the intricate processes flitting across the v-screens. "But I don't understand."

"It was night. My pa snuck into Gil Bodine's machine shed. He was... he was there to steal Gil's new generator, alright?"

"What?"

"Pa had gotten into debt. Way in. He was gonna sell Gil's genny, get some cash together. Like I said, it was night, dark. He didn't know Gil kept the two sandhog sows in there. They tore him up pretty bad."

"Liam..." Zenn's voice trailed off. She had no idea what to say to this.

She glanced up. Liam wasn't looking at her, but was standing, body rigid, staring a hole in the far wall, his fists clenched, knuckles white.

"We found him the next morning. He'd made it as far as our front porch. He was propped against the wall. And he was dead. That's how Gil lost those two sows. Pa never shut the gate behind him after he... We couldn't tell people what happened. No way I was gonna have the whole damn town think my pa was a thief. He was just doing what he thought he had to do. He deserved better."

He turned his face to her then, eyes brimming.

"You won't tell?" he said. "I'd appreciate it... if you'd not tell."

"Of course I won't," Zenn said, forcing her attention back to the screens. "I just wish you'd been able to talk to somebody about this. Before now, I mean. To carry this around inside you... Liam, it must've been..."

"Terrible. Yeah." He was in motion again, pacing. "But hey. We all have our secrets, huh?"

I can relate to that.

"I understand better, now. Your feelings... about aliens. But Liam, you know they didn't mean to do that. The hogs." She wasn't sure he wanted to hear this, but she felt like she had to say it. "They didn't kill your father on purpose."

"No? Well, that may be." He spoke quietly now, the rage drained from his voice. He sat heavily on the bench by the wall, elbows on knees. She looked up to see him rest his head in his hands. "But, it doesn't really make him any less dead, does it?"

EIGHTEEN

After Liam's admission about his father's death, they'd both gone silent for a long spell, the room echoing faintly with the hum and clatter of the Mag-Genis as it worked methodically from one shredded organ or bone to the next, Zenn making her minute adjustments again, then again, then again.

When Liam finally spoke, the sound startled Zenn out of the attentive trance she'd fallen into.

"Ya know, Scarlett, I guess people just don't really get the aliens, your animals, the way you do. I mean, know their personalities, get close to them and all."

"Well, I'm not really supposed to… get too close. Otha says they're patients, not pets. That it's important to keep a professional distance. But sometimes that's hard."

Liam had approached the Mag-Genis unit, and he bent down now to check on Zeus. The cat twitched slightly in the cushioning sling.

"Yeah. I can see how it could be. Hard." His voice cracked ever so slightly as he spoke. He rubbed one hand across his face. "So," he said, straightening up, the smirk back in his voice as he turned his attention to the v-screens, "what are you doing to my poor defenseless little alien now?"

"Just starting to knit together some capillaries. These supply blood to the right rear paw. See, they form a little net inside each toe…"

Twenty hours into the operation, the first of the damaged vertebrae had been rebuilt and the nearby spinal column nerves regenerated. After standing up for a quick stretch of her aching muscles, Zenn sat down again and began to guide the unit's work on the second shattered piece of Zeus' backbone.

Twenty-six hours in, there was a problem reforming the nutrient-absorbing cellular structures lining the small intestine. Zenn sent Liam to the ultratheer birthing pen to ask Otha for a work-around.

"Here," Liam said when he'd returned. "It's a v-film. Otha says this will show you what to do."

"Great, thanks," Zenn told him, taking her eyes off the Mag-Genis screens long enough to scan the film. "Yes. Perfect."

"Um, have you ever seen an ultratheer giving birth?" Liam asked.

"No. And I'm really sorry to miss it."

"No. You aren't. It's disgusting. Really disgusting."

She grinned at him. Her legs had fallen asleep again.

After thirty hours, Zenn's eyes burned in their sockets like tiny suns, her back muscles periodically spasmed with pain and she nearly nodded off at a particularly critical moment. When she actually fell asleep for a few seconds during the rebuild of Zeus' bladder, she knew she was in trouble and sent Liam to the refectory kitchen. He came back carrying a large thermos, a mug and a glass jar packed with a mix of leafy orange-brown plant material.

"What did you call this stuff?"

"Mettra yerba," Zenn said, her mouth dry, her vision starting to shimmer around the edges. She'd also had a headache for the past several hours. "Put it in the mug, and pour the hot water on it."

He did as she said and passed the steaming mug to her.

"The strainer? Did you..."

"Yeah, here it is." From his shirt pocket, he produced a short, silver straw that flared out at the end, where it was perforated with numerous small holes. She drew the hot, bitter liquid up the length of the straw, designed to filter out the small plant bits.

"So," he said, "if this yerba stuff is so full of that super-caffeine stuff, why didn't you have some before?"

"I didn't want to unless I had to," she told him. "Now I have to."

"What? You're too pure here in cloister-world to drink caffeine?"

"No. It's really acidic. Rots my stomach." She took another long pull on the straw, felt the warmth flowing through her, felt the sting in her belly. But it worked. She felt more alert almost immediately.

"Now, see that shelf? No, that one."

He went to the wall.

"Smallest white bottle at the right end. Yes. Would you bring that here please?"

Liam brought her the bottle.

"More meds for Zeus?"

"Meds for Zenn," she said, popping the lid and taking out two sovprin tablets. "For my head. It's splitting."

She took another pull on the hot liquid and swallowed

the tablets.

"So, how's that yerba stuff taste?"

"Like week-old dish water. Want some?"

Thirty-seven hours and fifteen minutes after Zenn had pushed the Mag-Genis start button, she leaned far forward on the stool and squinted at the control panel, no longer at all certain her eyes were being honest with her, no longer able to keep her mind on a single thought for more than a few seconds.

"I...can't... believe it," she croaked, her throat parched, the words barely forming.

"Huh? What?" Liam bolted upright on the bench, coming awake with his hair wild, eyes darting around the room as if he had no idea where he was. Heaving himself unsteadily to his feet, he staggered over to stand behind her.

"What is it?"

"It's over," she said, barely managing more than a whisper.

"What do you... No. Zeus. You mean he's..."

"I mean we're done. It worked. He's... going to be fine."

Zenn stood stiffly, stinging eyes blissfully closed, muscles exquisitely, deliciously sore. She reached out her aching hands, fingers, arms, stretched luxuriously, like a cat. The next thing she knew, she was lifted off her feet by Liam's unexpected embrace. The hug was quick, surprisingly strong. He set her down and stepped away, grinning, a swipe at his hair also meant to dry his watering eyes.

"Nine Hells. You did it, Scarlett." She was afraid he was going to hug her again. "You saved him!"

He turned from her and bent low over the unconscious cat. Zenn realized her body was prickling, as if charged with some exotic current. It was impossible to say if it was simple exhaustion... or the sense-memory of Liam's arms around her.

That was... *odd.*

So, was this Liam being more "friendly" as Hild said? Or was it just his entirely logical response to the long-shot survival of his favorite cat? The faint electric feeling lingered within her, and Zenn reminded herself of the Rule. It had kept her safe and pain-free in the past. There was no reason to start doubting it now. Was there?

NINETEEN

The following morning, Zenn had walked with Hamish out to the southwest edge of the compound, to the grouping of cages and fenced enclosures that occupied most of that corner of the grounds. After a full fourteen hours of blissfully dreamless sleep, she felt almost fully recovered from the Mag-Genis ordeal.

"Well, here it is." She gestured at the rows of cages. "Our Rogue's Gallery."

"They do not appear roguish," Hamish said, bending close to peer into a cage holding a pair of Akanthan axebill warblers. The eight-foot-tall, ostrich-like birds responded by bobbing their heads and opening their massive hooked beaks to produce a brief, bubbling measure of song together, their mournful tune delivered in perfect two-part harmony.

"I guess rogues in this case is more a term of affection."

Hamish's antennae fluttered in agitation. "Yours is a confounding language, if you don't mind my saying."

"You'll get the hang of it," she told him. "This is our bad boy, Rasputin." She gestured at the next enclosure, its woven wire fencing roofed over with a crisscrossing layer of heavy-gauge alloy chain. The area inside the fence was strewn six feet deep with shredded plant material, rocks and other debris. Unlike most of the other cages at the cloister, Rasputin's had a double door arrangement, with a space in-between. Anyone entering the cage had to close and lock the outer door behind them before opening the inner door. Both doors were secured with combination locks: an extra safety measure for an animal as fast as it was vicious. And if Rasputin ever escaped, there was no recapture plan. He would need to be put down, quickly and ruthlessly, before he set any of his five beady hunter's eyes on any other living thing.

"You probably know this, but Rasputin's from your neck of the woods..."

She gave the cage's chain netting a strong, noisy rattle – and the largest debris pile in the center of the pen instantly exploded in a blur of thrashing legs and writhing, tubular body. The thirty-foot creature that emerged threw itself into the cage wall in front of them with a loud, fence-shaking impact. Hamish leaped backwards in alarm, landing several body-lengths away in a defensive crouch, antennae rigid and quivering with fright.

"Bloodcarn!" he managed to gasp, his Transvox barely getting the word out.

Zenn hurried over to him.

"Hamish, I'm so sorry. I thought you knew we had one of these. I didn't mean to scare you like that."

"You... did not... mean," he muttered, still crouching. "Very... well. You did not... mean the scaring." He raised up slowly to his full height, mirror eyes riveted on the animal slithering back and forth on the other side of the fence. "I will state... that I was unaware of this slaughter-creature... confined here."

She felt terrible. Of course she shouldn't have provoked

the animal like that. Not without warning Hamish. Rasputin was a Sirenic *Scolopendra colossi* – a giant, multi-legged arthropod; more or less consisting of a huge, florescent-orange centipede back section with what looked like a tarantula growing out of its front end. With roughly seven hundred legs on the hind portion of its flattened, segmented body, and scimitar-sized mandibles in front, Rasputin's kind were the alpha predators in the densest jungle regions of Hamish's home moon. Voracious and swift, the big insectoids were ambush hunters, and careless coleopts – like Hamish – still fell prey to them from time to time.

"I'm really sorry," Zenn said again.

Hamish said nothing as they moved beyond the bloodcarn's cage, with Hamish giving it an especially wide berth. The creature emitted a parting hiss at them, then returned to the center of its cage. Vibrating its multiple legs in unison to agitate the leaves and rocks around it, it quickly submerged out of sight and was still.

"Here, Hamish," she said after they'd gone by several more cages. She'd stopped in front of one of the larger fenced enclosures. "This is where we keep the yotes." He eyed the pen suspiciously, and halted several feet away. She tried to sooth him: "No surprises here, I promise. Did you bring the syringes?"

He patted the satchel slung from a strap around his shoulder.

"I have them here, as instructed."

"Good," she said. "We'll be vaccinating Ernie today. He's the big guy, over there."

"Yes. He is a large… guy," Hamish said, taking one step closer and eyeing the yote dozing in the sun in the far corner of the pen. A little taller than an Earther buffalo, yotes looked to Zenn like morbidly obese hyenas, with short legs, a pig-like corkscrew tail and gray-green leopard-spots over bristly, dirty-yellow fur. "What do these mammal-yotes eat?" he asked.

"Not beetles, if that's what you're thinking," Zenn said, seeing the nervous twitching of Hamish's antennae. "They're scavengers, from the savannahs on Procyon. They eat carrion, dead animals left over from the kills of bigger predators. See those jaws? Yotes can snap an ultratheer's thighbone like a Solstice candy cane."

"You will feed him dead ultratheer creatures?"

"Not specifically. Otha saves stuff for the yotes from the surgery. Excised tissue, body parts, bones. And garbage from the kitchen. We put it all in here." Zenn went to the recycled fifty-five-gallon biodiesel drum that held the yotes' food. "It has to decompose in here for a few days. Otha calls it 'ripening.' Then we feed it to them."

"And they like it? All rotten?"

"You could say that." Zenn thumped the top of the drum with one hand, and Ernie came instantly awake. Spotting her, he galloped heavily over to the chain link fence, massive jaws already streaming ropes of thick saliva.

"Ernie, this is Hamish," Zenn said.

"Greetings, yote-Ernie. I am joyful to meet you."

Ernie ignored this, eyes locked on the food drum. Extending her arms as far as she could to maintain maximum distance from the stench of decayed flesh and kitchen slops, Zenn popped open the lid of the barrel. The smell was still overpowering. Ernie pushed up against the fence in anticipation. A globular, blue-veined pouch of exposed flesh protruded from the yote's throat. As Ernie shoved at the fence, it sloshed back and forth, producing a sound that always made Zenn slightly queasy.

"What is that, on his neck? The bulging?" Hamish pointed with one claw.

"That's his neck crop. It's still half-full from his last meal. Yotes like their food really rank. He stores it up there until it's broken down enough to swallow."

Zenn opened the small feeding door in the fence, then took the ladle hanging from the side of the barrel and sloshed some of the disgusting contents into the trough below the door. Ernie buried his face in the trough and, with a sound of slurping liquid and crunching bone, ate with gusto.

"Alright, he's occupied with breakfast. Hand me the syringe. The big one." Hamish gave her the pneuma-ject syringe she'd loaded with vaccine earlier that morning.

She pulled off the tip-protector and was just about to reach in through the feeding door and administer the first shot when her uncle walked around the corner of the nearest enclosure. She was surprised to see he had two boys with him – and they definitely weren't boys from anywhere on Mars.

"Here she is. Zenn, this is Areth," Otha said, gesturing at the older one. "And this is… sorry, I didn't catch your name, son."

"I am Fane, Fane Reth Fanesson," the younger boy said, looking past Zenn at the slurping yote.

"This is my niece, Zenn," Otha said. "She's a novice here at the cloister. And this is Hamish, our sexton."

The boys dipped their heads at them. Zenn raised her hand in greeting, felt suddenly awkward, and dropped it again. The younger boy looked about her age. Both had olive skin, high cheekbones and lean, muscular builds. Their appearance left no doubt: they were from the human colonies established over two centuries ago on the lone planet circling Procyon. Both had the same reddish brown hair, falling long and loose on one side of their head, the other side cut short in the Procyoni style. Each wore a long-tailed shirt of some rough, coarse-woven fabric belted at the waist and animal skin boots that reached to the knees – the older boy's tunic was tawny gold, the younger boy's forest green.

The older boy, she was interested to see, had several anitats. She'd seen these mood-controlled active tattoos once before, on the arms of the Indra groom who'd been there when her mother perished. The boy's anitats swirled and shifted on the skin visible at his wrists and neck, and he also sported an assortment of metal rings and studs on his face and ears. The other boy had no tattoos or ornaments, but wore colored beads and small feathers woven into his hair on the long side. Zenn realized she was staring, and quickly looked down, then at Ernie.

"Areth and Fane just came down on the ferry from the *Helen of Troy*," Otha said. "They're here to collect the whalehound."

"Oh... you work for the Leukkan royal family?" Zenn said. Of course they did; they were here for the Kiran's whalehound. She was flustered, having strangers on the grounds. Especially young ones. Especially Procyoni boys. She had to make an effort not to continue staring at them.

"We have the privilege of serving Princeling Sool," the older boy said, with a tone of voice and disinterested look that said this fact clearly elevated him above a lowly novice exovet. Zenn felt her face going red. "The Princeling has taken a deck of suites aboard the *Helen of Troy*."

"They've brought a bulk container-trailer for the hound; it's out in the front drive. And," Otha grinned at Zenn, "they've also brought us a little surprise."

Zenn was fully familiar with her uncle's "little surprises." Like when she was eight. Otha had carefully concealed a Dantean sulpher-newt inside a cast-off eggshell. He then placed the egg beneath a brooding axebill hen. When Zenn arrived and pulled the egg out, it cracked open to reveal the understandably annoyed little lizard, which promptly blew a defensive puff of shockingly bad breath at her.

"Look what hatched, unca," she'd exclaimed to him, holding her nose. "A baby dragon!"

Then there was the infamous case of the Encharan jumpworms Otha had hidden in her backpack. And the birthday cake that sprouted legs and walked off the table. He'd never told her what kind of animal he'd used for that "little surprise," but promised her repeatedly no harm was done to the creature.

No, she had good reasons for not liking the look of her uncle's mischievous grin.

"Otha?" she asked warily. "What kind of surprise, exactly?"

"You'll see," was all he said. "Now, I've got to go finish up the billing for the hound." He turned to the Procyoni boys. "When Zenn is finished here, why don't you boys show her what you brought down from the *Helen*?"

"Fane, you will show her," the one called Areth said to the younger boy. "And be quick about it. Groom Treth will be impatient to have the princeling's animal safely aboard. I will accompany the director-abbot and meet you at the vehicle." His tone indicated he was used to giving orders, and used to having them obeyed.

Otha and Areth walked off, leaving Zenn and Hamish with the younger boy.

"So… Fane… you have something for us, in the trailer?" Zenn asked.

"As the healer just said." The boy's expression was blank, his dark eyes unapologetically scanning her.

"Can you tell us what it is?" Zenn said, trying hard to be patient.

"It is an animal. A large animal." He made no effort to elaborate and, it seemed to Zenn, enjoyed keeping her in suspense.

Alright. Be that way. I don't care, then.

From behind her, Ernie crunched a particularly thick bone in the trough, reminding her that she had work to do. Giving the yote his shots was going to be tricky enough, even without some strange kid looking over her shoulder.

"Ever seen yotes? In the wild, I mean?" she said, affecting a casual tone and holding the pneuma-ject syringe up to check the dosage it held.

"They are from Procyon, my world. I am familiar."

Not exactly chatty.

She took a little longer than strictly necessary to check the syringe in her hand, thinking she probably looked very professional to this boy in his homemade tunic and rustic boots. Here she was, a Ciscan novice exovet, just going about her everyday duties, wrangling a big, male yote, expertly giving him injections, no big deal, really.

"They're prone to common distemper, you know." she said, gesturing with the syringe. "But we've never had a case here, at the cloister."

"Hm," the boy said, folding his arms. "Does this injection hurt them?"

"No. Well, not much, if you do it right." She moved close to the small door in the fence, breathing through her mouth to avoid the stench of the animal's breath, fetid with the smell of decaying flesh. When Ernie dipped his head into the trough again, Zenn darted her hand through the feeding door and touched the pneuma-ject tip to the back of his huge neck. He flinched and reared, but she had already stepped back – quickly, but not so quickly the boy might think she was afraid.

"And that's that," she said, trying to sound nonchalant. "It's not that tough. When you know what you're doing."

Ernie made a throaty, low-pitched groaning noise, his head suspended above the trough.

"Is he upset?" the boy asked.

"No. He's fine. Yotes often vocalize like that."

Ernie stood very still.

"He seems upset."

What? This Procyoni boy is going to educate me about my own yote?

"No. Actually, we've had this yote here for over a year," she said, taking a second syringe from Hamish and holding it aloft. "And I've never…"

A ghastly, retching sound suddenly detonated from inside Ernie, his jaws fell open, muscles contracted, and in a single, concentrated stream of thick saliva, rotting meat and half-digested body parts, he emptied the entire contents of his neck crop onto Zenn. A second later, she added to the reeking semi-liquid substance that encased her by vomiting too.

TWENTY

Both Hamish and the boy had jumped back out of the way and stood looking at her. The boy's mouth was slightly agape. Then he laughed. Not a long laugh. Just a short, derisive "*Heh*."

"Novice Zenn." Hamish came up to her, reached out, but stopped short of actually touching her. "Are you injured?"

"No," she said, attempting to speak without opening her mouth and being forced to taste the substance covering her face like a warm, wet mask.

"The yote was upset," the boy said. He laughed at Zenn once more for good measure, although, she also told herself later, this laugh might not have been as mocking as the first one.

It took Zenn a full ten minutes to clean up. And she still smelled foul enough to almost make herself gag. When she finally emerged from the small bathroom at the back of the infirmary wearing a clean pair of coveralls, the boy was standing by the back wall, reading one of the anatomical charts hanging there. Hamish had been called away to help Hild in the garden. He seemed happy to be as far from Zenn as possible.

The boy turned as she entered the room. Zenn wondered if he'd smelled her coming.

"We should go to the trailer now," the boy said. "Areth will want to get back to the ship."

She was almost over her intense embarrassment, but could feel her cheeks continuing to burn.

"So, what do you do?" she asked him as they left the infirmary and started across the grounds. "I mean, on the ship?"

"You are familiar with the term 'groom's sacrist'?" He came up close behind her as she walked, then dropped back a few paces, waving one hand in front of his face. She pretended not to notice.

She'd heard this term – the sacrist was some sort of assistant to an Indra groom. And she knew the position involved the rituals surrounding the groom's work as starship pilot, but that's all. The esoteric ceremonies conducted in a starship's Indra chambers weren't exactly public knowledge.

"You're an assistant, then. The groom's helper." She looked at him hopefully.

Maybe this will get him talking. Boys like to talk about themselves, don't they?

"A sacrist is no simple helper," he said, sounding offended at her ignorance. "They are the keeper of the Shuryn Dohlm – the sacred altar. They are also the chamber's mechanical worker and the speaker of the Path to Threshold prayer. They harvest the salviapine branches of offering that are placed on the Shuryn Dohlm, and gather the herbs bound into the incense that is burned. Without the sacrist, the groom would be unable to enter into commune with her Stonehorse."

"Yes, the incense," Zenn said. "I've always wondered why

you do that. Burn it in the Indra pilot room, I mean."

"Why burn incense?" He laughed another of his brief laughs. "Without the smoke to lift our prayers to the realm of the Ghost Shepherds, they would turn their faces from us. The Stonehorse would refuse the groom's communing. Tunneling would not be possible. Starships would go nowhere."

"The Ghost Shepherds. You really believe they watch over the Indra herds? That they're actually out there, somewhere, listening to you?"

"Clearly they are there. The proof is abundant. The Stonehorse tunnels at the groom's summoning, do they not? It is the Shepherd's blessing that permits this."

"But couldn't it just be the Indra, responding to the groom's intentions? I mean, the groom visualizes the destination, and the ship's computer interface transmits this to the Indra, and then it tunnels."

"Without the Shepherds' blessing? Impossible. The groom's thoughts would be... gibberish without the Shepherds' guidance. Humankind is too lowborn to commune with the Stonehorse without the Shepherds' intervention. This is the way of things. This is the truth passed down every generation within the Procyoni people."

"Yes, but just because your elders say it's true, doesn't make it so," Zenn said, growing exasperated with the boy's apparent unwillingness to argue according to her idea of the facts. "New research shows that Indra are responding to cortical theta waves – to the electrical activity inside the brains of their grooms. The nav-computer records the waves and..."

"Waves? Heh." The boy laughed. "We need no waves to show us the truth of the Ghost Shepherds. The fact that the communing allows travel among the stars is all the proof we require."

"Yes, but that's my point," she said. "Things happen for a reason. If you just accept somebody's word, and they just accepted somebody else's word, you're just believing things because you're told to. Not because you actually know the original cause."

"The original cause of the Stonehorse's power? That is hidden from us. It lies in the hearts of the Shepherds, and we cannot know it. It is much too awesome a thing for a lowly human being to comprehend."

"But..." Zenn fought to keep her voice from rising to a shout. "You might as well believe in magic then. And... and... garden fairies."

"Fay-reeza, yes," the boy said, looking solemn. "I have heard of these beings. On Tandua. They lurk in the dens of swamp sloos and are known to turn men into mud-hoppers."

"No! No, they do not live there, and they do not turn men into mud-hoppers!" Zenn's exasperation had now reached the point that she hardly knew how to respond.

"Oh? And you can bring me proof that a certain mud-hopper was not once a certain man?"

"No, I can't prove that. You can't prove a negative, alright?"

"Ha! As I thought."

Zenn was fighting to cool down enough to marshal a counterattack when they stepped through the side gate into the cloister drive. In the center of the gravel expanse, the container-trailer was parked behind the separate truck cab that pulled it. The trailer was about one hundred feet long, and consisted of a thick-walled, rectangular metal structure that could be lifted off its wheels and stacked in a starship hold. The gleaming white trailer appeared brand-new and bore the shield-like coat of arms of the Leukkan Kire royal household. The truck that pulled the trailer was, however, obviously Martian – old and rusted, but looking as if someone had at least taken the effort to hammer out the larger dents.

The boy walked around the side of the trailer, and she followed.

"Oh," she said, pointing. "You've got vomit. On your boot."

He stopped, looked down at his feet.

"I do. I have yote vomit on my boot." To Zenn's surprise, he laughed again. At himself? "The vomit of a yote. To approach groom Treth's chamber in this condition. She would beat me." When he laughed, she noticed that he had a slightly crooked smile, and very white teeth.

"Would she?" Zenn was taken aback. "Beat you?"

"No, of course she would not," he said, wiping at one eye. "A joke. I exaggerate. We are treated with the respect we are due, naturally."

"Oh, I'm glad to hear it."

"Grooms and those who share the workings of the chamber are a fellowship. Like you healers, in a way. You in your cloister here, we aboard our ship. The Indra chamber is our cathedral."

Zenn rather liked this comparison. And it brought to mind questions this boy might have answers to.

"So, have you heard anything lately about the Indra problem? About the ships that have disappeared?"

"The takings?" He frowned, one hand going to the feathers in his hair. "We have heard little, for there is little to know. The taken ships send no distress signals. And there is no debris field afterwards. It is curious. And it seems to be worsening. The grooms' union has assembled their own commission of investigation. But they have found nothing to report. Why do you ask?"

"The Indra ships are really important to us here. The ships bring our client's animals to Mars from the rest of the Accord. And of course we treat the ships' Indras, too. At least we did when the ships still came regularly. If things keep going the way they have been…"

"I see. The takings have affected your livelihood. As they will affect many more if the truth of the matter is not found."

"Does it worry you? To be a sacrist on an Indra ship? I mean, you never know. Your ship could be next."

"We… do not think of this," he said, but his hesitation said otherwise. After a short pause, he went on, "I should clarify one thing. Areth is, in truth, sacrist aboard the *Helen of Troy*. I am under-sacrist."

"Oh, I see."

"But I have expectations. Of promotion. To full sacrist. And very soon, Ghost Shepherds willing."

"So, you're a novice, like me." His expression told her he wasn't familiar with the word. "Right now, I'm a Novice, Second Order. When I pass my end of term tests, I'll be a Novice, First Order, for the next half-year term. Then, more classes, more testing, and I'll move up to Acolyte. What I mean is, right now, we're both just beginners."

"A beginner? No," he almost snorted at her. "That would not be true. I have almost a full year on the Helen. I have proven myself capable. When I am made sacrist, I will be allowed to choose the ship I serve on. No beginner underling would be allowed such an honor. Never."

Sorry I asked.

"And you," he said, scuffing his dirty boot in the sand to clean it. "What are your expectations, here on your world?"

Zenn looked up at the trailer, hoping he'd take the hint. He didn't.

"I want to become a fully licensed exovet."

"This is a long procedure?"

"Sort of. But I've had a head start. Living here in the cloister. So I'll be able to get through my basic courses here in just a couple of years. Then I'll do a year-long apprenticeship, take the final board exams and get my license. Unless I decide to go on to do a residency program in some specialty area. Like neurology or in-soma surgery or something."

"But it is a long procedure. To do what you want. To endure all those years of study."

"It's what I've always wanted to do. So, no, it doesn't seem so long. Not really."

"I would not be willing to wait such a period," he said. "To delay doing what I wanted."

"That's just how long it takes," she said, beginning to resent his curt attitude. "Learning the science behind the treatments, the biochemistry, the anatomy of all the different animals and the conditions they live in. You don't pick that up in a few months."

"Yes, but my kind come to know their Stonehorses without being shut into a room with a book," the boy said, waving one hand in the air, dismissing her argument. "We know these things by doing them. We learn from our closeness to the Stonehorse, and the miracle of tunneling. To do this requires no anatomies or book words. It is granted to us by the tuning of our senses, by opening our soul's-eye to the mystery of the Stonehorse."

"Right. I'm sure you know a lot about your Indra. But that's different." Zenn said, impatience growing inside her. For some unknown reason, she suddenly found herself comparing this arrogant off-worlder to Liam. She realized to her surprise that she'd much rather be talking to Liam Tucker, smirking, joking and all, rather than arguing the obvious with this superstitious young Procyon. At least Liam seemed to have some capacity to adjust his views when exposed to incontestable facts.

"Different? Yes," he scoffed at her. "The difference is I have journeyed among the stars, and you have read words on paper."

"The difference is you don't know how it works! Like how your Indra uses dark matter, the physics and biology of it, or the things that can make an Indra sick."

"Heh. We know all of these things, in here." He thumped once on his chest. "We know by living in the blessed aura of the Indra all our lives."

"Yes, but you're here on Mars now, aren't you?" she said triumphantly. "You're here at our cloister to get the whalehound. We're the only ones who could house it, take care of it. Or if your Indra, your stonehorse, gets sick, you'll bring it here to cure it, won't you? And the reason we can do that is the science we learn, all the studying, the training that exovets go through. All those years."

The boy glared at her, but had no ready response.

"So," he said then, looking at the trailer and sounding for all the world like he hadn't just lost an argument. "Do you wish to see what is inside, or not?"

Finally!

She nodded, and he climbed up on the side of the trailer where there was a small, moveable metal panel. She climbed up beside him, and he slid the panel open.

She looked inside, but it was too dark to see anything. Then, slowly, her eyes adjusted to the dimness. Something moved, too close to make out its shape, just the sense of a large mass, alive, breathing. It shifted position, but despite the thing's huge size, the trailer didn't sway or bounce. Now it moved away from her, and she could make out parts of a huge body, an expanse of tawny skin stretched over the sharp keel of a breast-bone, great wings folded in, a head, dark, oblong – no, two huge, dark heads, on two long, sinuous necks attached to... It couldn't be, could it? Yes. That would explain it. The trailer wouldn't react to the movement of an animal... if that animal was floating. Zenn's eyes widened, she pushed her face against the cold metal to see better. Yes, yes! This could only be one thing, only one creature in all the universe. And now it was here. On Mars. At their cloister. *Solsolis assassina magnus*. A Greater Kiran sunkiller.

Several hours later, after they'd made the switch and finished loading the whalehound into the recently emptied container-trailer, Zenn still couldn't believe what was, at that very moment, housed in their infirmary. A sunkiller. A living, breathing sunkiller. This one was young, just a fledgling; a fraction the size of a full-grown adult. But it was still any exovet's wildest dream. It was, after all, an animal so revered, so sacrosanct, few non-Leukkans had ever even seen one up close, let alone been allowed to touch or, in this case, to treat. Zenn's face was actually beginning to ache from smiling.

"My groom aboard ship will see to the transfer of funds concerning the whalehound, if that suits," Areth said to Otha, brandishing the v-film invoice he held in one hand before tucking it into his tunic.

"Suits fine," Otha told him. "Let us know if you have any trouble transporting him up to the ship. And don't be afraid to give him more of the ambicet." Otha gestured at the box of sedative biscuits Areth carried. "They're low-dosage and he likes the flavor."

"We will have no trouble with the hound," Areth said confidently, walking past Zenn toward the truck. As he passed, he wrinkled his nose and looked off toward the animal pens, frowning. Zenn took a step away from him.

"Thank you again," he said to Otha.

"Our pleasure. And please remember what I said, about thanking the princeling, for trusting us with his sunkiller. We're well aware of the honor."

"The princeling simply appreciates the Ciscan reputation," Areth said. "I'm sure you will bear out his trust by repairing what ails the beast." He nodded then at the younger boy, who immediately jumped up from where he sat on the ground and went to climb into the truck's passenger seat.

Otha started out in the direction of the infirmary.

"We'll see you in a few days, then," he said, lifting one hand in the air without looking back. Zenn was eager to follow him, to be in the same room with the sunkiller again. But she shouldn't just go, she told herself. She should see the Procyons off first. It was the polite thing to do, after all.

"So," Zenn said to the older boy. "Where do you go next? On the Helen?"

"Once your director-abbot has repaired the sunkiller, we will retrieve it and return to the princeling's home port, on Kire Secunda." Walking to the driver's side of the truck, he jerked open the door.

She let her gaze wander to the younger boy.

"Nice meeting you… both."

"And you," Areth said, climbing into the seat and shutting the door.

"So. I guess we'll see you again when the sunkiller is ready." She could think of nothing else.

"Shepherds willing," Areth said, and he started the truck.

"Yes," Fane Reth Fanesson called to her, turning to the truck window to give Zenn his bright smile. "And take care you do not upset your yote. Heh."

Before Zenn could respond, the truck pulled out of the drive and into the road, then shifted gears before roaring west toward Pavonis, a long rooster tail of rosy, sun-struck dust chasing along behind.

TWENTY-ONE

"What a specimen!" Otha declared as Zenn entered the infirmary. He was standing on the catwalk that ran around the interior walls, hands on hips, gazing up at the animal floating near the ceiling of the cavernous main room. The sunkiller's fully extended wings almost brushed the opposite walls of the building. Suspended beneath its body on a webbing of thick ropes and woven padding mats that ran up around its back was the gondola, a narrow structure that resembled an ornate, oversized sort of canoe built of interlaced reeds and bones, the stern and bow rising up to points at either end. The gondola, in turn, was firmly attached to the floor by four braided wire cables hooked to massive anchor bolts sunk into concrete footings.

"Only twelve years old, but look at that wingspan. Must be sixty, seventy feet already."

"Why did the Leukkans send it to us?" Zenn climbed the metal stairs to join him. "I mean, what's wrong with her... with them?" She was unsure of how to describe a single creature that bore two heads. Each of the massive skulls was eight or nine feet long, with blunt noses, large, toothless jaws equipped with baleen-like filters, a pair of deep-set hooded eyes and boney skull crests that arced backward from where the heads joined the necks. The overall effect was something like a double-headed pterodactyl crossed with a colossal manta ray.

"It's her methane plexus," Otha said. "She's not getting the right mix of gases to her wings. See how the bladders are stretched tight?" He pointed to the hundreds of small, gas-filled skin bubbles covering the underside of the creature's wings. "She's producing excess methane. Makes her too buoyant. The Kirans saved her life, kept her tethered since she was born. If they hadn't, she'd just have floated up until the atmosphere got so thin she'd suffocate."

"So, what's causing the problem?"

"A birth defect. I suspect it's a malformed valve in the plexus, but we won't know for sure till we do a scan."

Beneath the broad, legless body, curving down to almost touch the hanging gondola, was a scorpion-like tail that ended in a single, immense boney hook. The sunkiller used this when it wanted to anchor itself to the ground, which wasn't often. The buff-colored skin had no feathers or scales, but was leathery and dimpled, with darker coloration at the wingtips and intricate patterns of spots radiating up the dual necks onto the heads. The two necks, long and thick as giant pythons, twined and arched in the air as they bore the heads this way and that, the animal seeming to taste the air in this strange, new place.

Giving birth aloft in the upper atmosphere of Kire Secunda, sunkillers lived to be over five hundred years old, and spent almost all of that time drifting on the air currents, feeding on huge shoals of airborne strato-plankton. The only time they approached the ground was during the planet's ferocious, annual wind storms. Then they would descend, anchor themselves to mountaintops with their tail-hooks, and ride out the tempest.

"Otha," she said. A thought had suddenly occurred to her, and she decided on the spur of the moment to go ahead and voice it. Nothing ventured, nothing gained.... "Would you let me do it? The procedure?"

"On the sunkiller's plexus?" He was clearly startled. "You think you're ready for that?"

"I think so. Yes. I'm sure I can do it."

He considered, but only briefly, chewing at his cheek.

"No," he said then. "The operation is highly complex, Zenn. And the creature is just too... important. To the Kirans. And the Kirans' business is too important to the cloister. You know that."

"But Otha," she complained, unwilling to accept his evaluation of her skill level. "I am ready. I've assisted on three or four procedures that are almost identical to a plexus bypass."

"Oh? Looking over my shoulder as an assisting Novice Second Order has made you a Master-Surgeon? And a sunkiller specialist to boot? Well, that's good news. We can just skip you right over the next three or four years of training you seem to think you no longer require."

Her uncle was joking with her, but Zenn wasn't in the mood.

"I can do it, Otha. I could show you, if you'd let me do more than watch you, more than just put in a stitch here and there or mop up the bloody floors when you're done."

"So it's my fault now? I'm the one holding you back?" He actually laughed at her, shaking his head.

"Otha, how can I make any real progress if you won't let me try? Half the time you treat me like I'm still a little girl, playing exovet with my stuffed animals."

"Zenn, the fact of it is you are not an exovet. Not yet."

He lowered his eyebrows, holding her gaze. "That's what being a novice is about. You go step by step. You don't over-reach. So, no, I'm sorry, but you won't be operating on the royal family's sunkiller. Save that for your surgical apprenticeship. Save it for when you're ready."

Another thought returned to Zenn now. And she was just angry enough to let it out.

"Actually, I've been thinking about that. My apprenticeship."

"Oh? Have you?" He turned his back on her and went to check the cables that secured the sunkiller's gondola to the infirmary floor.

"Hild says the Ciscan hospitaliers at the cloister on Bhranthis have put out a notice. They're accepting acolytes for their pre-surgical program next year."

This had the desired effect. Otha stopped and turned back to her.

"Bhranthis? That's halfway across the Accord. We've always assumed you'd be doing your acolyte year here on Mars. With us."

Yes. Exactly. You assume I'll always be here. Always be a stable girl on the bottom rung of the ladder. Maybe the Procyoni boy was right about being shut in a room with books.

Zenn wasn't sure she was serious about Bhranthis. The truth was, until recently, she too had always seen herself staying on Mars for her acolyte year, and possibly beyond. But if Otha was going to treat her like a child, she was going to rebel like one and let him stew.

"Well…" Otha looked as if he wasn't quite sure himself if she was having him on. "Maybe we'll let you do a bit more than assist on the sunkiller's plexus. But, just a bit. Let's not get ahead of ourselves here."

"Fine," she said, feeling she'd just achieved a surprising victory. "I guess I'll settle for a bit."

"And we'll... keep an open mind about where you'll do your acolyte year, eh?"

Zenn let him worry for a few seconds more.

"Yes, alright," she said. She couldn't resist adding: "But the Sister says the Bhranthis pre-surgical practicum is the best program she's ever seen."

"Hmph," Otha snorted. "She says that, does she?"

Zenn heard the infirmary door open behind her. It was Hamish.

"This is an impressive variety of beast," the coleopt said, stopping at the base of the steps. "Do I have approval to ascend the steps and observe it more closely?"

Zenn sighed. "Hamish, what did we talk about? About approvals?"

"Ah, that I am not to ask another's approval every single time. That I am to think for myself, and take action based on my thoughts. Correct?"

"Yes... and so...?"

"I see. This is one of those times. Very well. I will... come up the stairs? Yes. I am coming up. So," he said when he was next to her, "the Sister tells me this flying-life-form is young. How big will it grow when old?"

"Very big," Otha said, going past Hamish to descend the stairs. "Zenn, I'll let you introduce the sexton to our new arrival. I'm going to warm up the Q-scanner, get it calibrated for a solsolis. Hamish, stick around. We'll need your help positioning the scan sensors."

"Yes, director-abbot," Hamish said, not taking his eyes off the creature. "I will remain here. Novice Scarlett... how big will this creature become?"

"A full-grown adult will reach fifteen-hundred feet,

measured across the wings."

"That large? It's difficult to envisage such a thing."

"They blot out a pretty big piece of sky when they fly over. That's why the Leukkans first called them sunkillers."

"It is so still, resting in the air." It was true. The sunkiller, despite taking up most of the infirmary, was almost silent, the two heads emitting only a quiet thrum of barely audible vocalizations. "The wings do not flap. How does it fly?"

"See the bladders?" She pointed to the underside of the wings. "All those little bubbles are filled with a mix of gases. The sunkillers produce hydrogen, methane and some other gases as natural by-products. The gases are lighter than air, so that's how they stay up. They mix in oxygen, too, which is heavier and helps them control their altitude. This one has a problem with its methane plexus. That's the organ that routes the right gases to the right places. It's up on top of her back, running along her backbone, a big, sack-like sort of thing with tubes running out of it down to the bladders under the wings."

"I understand. So this is why the wings remain in one place."

"Yes. And since they don't flap, it makes their body a stable platform for the Leukkans to live on."

"The beings of the Leukkan Kire live on top of sunkillers? You jest with me."

"No. Really, it's true," Zenn said. "You've never heard of the Kiran sky-forts?"

Hamish shook his head.

"Well, a long time ago, like a thousand years or something, the surface of Kire Secunda was crawling with predators – dire-cats, vampiric fungi, huge packs of giant eviscerenni. Big, hungry things. The Leukkans had to wage a constant fight just to keep from being eaten. Then they tamed the first sunkillers. They realized they could escape the hunters down on the surface by staying up in the air. So, they started building little shelters on the sunkillers' backs. Then they made forts, then palaces, then entire villages. They've been living on them ever since."

"Imagine that," Hamish said. "To make one's home on the back of such a beast. Does it not pain the animal?"

"No, apparently not," Zenn told him. "The Leukkans usually put the first light-weight structures on the sunkillers when they're small, to get them used to it. That's what that thing is." She pointed to the suspended gondola. "They start out by hanging one gondola underneath them, then they add more. They're really light, woven from reeds and the hollow wing bones of giant Kiran vultures. After a few years, they start putting buildings on their backs. By then the animals are so big they hardly notice. Kind of like a saddle on an Earther horse."

"Yes, but a saddle that stays on always. And has organisms living on it."

"Alright, Zenn, Hamish." Zenn looked down to see Otha wheeling the Quark Resonance Scanner into the room. "Let's see what's ailing this little girl and get her fixed up."

TWENTY-TWO

After Otha confirmed his suspicion about the sunkiller's defective plexus valve, hunger finally forced Zenn to tear herself away from the infirmary and head for the kitchen. Crossing through the center of the cloister walk, she caught sight of the sundial. If she hurried, she had just enough time to grab a quick snack before Sister Hild's lecture on the anatomy of Indra brain ventricles. No sooner had she started for the kitchen when it dawned on her: in the flurry of activity she'd almost forgotten her second assignment for the morning. She never forgot assignments. Well, almost never. But the fact this very important one had almost slipped her mind made her more than a little irked at herself. She changed direction and headed toward the main storage shed.

Entering the shed, she flicked on the light – only to have the bulb crackle, pop and burn out.

"I do not have time for this," she said to no one at all.

No matter, she decided. She knew the layout of the room well enough to do what she had to do in the semi-darkness. She went to the largest of the three wheelbarrows parked there and rolled it over next to one of the large metal tubs lining the far wall. She could just make out the label, "Dried Tanduan Rhina Grub." Prying off the lid, she rapidly scooped out enough to fill the barrow half-full. Pushing the barrow over to the tub that held powdered sweetbark, she dug out half a scoop's worth and added that to the barrow's contents. Then, she unlooped the water hose from its hook on the wall, cranked on the spigot and propped the hose so it would slowly fill the barrow as she mixed the contents.

Thinking about what the wheelbarrow's contents would be used for tomorrow, her breath came a little faster.

It's alright. I'm ready. She'd been giving herself the same sort of pep talk all week. She'd gone over the in-soma procedures until her brain hurt. *At least, I think I'm ready... No. I'm ready.*

Using a discarded piece of pipe, she stirred the mixture until she had what she thought was the proper gooey consistency.

A sound at the door made her turn. It was Liam Tucker.

"Scarlett," he said. "Didn't see you. What're you doing in the dark?"

"Bulb burned out," she said, mildly flustered by his arrival. The breeze through the door carried a familiar scent to her: the pleasantly sweet, dry-grass smell of baled alfalfa. She realized why she recognized this. It was Liam Tucker's scent, from his work in the cloister fields and barns.

"I, uh, never really said thank you, you know?" he said. "For Zeus. What you did."

"I got the idea you were grateful." She relived the press of his arms around her, something she'd done more than once since that moment in the surgery.

No harm in that. Not breaking any rules. Rule intact.

"No, I mean, I didn't really say what I meant. You saved his life. And I... I don't know if I really said thanks so you'd know I meant it." He turned sideways in the doorway. She breathed in the scent of him as she squeezed past. It wasn't intentional. She was just breathing. It was only the smell of alfalfa. But she suddenly felt she was too close. She moved a few safe steps away.

"Sorry," she said, nodding her head in the direction of the scriptorium. "I have a lecture, with Hild. I should go."

"Yeah, right," he said. "Sister Hild. Don't wanna keep her waiting."

"Were you looking for Hamish?" she asked. She really didn't have time for this. Didn't have time to be distracted. But she was strangely reluctant to leave. There it was. No point in pretending. Just now, standing in this spot, she was distracted. The Liam-virus-thought, propagating, spreading. This was exasperating. But not in any way she'd been exasperated before. She breathed in the scent of sun-dried alfalfa that seemed to radiate from the boy. And she was... distracted.

"Oh, yeah. I was. Looking for Hamish," he said. "But... I don't really mind running into a novice exovet now and then." He was smiling at her. Not his Liam-smirk, either. An actual smile-smile. Zenn's mind was quite blank, then sputtered pathetically to life.

What? What did he just say?

"I mean," he said, "I'm always wondering what poor creature you're gonna pick on next."

Oh, that's what he meant.

"So, you know where the big bug is at?"

"Yes. Hamish. He's at the infirmary. Helping Otha." She'd never noticed before, but she really liked the smell of alfalfa. Really. Liked it.

"Right. Well, I'll go track him down."

Zenn just nodded, then stood there until she felt foolish.

"Right. Goodbye." She turned and headed toward the scriptorium. She'd said "Goodbye." That was idiotic. Why did she say that?

The *Rule*, Zenn. Obey the Rule.

And now, there would be no time to steal a bite to eat. But she was no longer so hungry.

The Rule. You're disobeying. *Bad Zenn.*

But was she? Being bad? Recently, she'd been toying with an improper new thought: what if the Rule... was wrong. Could that be? What if, for instance, newly discovered information rendered the Rule obsolete, or called for exceptions?

Liam is... interested. Am I interested? And if I am, is it only because he was interested first? Should I like Liam Tucker? Can a person make a decision to like someone? Or is this sort of thing... involuntary?

No doubt about it – she was adrift now in foreign territory. She felt weightless and unsighted, so much so that she almost tripped over a water spigot at the side of the path. She stopped and stood still. She heard the sound of her own breathing. She crossed her arms and looked down at the spigot.

Thinking like this was against more than the Rule, of course. There was also the rule about theories and their supporting evidence. But, lately she'd found herself considering that under specific circumstances dealing with emotions, the values in the equations could be changed, more or less at will, producing answers that were just what you needed them to be. It all... depended on how you felt. On your feelings. Stunning. But should she just let this new model of thinking go into effect without further scrutiny?

Probably not smart...

It was the water spigot at her feet that finally reminded

her: *The water in the shed. It's still running.*

Berating herself for this latest lapse, she hurried back to the shed. She'd just stepped through the door when a movement in the darkened interior brought her up short.

Liam came out of the shadows abruptly, seeming momentarily as surprised as she was.

"Scarlett," he laughed. "You... following me around now or what?" He laughed again.

"No!" she said emphatically. "It's the water. I was filling the barrow. Forgot to shut it off."

"Yeah, you did," he said after a slight, bemused pause. "I heard the water running. I shut it off for you. You're welcome."

She looked past him to the wheelbarrow. It had only overflowed onto the floor a little. She wouldn't have to re-mix the paste. "Well, thank you."

"That goo." He nodded at the barrow. "That for your in-soma thing tomorrow?"

"Yes. It goes on the pod. It'll attract the sloo when it's time for the insertion."

"Yeah, better you than me," he said as they both walked out into the sunlight. "Well, I better go track down the boss-bug. Make sure he hasn't strained himself doing some actual work."

Zenn laughed at this. It was true. Hamish did avoid physical exertion whenever possible. The odd thing was that generally speaking, Liam was just as bad, except when it came to lending Hamish a hand. She watched him go. She thought of Hamish's friendship with Liam. Whatever it was, Hamish had Liam wrapped around his little finger. Or little claw-digit. She imagined the towner boy lugging bales of straw, Hamish reclining nearby, complaining about having too many chores.

Hamish owes me one, she told herself as she again made for the scriptorium. Then she allowed herself to consider the scent of new-cut alfalfa once more, and Liam's smirk-now-a-smile, and the sight of his broad back beneath his torn red shirt as he had walked away from her. She forgot about Hamish and what she was owed.

TWENTY-THREE

Early the next morning, Zenn muttered to herself as she moved at a rapid clip toward the cloister's treatment and nesting pools. She was running through the details of the insoma insertion one more time. Rather, she was attempting and failing to concentrate on this all-important second test in the end of term trio. Her mind was on the verge of grinding to a gridlocked halt. She felt under siege from all angles: her increasingly disturbing interactions with the animals; Ren Jakstra's alarming news about the cloister lease; and the unexpected, entirely unintentional way her opinion of Liam Tucker was evolving, like some newly emerged life form. All combined with the usual roster of studies, and chores...

In the end, desperate, she'd resorted to talking to herself out loud to clear her head of anything besides the day's upcoming trial.

"...and keep a light touch on the polycilia throttle," she intoned, calling up an image of her lecture notes on the subject. "Engage propulsion only when forward progress has ceased. Toggle regularly between bow and stern view screens to maintain locational awareness and gauge proximity to internal organs…"

She found Otha pushing the wheelbarrow of rhina grub and sweetbark paste down to the edge of the largest treatment pool. It was chilly that morning, causing thick fingers of fog to drift like phantom hands reaching out over the collection of shallow ponds where various aquatic species were housed.

"Sure you're ready for this?" Otha nodded at the in-soma pod, its sleek, downy surface shimmering in the slanting morning light.

"Ready? I can't wait," Zenn said, wanting to let Otha hear in her voice that she was focused and confident. She had spent all her free time during the past week studying the digestive tract of swamp sloos and practicing with the in-soma controls. She was ready now to show Otha the disaster with the hound was just a fluke. Yes, she was ready for this test.

Mounted on a pair of old, reclaimed railroad tracks that led down into the sloo's pool, the in-soma pod was about seven feet long, barely three feet wide, and shaped like an elongated pumpkin seed. The streamlined surface displayed the silky sheen of artificial polycilia – a layer of microscopic hair-like filaments. Beating in unison, the cilia would silently propel the pod through the interior of whatever gargantuan creature happened to be the subject of the in-soma procedure. Today, that would be the interior of a female Tanduan swamp sloo.

Otha went to the edge of the pool, kneeled and slapped the surface with his open palm, as he did whenever he fed the sloos. A splashing sound came from the distance and the animal appeared, paddling into view from a great cloudbank of mist on the pool's far side. This sloo was roughly two hundred feet long, and about forty feet tall.

With its slender, tubular snout and long, graceful neck mounted on a body propelled by four, big paddle-like flukes, the sloo struck Zenn as resembling a prehistoric plesiosaur mated with a giant anteater. In any case, it was ideally adapted for invading the huge hive-mounds of the human-sized insects it fed on in the coastal swamps of Tandua.

The sloo looked on with interest as Zenn and Otha prepared the pod for insertion, tilting its great head this way and that as it watched.

She knelt to activate the pod's door mechanism and it split open, hinges squealing. Inside was a padded bench.

"Sounds like it could use a little oil," Zenn said.

"Well now, this unit has served both your mother and me well enough over the years."

It occurred to Zenn the pod was a good deal older than she was.

"It's been through a lot though, huh?"

"No worries there," Otha said, shifting the wheelbarrow closer to the pod. "Hull plating and software are all fully functional. Truth is, these early Gupta-Merck models were built better than anything on the market now. You can't get this kind of craftsmanship these days." He patted the open lid of the pod to demonstrate its soundness, but his touch only made the hinges screech even louder.

"Changed large animal medicine forever, these first in-soma units," Otha went on, attempting, Zenn assumed, to distract her from the pod's age. "Before in-somas, major surgery on the big animals was a real nightmare. You should've seen it. Took four, five exovets at once. Incisions twenty feet long and yards deep. Of course we lost most of the patients – massive bleeding, post-op infection, shock."

Otha pulled the pushbroom out of the wheelbarrow's load of watered-down grub bits and smeared the substance on the side of the pod.

"And the experience of it. An in-soma run is like nothing else, I can promise you that."

"I guess today I find out for myself," said Zenn, trying not to sound giddy.

"That's the spirit. So, how are you feeling now, about being inside?"

"I feel good," she said, nodding her head and doing a fair job, she told herself, of looking self-assured. "This past week, I spent lots of time in the pod. Closed the lid and ran through procedures. Piece of cake."

Otha patted her arm. "You are your mother's daughter, true enough."

A high, fluting cry came from the pool. The sloo's mate was calling to it from somewhere inside the wall of fog. Otha stepped over to a control pad mounted on the side of the small tool shed next to the pond and flipped a switch, activating the energy fencing behind the female. This would keep her penned up where they could work with her.

She watched the creature's long, tubular nose waving in the air. The sloo had picked up the scent of the paste-covered pod. Zenn was only mildly reassured by the fact that sloos had no teeth. They devoured their prey whole, licking them out of their hives with a sticky, thirty-foot tongue. This animal was selected for Zenn's in-soma exercise because it was both larger than the male and relatively docile. As she contemplated being swallowed by a two-hundred-foot-long insectivore, however, "relatively" was a word that carried little comfort. Still, she was thrilled to be on the verge of her first in-soma run. She stepped into the pod and lay face down on the bench.

"Otha." The shout came from a short distance away. Zenn raised up in the pod and saw it was Ren Jakstra. He stood beyond the tool shed, eyeing the sloo. "Is it safe to come down there? Got these for ya." He held a sheaf of v-films aloft.

"It's safe, Ren," Otha said, waving him on. "This big girl's gentle as a baby."

"Glad to hear it," the constable said, watching the sloo as he approached them.

"So, what's this all about?"

"The cloister mortgage docs. Bank in Zubrin sent them via my office. They're gettin' antsy."

Otha took the films from him and scowled.

"I'll look these over later. Our novice here is about to take her first in-soma run."

"That so?" Ren gave the pod a skeptical look. "Hmph. She really gonna go inside that behemoth? All the way in?"

"That's the idea," Otha said. "You're welcome to stay and watch. In fact, I wish you would."

"Oh?"

"It's something I've been mulling over lately," Otha said, rolling up the v-films and putting them into his back pocket. "I think we could be doing a better job of reaching out to the community. You know, get folks in Arsia more familiar with what we do out here. I'd like to have some groups come out and observe now and then. Might defuse some of the... well, might make people a little more comfortable with having us as neighbors."

"Yeah, couldn't hurt, I guess," Ren said, not convinced.

"If you'd mention the idea to the council I'd appreciate it," Otha said. He gestured at a nearby bale of hay. "So, have a seat. You can be our guinea pig."

"Not sure I like the sound of that," Ren said. But he sat down on the bale. "Can't stay long, though. And speakin' of pigs, I hear your novice here has quite a talent with sandhogs."

"Oh? How's that?" Otha said.

"From what Gil Bodine says, she does indeed." Zenn looked at Otha, who just raised an eyebrow at her and turned back to Ren as he continued: "Gil says that big sandhog boar of his was about to come down on you like a ton of bricks. He says…" Ren smiled. "He said little Zenn here put the evil eye on that hog. Turned the thing meek as a puppy, just like that." He gave her a sly look. "Quite the talent."

"Gil is a bit of a storyteller, as we all know," Otha said. "That hog just moved a little slower than I could run, that's all. That and some bad feed."

"Well, whatever happened out there, it didn't do you any good, with the council, if you get my drift. A sandhog boar on the loose? Bad timing for something like that."

"What are you getting at, Ren?" Otha said, frowning at him.

"Just that you people out here might want to… *re-evaluate* your priorities. Far as selling the cloister. Council votes against you, your rights to the land get revoked. Leaves you all in a bad way."

"Our priorities are just where we want them, Ren," Otha said, leveling his gaze at the constable. "You know where I stand on selling out. And I've done some thinking about what you said, about talking to the council. If Warra could do it, I guess I can too."

"Well, the council will be all ears." The constable looked around then, surveying the surroundings, seeming to measure the weight of what he was about to say. "About Warra – look, I understand what he went through after Mai… after the accident. But your brother's making some people pretty unhappy. With what he's up to out on

Enchara."

"What do you mean, 'what he's up to'?" Otha said, squinting at him.

"You know. Refusing to let things go. Stirring things up, making the Authority look bad, just when Earth is trying to get back into contact with the other planets in the Accord. And with Mars. It's politics, Otha. Big boy politics. People are noticing, and not in a good way."

"So, you're in direct contact with the Authority on Earth now? Didn't know that was in your job description. Ren."

"Hey, I'm a public official. When higher ups on the food chain ask me questions, I give 'em honest answers." He lowered his voice. "Do Warra a favor. Tell him he's in over his head out there."

"Warra's a big boy, Ren. I don't see how he needs any advice from you or the Authority. They may run things on Earth. But they don't run things on Mars."

"No, they don't... yet." He sucked his mustache. "But," he gestured at Zenn, "don't let me hold ya up. On with the show."

Otha gave Ren a look, seemed about to say something, but instead turned to Zenn.

"You all set?" he asked her, kneeling by the pod.

"Yes. All set," Zenn said, though she could do without Ren's presence. Still, the prospect of the coming procedure outweighed that minor irritation. She lay down again, rested her chin on the bench's forward cushions, tested the tension of the seat-belt harness and made sure the two view screens were functioning. One screen could be switched between the view straight ahead of the pod and behind the stern. The other screen's signal came from a camera mounted on the roof of the tool shed, and showed a wide-angle shot of the entire pool. This allowed the one piloting the pod to see how the patient was reacting from the outside.

"Take it slow, don't rush," Otha told her. "Let the peristalsis action carry you whenever possible. Only engage the cilia if you have to."

"Yes, Otha, I know," she said, her voice breathy with excitement. "See you on the other side."

"You mean 'at the other end'," Otha said, grinning.

"Yeah... right," she answered, in no mood for his breezy exovet humor about the obvious conclusion to a two-hour journey through a sloo's intestines

Zenn toggled the lever next to her right hand and the pod lid closed, hinges complaining all the way, the wrap-around cushions gripping her body in a firm embrace. Otha slid the pod down the ramp's tracks. Zenn watched the outboard monitor screen, and saw the sloo respond to the pod's motion, raising its head for a better look.

The pod hit the water, and the bow screen darkened momentarily as the nose cam was submerged, then brightened as it bobbed to the surface. She lost sight of the pod's position in the pool when the sloo's body blocked the outside cam view, but the next instant, she knew the sloo had seen her.

With a powerful jerk, the pod was lifted free of the water by the sloo's muscular tongue and pulled into its mouth, as if a huge rubber band had been stretched and snapped back. The viewscreens went black and flickered on again, the pod's bow light switched on, and Zenn saw the sloo's oral cavity displayed on the view screen, yawning ahead of her like a narrow, fleshy cave.

The sensation of being crushed hit Zenn almost at once, and she reminded herself this was normal, everything was fine, no problem. But it didn't help that the pod was jammed up against the roof of the sloo's mouth, the huge tongue trapping it.

"She'll hold you there a moment," Otha's voice in her earpiece was calm and reassuring. "She's just making sure you're something worth swallowing. Doing alright?"

"I'm good," she told him. It was a lie. Her mouth was dry, and she had the distinct sensation of being suffocated. She made herself breathe slowly, regularly. In, out, in, out. The trapped feeling subsided... a little.

Zenn focused on the instrument readings. Her hands reached out until they contacted the controls, unseen beneath her on either side. She'd spent hours memorizing the pod's instrument layout, testing herself until she could visualize every detail. Now, she conjured up an image of the control surfaces and manipulators of the various instruments.

Right hand: forward viewscreen and zoom, toggle to rear viewscreen or outboard cam, hypojection arm, biopsy collection arm and maser-cauterizer. Left hand: polycilia propulsion, pod enviro controls, patient vital signs monitors and sensor probes.

"When she's ready," she heard Otha say, "she'll push you into her laryngeal opening. Wait for it."

Zenn now heard another sound beneath the hum and tick of the pod's various systems. Like creaking, or... metal bending? Yes, it must be the outer hull, stressed by the pressure of the sloo's quarter-ton tongue.

Normal sounds. Not a problem. Perfectly normal sounds.

But the sloo wasn't cooperating. For some reason, she was refusing to swallow the pod. Instead, she gripped it tightly in the rear of the oral cavity. Zenn wanted to ask Otha what to do. He would be waiting for her to do that, to fall back on him for guidance, reassurance. Of course, she couldn't ask. Not if she wanted to get the score on this test that she needed. A few more stomach-knotting moments dragged by, then she made her choice, toggled the cilia propulsion on, and, almost imperceptibly, the pod began to slide forward. She felt her tensed body relax.

Good. We're moving. Good decision.

Now, it was simply a matter of making sure the sloo's epiglottis was in the closed position, blocking the entrance to the trachea and the lungs. This would give her a clear shot at entering the esophagus and continuing on to the upper digestive tract.

As she moved from the oral cavity into the throat, though, the sloo's muscles constricted again, halting the pod. Zenn increased the cilia rate.

Abruptly, the creaking sound of the flexing hull increased alarmingly, accompanied by another noise, guttural and grating: the sloo was gagging.

Problem!

The next moment, Zenn was thrown hard against the pod restraining straps and the external monitor showed the sloo shaking its massive head back and forth. The force of it made Zenn's hands lose their position on the controls. Frantically, she groped to relocate the instrument pods.

This isn't right. Why is she doing this?

The shaking grew so violent that Zenn had to give up trying to find the controls and simply clutch the padded bench with both hands. Next thing she knew, the remote cam monitor showed the sloo heaving itself up out of the water, throwing its great, green-and-gray speckled body up onto the shore, its front flippers clawing at the muddy bank. She saw Ren leap up from his seat. The sloo waved its neck and head toward him – and she saw Ren pull his pistol from its holster.

No! Don't shoot! Don't attract its attention.

But when the sloo whipped its huge head closer to him,

Ren pointed the gun into the air and fired. The sloo reacted instantly to the sound. Zenn watched in horror as the long tongue lashed out and wrapped itself around the constable's midsection. Ren got out one short, high scream before he was whisked up and into the animal's snout.

Zenn stared at the monitor in disbelief. Before she could even begin to think what to do next, there was the distant, muffled sound of another gunshot and a loud hoot of pain from the sloo. The monitor from the tool shed cam showed a small, red cloud of blood and tissue puff out into the air from inside the animal's snout. Ren had fired again.

And then the sickening, familiar feeling hit her, like a fierce wind gusting up out of nowhere, like her body and mind had been instantly submerged in some deep well of unnamable sensation. She was gripped by two strong, distinct impressions: heat, searing her mouth; and intense, stinging pain in her nose, as if her nostril had been pierced by a thick needle. But even as her eyes teared from the pain, she knew the sensation wasn't coming from inside her mouth, or from her own nose. At that second, she was feeling what the sloo felt.

Then, the sloo gagged again, jolting Zenn back into her own head, the spasm rotating the pod until it was upside down. Fumbling frantically, her hands again found their way to the controls – but which was the propulsion toggle? Inverted, disoriented, she was suddenly unsure of the instrument layout. First toggle on the left? Or second? Which side was her left?

Now, the suffocating sensation rushed back, worse than before. The walls of the pod pressed against her from above and below – the hard metal pushing in, crushing the breath out of her lungs. The viewscreens dimmed – or was she blacking out? Was that smoke in the cabin air? Yes, smoke.

Almost invisible, but she was sure it was smoke, curling up from the instrument panel. Her head was swimming, panic rising. Then something stung her in the small of her back: a tiny pinprick of heat, growing, radiating outward – acid. Digestive fluid, leaking in from outside. Hull breach.

"Otha," she gasped into the mic. "I need to come out. The cap..."

Her voice was drowned out as the sloo produced a deafening retching sound, and the shaking increased. Zenn punched at what she thought must be the polycilia control. It was. The tachometer red-lined and the pod lurched – backwards. She'd moved the control the wrong way. The pod shoved itself into the soft palate at the rear of the sloo's mouth, and the animal reacted. With an explosive hacking sound the pod shot down the long snout – and out into the air.

For a split second, the in-soma pod was in silent freefall. This ended with a skull-rattling impact as it hit the ground, bounced into the air again, then hit something else that made a horrible, splintering sound. Finally, it struck the ground with a painful jolt, rolled several times and stopped.

A few moments later, the lid creaked open, and Otha was standing over her, pulling at the straps that held her, lifting her up into the bright light and fresh air. As she was raised upright, pain radiated out from several different points on her body. One elbow was bleeding, probably, she thought dully, ripped by the edge of the control toggles. Her left hip ached from hitting the side of pod when it hit the ground; her ribs felt badly bruised.

"Zenn! Are you alright, girl?" Otha held her at arm's length, rapidly scanning her up and down, turning her around to examine her for injury. As he turned her, she saw what remained of the shattered tool shed she must've hit, saw Ren Jakstra, sitting half-sunk into the mud at the edge of the pool, covered in sloo saliva, clasping one arm, grimacing in pain.

"Acid. I felt acid," she told Otha, breathing hard. "It was collapsing – a hull breach."

"No, girl," Otha said. "I monitored you every second. There was no problem with the pod."

"But... smoke. I saw smoke from the panel. Acid, burning my back."

She stared at the pod in disbelief, looking for the rupture, the crumpled metal, the residue of acid. The pod looked intact. She realized her back was one of the few parts of her body not hurting. It struck her at once... Of course. There was no acid in the mouth of a sloo. Only saliva and mucous. She'd imagined it. The smoke, the burning sensation. When the pod flipped upside down, she'd lost her bearings – and panicked. She wasn't ready... nowhere near ready for the test. She turned away from Otha, her face flushing. She saw the sloo then. It had re-entered the pool, and was still shaking its head.

"Damnation, Scarlett." It was Ren, on his feet now, walking rapidly toward them, spitting and coughing as he came. "That thing... damn near... killed me."

"Ren, I don't know what happened," Otha said. He gestured at the constable's arm. "Are you alright? Here, let me take a look at that."

Ren pulled away sharply, shielding his arm from Otha's touch. "You? Are you *kidding*?" He glared at Otha, then at Zenn, and stalked off, shoes squelching with every step.

"Ren, you need to get that attended to!" Otha yelled after him.

"I'll send you the damn bill," he shouted without stopping. "Damn straight I will."

TWENTY-FOUR

"Blister-gnat?" Zenn said, setting her mug down so hard it slopped tea onto the kitchen table. She was still adapting to the thick flex-skin bandage constricting the movement of her injured elbow. "That's impossible."

"I analyzed the residue in the wheelbarrow," Otha said, frowning down at her where she sat. "Almost thirty percent pure blister-gnat. That's what made the sloo go ballistic. Must've set her mouth on fire. Ren has a broken wrist. We're just lucky no one was killed."

"But I mixed that paste myself – rhina grub and sweetbark. How did blister-gnat get into it?"

"That's what I'd like to know, novice." He pulled a chair out from the table and sat, leaning forward to address her. "You certain you didn't mix up the containers, something like that? You double-check the labels?"

"Yes, well, no. I…" She thought back. "The light was burned out. In the storeroom."

Otha ran one hand over his eyes. "Uh huh. So it was dark when you were making up the grub-paste. Too dark to see?"

"Kind of," Zenn grimaced. "But I know exactly where everything is in that shed." It was a weak defense, but she was sure she couldn't have made such a blunder. Almost sure. "I don't see how I could have gotten blister-gnat by mistake. I mean, it looks completely different from rhina or sweetbark."

"If there's light to see by, maybe." Otha sat for a moment, then rose heavily with his coffee mug in hand. He went to look out the open window overlooking the garden. "And as for what happened once the sloo went berserk..." He turned back to her. "You lost control of the pod, Zenn."

She knew he was stating the simple fact. But that didn't make it any easier to hear.

"I should have practiced more." It was all she could think to say. "I should have been better prepared."

"You think?" He wasn't joking, and let the comment hang in the air. "This... feeling you supposedly get sometimes. Did that happen again? Was that the problem?"

"No, it wasn't that." This was no time to have him questioning her mental stability. "I just lost my grip on the controls. Sorry."

"Don't apologize to me. It's Ren who's nursing a busted wrist, convinced our animals are running wild out here. That we're a menace to the community. And you can be sure he'll express that to the city council."

Of course he would, she thought. The constable didn't try to hide his feelings when it came to the Ciscans and their "monsters." He was just like the rest of the towners. Yes, just like the rest... The thought caught her attention, held it. And Ren was there when the sloo went crazy. But when had he arrived? Early enough to doctor the paste mix before Otha went to get it from the shed?

And why did the constable pick that day to bring the mortgage docs out, the very day of her in-soma test? All he'd need was thirty seconds or so. More than enough time to dump blister-gnat in the rhina-grub paste. On the other hand, there was the fact he'd gotten himself sucked up by the sloo. But the only reason for that was because Otha asked him to stay. The idea prodded at Zenn. It certainly made more sense than her using blister-gnat by mistake.

She twisted in her seat, grit her teeth as her arm flared with pain, and glared down at the table. What about the other times? Was that Graad with the whalehound, and Ren now, with the sloo? Could they be working together? Several trains of thought sped off in different directions inside her. Maybe it was time to bring her theory out in the open. Yes. Even without definite proof, it was time to tell Otha, before something even worse happened.

"Otha," she said. "What if someone else, someone from outside was tampering with the animals?"

"Someone from the outside..." he said. "Tampering? What do you mean?"

"What if someone didn't want us to get our lease renewed? They might try to make us look bad. Like we couldn't control our animals. That would give the council a reason to vote against us."

Otha scowled.

"Zenn, does that really make sense?"

"Yes! If people thought the animals were dangerous and they wanted to make it look like we... I mean, what if Graad Dokes was doing it?"

"Dokes?"

"Or Ren Jakstra. He was just out here. And they both hate our animals and..."

Otha put a hand up.

"Zenn, stop. There's no indication anyone's sabotaging our animals. And accusing Graad and Ren..." He heaved an exasperated sigh. "Listen to me now. I know the pressure on a novice at end of term. And you've made some mistakes lately. But we all make mistakes. Sometimes it's hard to own up and take responsibility. But inventing fantasies…"

"These aren't fantasies, Otha." Zenn said, feeling she'd made a serious error thinking he'd understand.

"As I was saying, inventing fantasies to excuse your mistakes is no way to be, girl." The worry clouding his face was actually worse than if he'd been angry. "You hear what I'm telling you?"

Once again, she'd opened her mouth too soon, with no evidence. She wasn't going to convince him. All she could do was nod, avoid his gaze… and seethe inside.

"Good. Enough said." He seemed to relax a bit, sipped at his coffee. "I shouldn't have to stress what a dangerous situation that was, Zenn. There's no margin for error with creatures that size. When you said you were ready for the in-soma test, I had to take you at your word. But you can't let your concentration falter. Do that, and you'll end up thinking about yourself, about your fear."

He set his mug down and leaned on a chair back with both hands.

"Whenever you're treating a patient, it's only about one thing: that patient," he said. "It's about what you need to do, at that moment, to help that animal. It's about exercising simple, common sense while you do it. You keep yourself safe, you keep the animal safe, no exceptions." He looked at her to make sure she was hearing him. She nodded again. "If your thinking isn't one hundred per cent on task…"

Her stomach churned with self-reproach – at her impatience to prove herself, at her over-confidence, most of all at the tone in her uncle's voice.

"Will she be alright?" she asked.

"The beast is fine. I dropped an antibiotic plug into the

hole in her snoot. Mucous membranes are a little inflamed, but no permanent harm. And Ren will heal. Probably make more of a fuss than the sloo while he's at it." He regarded her for a moment. "How's that arm?"

"Fine. A little sore."

He nodded, went to the stove and refilled his chicory coffee from the pot before walking to the door. "So. Third test coming up. You'll do better, won't you." He wasn't asking.

"I'll do better." She counterfeited a smile, and tried hard to believe that with this last statement, at least, she'd told him the truth. "Um…" she hesitated, then decided to risk the question: "Any chance of a hint about that?" She'd convincingly failed the first two tests. A perfect score on the final challenge was her only hope; a distant, unlikely, pathetic hope. But, at this point, she had nothing to lose.

"You know that's against the rules, Zenn." The look he gave her before stepping through the doorway told her, yes, she'd made yet another mistake. She was beginning to get used to that look.

TWENTY-FIVE

The sun was just dipping below the canyon wall when Zenn arrived at the maintenance garage where the in-soma pod was kept. The valley was deep in shadow, except where shafts of late afternoon sun cut through clefts in the cliff, producing dusty shafts of ruby light angling down to the valley floor.

She was intent on going over the in-soma procedures one more time. She lay down in the pod, but got up again almost immediately. It was no use. She couldn't concentrate. Yesterday's dismal test kept playing over and over in her mind. Could Ren really have been responsible? Sure, he was a towner, he thought like a towner. He had it in for the cloister. But he'd been hurt, and the animal that did it was her patient. He could've been killed. What if it was her fault? All of it? This idea terrified her even more than the other possibilities. But the fact was, both Ren and Graad had potential motives. She refused to trust Otha on this, refused to accept his dismissal of her suspicions.

Her failure with the sloo brought thoughts of her father to mind. She wouldn't be sending a victorious shard to him on the next starship after all. And then there was Ren's comment about Warra being "in over his head" on Enchara. What was that all about? She needed to try talking to her uncle again.

En route to find Otha, she encountered Hamish on the south side of the calefactory hall. He was pulling a hay wagon piled high with a loose mountain of bedding straw.

"Novice Zenn, good evening," he said, dropping the wagon tongue and pausing, claw-digit raised in greeting.

"Hamish, have you seen Otha?"

"The director-abbot is at work in the infirmary surgical room. I assisted him in bringing the long-neck leaf-chewer life form to be cured of its ailment. I did not wish to see the medical cutting involved. I elected to bring this sleeping straw to the slaughter-creature Rasputin instead. The director-abbot has entrusted me with the lock-combination to open the caging door. I have never done this, but he tells me it is not difficult." Hamish brandished a slip of yellow paper in one claw. He didn't sound especially thrilled. But apparently tending to Rasputin was better than watching Otha operate. Maybe Hamish, like most humans she knew, had an aversion to the sight of blood.

"Would you like some company?" she asked.

"Yes. Very much," he answered quickly. "Your companionship is welcome."

She'd be going in that direction to reach the infirmary anyway. And she had other reasons for wanting to walk with the sexton.

"So, Hamish," she said as he lifted the wagon tongue and leaned ahead, tugging the wagon into motion. "Did you happen to notice Ren Jakstra anywhere around the cloister yesterday, in the morning, maybe? Down by the treatment pools?"

"The constable person? No, novice Zenn. I did not."

"You didn't... smell him?"

"I detected no novel odors."

A possible defect in her latest theory.

"What about Graad Dokes?"

"No. I did not sniff up his smell or hear sounds of him within the cloister."

"But you might've missed the signs, right? I mean, you could've been out of range, or not paying attention."

"There is an amount of truth to this. The wind velocity yesterday was greater than average. This may have made it difficult for me to detect an unusual presence."

Zenn considered this new information. The fact Hamish hadn't noticed anything unusual wasn't helpful, but it didn't rule anyone out.

Hamish turned his head toward her as they walked. "You are thinking over your concept of who is interfering with the cloister animals, are you not?"

"Yes, and I'm not really getting anywhere. At least as far as turning up any evidence."

"What if this lack of evidence indicates lack of the thing that would leave evidence?"

"Oh?" She stopped, and he brought the wagon to a halt. "So, you think I'm just inventing fantasies, too? That all this is just a wild goose chase?"

"Are there untamed water fowl loose in the grounds?"

"No, no, that's just a saying. It means you think I'm imagining things. Which is pretty much what Otha thinks."

"So, you have spoken of your theory to the director-abbot? And he remains skeptical in the matter?"

"Yes, very skeptical. And he'll stay that way until I come up with something to convince him."

Zenn started out, and the coleopt again forced the wagon into motion. "Hamish," she said after they turned onto the path leading to the infirmary. "I want you to do me a favor. When you're on patrol in the cloister grounds, like at night, if you do sense something strange, someone in the compound who shouldn't be here, I want you to come and tell me. Not Otha or Hild."

"I should not alert the director-abbot? Should he not be informed of such an event?"

"You know how Otha is when you wake him up for no reason," she said, feeling a momentary tug of conscience as she formulated her argument.

"He dislikes this. His voice becomes loud and insistent that this must not occur."

"Yes. But if you come to me, I can decide whether to tell Otha or not. So you won't have to worry about making him mad. Alright?"

Hamish's antennae did a brief dance above his head as he reflected.

"Yes... if you wish this. I will come to you first with news of strangeness in the grounds." Even via the Transvox, Zenn could sense his unease at the arrangement. She forced herself to overlook his discomfort. She needed information if she was to have any hope of unraveling what was happening. And she needed the raw data, unfiltered by Otha or Hild.

"So," Zenn said brightly, steering the talk to something else. "How about this? At Rasputin's cage, I'll handle the gate combination. You get up on the hay-rack and fork the straw down to me, and I'll fork it into his cage."

Hamish agreed that this sounded like a highly satisfactory plan.

A half-hour later, Zenn found Otha in the infirmary's main operating theater, up to his elbows in the abdomen of an anesthetized Gliesian mountain raff.

She tapped on the observation window. Otha looked up and nodded for her to enter. After hastily scrubbing, she gloved, gowned and masked-up before stepping into the brightly lit room, her thoughts about everything she wanted to discuss with her uncle jostling for position within her.

Too heavy for the largest op gurney, but too gangly and delicate to suspend from the overhead track-and-pulley system, the raff's boney form was laid on a succession of foam pads, strung out in a row to accommodate the animal. Coupled with its long, sinewy neck, the raff's body configuration gave it the incongruous look of an Earther camelid of some sort but outfitted with the immense hind legs and tiny forearms of a tyrannosaurus rex. But besides being clearly mammalian, the triangular head displayed the blunt teeth and heavy jaw structure of a herbivore. Surgical drapes covered its midsection, with a square opening in the draping where the incision had been cut and the chest flesh peeled back. The metal tines of a Garrigson rib-spreader protruded from the glistening, red cavity. In the background, the rhythmic sound of the ventilator compressor puffed quietly as it forced air in and out of the raff's four lungs.

"Good timing," Otha said, his words muffled by his surgical mask. "Hand me that synlast-graft. The number twelve." He nodded his head toward the stainless steel instrument tray next to him.

She peeled the wrapping from the foot-square patch of synthetic grafting tissue and passed it to him. Leaning into the body cavity, he wrapped the graft around the garden-hose-sized artery connecting two of the three hearts that raffs needed to pump blood all the way up their lengthy necks to their brain.

"There," Otha grunted, leaning away from the animal and admiring his handiwork. "That should do it. He'll be cropping the high branches again in no time. Want to close?"

Zenn's stomach flipped. "Yes! Thanks."

She picked up the protein-stitchgun from the metal tray and checked that it was fully loaded. Standing on her tip-toes to look down into the operative field, she drew together the two edges of the delicate visceral pericardium membrane and placed her first sutures.

"Good," Otha said, looking over her shoulder. "Keep your spacing even... nice work."

"Otha," Zenn said, not looking up. "What Ren was saying before, about Dad. What did he mean about politics?"

Otha stood for moment, watching Zenn methodically stitch together the thin veil of tissue surrounding the raff's hearts.

"It's about your mother," he said finally. Zenn turned to look at him. "No." He motioned at the raff. "Keep at it. Get him closed up." She turned back to the opening. "Your father has this theory about... what happened to Mai."

"A theory?" Zenn looked at Otha again. "What kind of theory?"

"There was an investigation after Mai... after it happened. There were irregularities, with the in-soma operation. Facts that didn't quite seem to add up. At least not to Warra."

"What facts?"

"Are you sure you want to hear all this? Now?"

"Otha..." Zenn stopped her work, but didn't look up. She waited.

"I don't know if you remember this. But there were several kinds of equipment that malfunctioned during Mai's in-soma run on the Indra that day – monitors, navigation system, the autopilot."

"Yes. The radiation knocked them out."

"That's one of the issues. For Warra," Otha said, going to the instrument tray. He picked up a las-scalpel and began to clean off its cutting tip. "When the pod's problems began, the Dahlberg radiation levels the Indra was producing weren't dangerously high. And Mai's in-soma unit had all the appropriate shielding and D-rad repulsers. Warra thinks it's just too much of a coincidence that all these things went wrong at once."

"Was it? Coincidence?"

"Not necessarily. You know as well as I do how in-soma insertions can go bad." He gave her a look, but didn't say anything about the sloo. He didn't have to. "They're always risky, one way or another."

"What does Dad think happened?" She was suddenly finding it hard to keep her sutures lined up.

"He thinks somehow, someone meddled with the pod systems. He thinks somebody wanted that in-soma unit to go off course, into the Indra's skull."

"On purpose?" Zenn stopped her work and faced Otha. "Who would do that?"

"Well, that's the question I've put to Warra. And despite the final report, despite what we know... Zenn, your father thinks Mai's death wasn't an accident."

TWENTY-SIX

Zenn felt as if the floor had dropped away, as if she was falling into empty space. She stood staring at the pattern of stitches she'd placed, unable to think.

Otha took the stitchgun from her. Wordless, Zenn went to the bench by the far wall and sat while Otha unclamped the raff's aorta, removed the rib-spreader and placed the final sutures to close up the creature's chest.

"That's why Warra took the job on Enchara, after it happened," Otha said, turning away from the raff and pulling off his mask. At the wall, he pressed the switch that shut down the machinery that had been re-circulating the animal's blood, and simultaneously sent a small electrical charge to start its hearts beating again. "Warra thinks Mai's death is connected somehow to the Indra disappearances. And Enchara is the last system before the Outer Reaches, where most of the ships have been lost."

Zenn took her own mask off, stared at her uncle – she was getting too much input, too quickly.

"He thinks someone reprogrammed the in-soma pod's autopilot, sent it into the animal's skull." Otha came to stand close to her. "And he thinks Mai's lab assistant might have had something to do with it."

"Vremya?" Her mother's long-time assistant came from the Russo-Asiatic sector on Earth. Beyond that, all Zenn had really known about her was that she had specifically requested to be her mother's lab tech, and that she'd had to get special clearances of some kind to leave Earth and come to Mars. Eventually, she'd become Mai Scarlett's right-hand women, almost a partner in her Indra research. "But she was killed too," Zenn said. "When the radiation spiked."

"Yes. But, Vremya was also with your mother earlier, during the contamination scare in Mai's lab. Warra thinks that fact is... significant."

Zenn had heard all about this incident. It was a year or so before Zenn was born. Her mother was trying to grow a culture of Indra brain tissue. Vremya was assisting, and had her respirator on; Zenn's mother was just putting her breather on. The culturing flask of Indra neural cells ruptured somehow, and tissue particles became airborne. Everyone was terrified her mother had breathed in some of the brain tissue. No one knew what effect that might have had on her.

"But you ran tests, afterwards," Zenn said. "No traces of Indra tissue were found in Mom, right? She was clean."

"Yes. Exactly. Warra, however, is still convinced there's a link between that event, the missing Indra ships and the in-soma pod malfunctioning."

"But the missing Indra ships have disappeared with all their passengers and crews. Mom's accident was completely different."

"That's what we've tried to tell Warra. Your father is a stubborn man."

"It doesn't make sense," Zenn said. "Mom was trying to cure that Indra. Why would anyone want to stop her from doing that?"

"Well, there are people who would like to see the entire Indra fleet out of commission. Permanently."

"The Authority on Earth?" Zenn said. "I thought they were ready to start up contact with other planets again, end the Rift."

"Warra doesn't think it's them. He thinks it's the New Law, behind the scenes."

Zenn thought for a second. "The New Law? You always said they're just a noisy little bunch of Earther fanatics."

"Hateful, anti-alien fanatics. Yes. I still say that. Warra thinks they've got more influence than we know."

"But without the Indra ships, the whole Accord would just... fall apart. There'd be no interstellar travel, no communication between star systems. Every planet would be totally isolated. It would be chaos, the Dark Ages all over again – forever. Even the New Law types aren't that crazy. Are they?"

"I don't know, Zenn. The main point here is that there's no evidence Mai's death was anything but an accident. Or that it's related to the Indra problem." Otha picked up his episcope from the counter, inserted the ear-buds and went to stand near the raff's upper thorax to listen to the animal's breathing. "Warra's ideas about this may just be his way of dealing with the pain. In his mind, a random accident makes Mai's death senseless. But if he could find a reason for what happened... Well, maybe that's what's kept him going lately." Satisfied the raff's lungs had taken over respiration, Otha turned off the ventilator, and the rhythmic pulsing of the compressor died away. "What he's doing now, trying to reopen the investigation, that's put him on the wrong side of some influential folks on Earth. The negotiations to end the Rift are at a delicate stage. There are people who don't want anybody rocking the boat right now. That's what Ren was talking about." At the raff's head, Otha now removed the ventilator tube from its throat, then stood a moment, stroking the sleeping animal's muzzle. "Your father may just need more time to sort things out, to learn to live with the past and move on."

"But why won't he talk to us about it? Why hasn't he gotten in touch? What if he's… I don't know… sick or hurt or something?"

"Zenn, I know you're concerned about him." Otha turned to face her. "But you mustn't let your imagination run away with you. There's no sign that Warra is in any kind of trouble."

"But that's just it," Zenn had to keep herself from shouting. "We haven't any sign at all, for over a month."

"I've sent a shard to the ferry port. It's probably been shipped up to the *Helen of Troy* already. Warra will get in touch when he receives it, I'm sure." Otha went back to the instrument tray. He gathered up the remaining surgical instruments, put them into a large, metal basin, set the basin in the autoclave and switched the sterilizing field on. "So, you need to stop tying yourself in knots over this. And, besides, we've got… you've got more immediate things to occupy you right now."

"I know," she told him, a little too forcefully. "I'm just…"

He looked down at the instrument tray and chewed at his cheek.

"Zenn. Third and final test coming up. You need to clear your head, go over your course notes for the past term, and be as prepared as possible. Right?" He arched his eyebrows at her, waiting for an answer.

"Yes. I'll be ready."

As ready as I can be without having any idea what I'm

going to be tested on...

He nodded, turned and stepped through the door, leaving her alone with her tumbling thoughts and the soft, regular breathing of the sleeping raff.

TWENTY-SEVEN

Bleary-eyed from sleep deprivation, Zenn was at her desk bent over a v-film detailing the complex pulmonary plumbing of Kiran sunkillers when a loud ping at her window made her levitate a good two inches up out of her chair. It was late; everyone else had long since turned in. But with the removal of the sunkiller's bandages being scheduled for the next morning, she wanted to make sure she understood every aspect of the valves directing the airflow in the creature's wings.

At the window, she looked down to see Hamish winding up to toss another pebble. She pushed up the sash.

"Hamish," she called softly, not wanting to wake the Sister, sleeping just down the hall. "What is it?"

"I have detected an unusual event. Within the cloister walls," he half-whispered, craning his head up at her. "As instructed, I am coming here to speak of this to you. What would you wish me to do now?"

"Wait there. I'll be right down."

Less than a minute later, she was next to him in the cool air outside her dorm room. The night was spiced with scent of rosemary from the garden, and the usual tang of the animal pens.

"What did you hear?" she asked.

"It was not an audible signal. I detected a scent. Born on the breeze currently blowing from east to west, and enhanced by the evening's rather high humidity, which increases the carrying distance of…"

"Hamish," she whispered harshly. "What was it?"

"It was the scent molecules of masticated addictive tobacco and goat manure."

"Chewing tobacco… Graad Dokes. I knew it!"

"As well as a second array of scents I could not distinguish, due to the overwhelming potency of the tobacco resin odor."

"But it was Graad? You smelled him?"

"I cannot attach person names to these odors. I simply state the molecular signature I detected."

"Where did the scents come from?"

"From the area to the southwest. I would say the far corner where the cloister walls intersect."

"The Rogue's Gallery. Come on."

Zenn started out at a half run. After a moment's hesitation, Hamish fell in behind her. Framed by the canyon walls on either side, the narrow strip of black sky above them was bridged by the arc of the Milky Way, its faint, cold light painting a wash of star shine on the shadowed cloister grounds.

Chewing tobacco. That could only be Graad.

She was running flat out now, the packed gravel path hard beneath her feet, arms pumping, the air burning her throat. She sped past the refectory, past the infirmary and out into the soft, recently plowed ground of the open field beyond.

As they neared the edge of the Rogue's Gallery, Zenn raised a hand, and turned to make sure Hamish had seen her signal. They both stopped. She bent, hands on knees and tried to listen, breathing hard.

"Sense anything?" she whispered between breaths.

"There are voices. Two speakers. In that direction." He lifted one claw to point.

"Who is it?" she asked.

"The sound volume is too low for me to discern this."

She crouched and crept forward, past the darkened cage of the axebills. The two birds huddled together, sleeping with their bodies so close they looked like a single animal. She skirted as far from their cage as possible, not wanting to wake them and have their alarm calls draw attention.

"The voices," Hamish was very close behind her, his Transvox almost inaudible. "They spoke from... just there."

It was Rasputin's cage. Zenn was startled to see the outer door standing open. But from their position, she couldn't see into the holding space between the two doors. The sound of rustling debris and angry hissing from inside the cage made it impossible for her to hear anything else.

"Stay here, out of sight," she told Hamish. "I'll get closer."

"Very well..." Hamish seemed perfectly content with this suggestion.

Leaving the sexton in the shadows, Zenn made her way silently to a row of water barrels lined up against one wall of Rasputin's cage. Hidden from view by the barrels, she knelt in the dark and listened, breathing deep to settle her racing heart.

"...and I say quit stallin' and unlock the damn door."

There was no mistaking that voice. Graad Dokes. The second voice sounded out of the darkness then, and Zenn's breath caught in her throat.

"I told you already. This won't work." The other voice was a low, anxious whisper. Zenn knew its owner. She tried to tell herself she was wrong. But she knew. "You see how that thing moves? We let it loose, it'll be on us before we go ten feet."

Liam... No!

Zenn slumped back against the nearest barrel, her eyes squeezed shut against the sensation of a hot steel band suddenly constricting her chest.

"And I told *you*," Graad snarled. "We just open the door a crack and leave. By the time the monster finds its way out, we'll be long gone."

A sour taste rose in Zenn's mouth, and she felt she might be sick. She turned to peer between two barrels. Liam and Graad stood in the narrow corridor between the two cage doors. Just beyond them, in his cage, Rasputin undulated back and forth, his black-dot spider eyes watching the two men with a murderous, single-minded intensity.

"No," Liam said, shaking his head, a new firmness in his tone. "We can't. People will die."

Graad made a disgusted face, then stepped in close to Liam, menacing.

"Then they die. And their monsters with 'em."

Graad lashed out and snatched something from Liam's hand. It was a piece of yellow paper. The combination Otha had given Hamish. The coleopt must've dropped it, or thrown it away... or, the thought stung her: Liam had talked Hamish out of it. Liam. The fact that he was here, with Graad, was something simply too unthinkable, too horrible to be real. But there he stood. Zenn felt sick to her stomach again.

"If you won't do it, I will," Graad said, pushing past Liam to the inner door.

"This thing isn't like the others," Liam said. "It'll kill everything in sight."

"Your heart has just never been in the right place on any of this, ya know?" Graad said, reading off the paper and then punching numbers into the door's keypad. "Look, kid. The Authority won't never end the Rift long as this place and their freaks are here. We get rid of the monster-church and its monsters, Earth opens up contact with Mars, and I get a one-way ticket off this rock and back to where I wanna be. Pretty damn easy to understand."

The realization hit Zenn instantly. That's why Graad hated the cloister and its animals. He thought the presence of aliens on Mars was why the Earthers refused to end the Rift. And, she had to admit, he might be right. Especially if the New Law had anything to say about it.

"Dokes, I did what you asked, before. Right?" Liam tried to wedge himself between Graad and the door. "But the whalehound, the sloo thing, they weren't man-killers. Not like this one."

"Yeah, you did what I told ya. Cause I explained what would happen if you didn't." He pushed Liam roughly out of his way. "And like I've said, this here is a dangerous place. Be a pity if your little red-headed freak-doctor pal had herself a nasty accident."

"I told you to leave her out of this. I swear, Dokes…"

"Ah, too late for those kinda sentiments, kid." He flashed an evil grin at Liam, and cracked open the inner door. "Way too late."

"Don't!" Liam lunged past Graad, trying to shut the door, but the big foreman jammed his elbow viciously into Liam's midsection, doubling him over. Then he brought his knee up hard into Liam's face, and the boy staggered backwards through the outer door and crumpled to the ground, clutching his head and moaning.

By the time Zenn had scrambled to her feet and run out

from behind the barrels, Graad was already disappearing into the darkness on the other side of the cage, running fast. Liam was still on the ground, gasping for air. A cold terror froze Zenn in her tracks: just beyond Liam, Rasputin's inner door stood wide open.

"Liam!" she screamed, rushing toward him. "The door. Shut the door!"

Liam's bloodied face tilted toward her, his expression one of dazed pain and confusion. In the cage, Rasputin's fore-section rose up at the sound of Zenn's voice, long, spider legs waving in the air, small head turning rapidly back and forth as it scanned for a way to get at them. Liam staggered to his feet, stumbled toward the outer door, and went down again, sprawling onto the ground. Rasputin spotted this and responded, scuttling for the open doors. There was no time. The creature would be out before she could stop it.

"Hamish!" She yelled, still running, not turning to see if the sexton was there or not. "Distract it. Draw it off. Other side of the cage."

She didn't want to believe what she heard next.

"Do I have your permission to…?"

"Yes! Do it!"

She saw the black beetle shape heading toward the far cage wall. Rasputin saw the movement and immediately turned in pursuit.

Then she was next to Liam, who was almost up on his feet again. She raced past him, arms extended, reaching for the outer cage door. But the bloodcarn had already lost interest in Hamish. The orange blur of its immense body scurried into her peripheral vision, coming with uncanny speed. The creature dove for the opening, but was moving too fast, and overshot. With a hideous, sputtering scream, it skidded in the loose litter of its cage, then coiled back on itself, hundreds of feet scrabbling to gain traction and reverse direction. A second later, it found the open inner door, and pushed the front half of its body into the narrow corridor, jaws snapping, thrashing its way toward her.

At the last possible second, Zenn's fingers wrapped around the chain link of the outer door. She flung her entire body against it, slamming it shut. Before she could pull away, the bloodcarn crashed full-speed into the door, one huge mandible pinning her fingers to the wire mesh. The entire doorway bulged out with the force of the impact and for a horrifying second it seemed about to burst from its hinges, as the creature, inches from Zenn's face, hissed and sputtered, its bitter, sulphurous insect smell sharp in her nose and throat. With the last of her remaining strength, Zenn pulled back with all the weight of her body, ripped her hands from between the bloodcarn's mandible and the wire mesh. She fell to all fours on the ground. The bloodcarn backed out of the corridor, then seethed and writhed along the fence line, hissing loudly.

Zenn raised her head. Liam had managed to sit up. His face was ghostly white in the thin starlight. Blood streamed from a gash over one eye, which was already swelling shut. He ran a hand over his face, smearing his forehead with red.

Zenn stared at him, unable to arrange her thoughts into any sort of meaningful order. She felt the light pressure of Hamish's claw on her shoulder.

"Novice Zenn," he said, bending low. "You are damaged there."

She looked down at her hands; the knuckles on both had been skinned badly. Blood oozed from the crushed flesh.

"I'm alright, Hamish," she said, her voice as shaky as her trembling body. She moved gingerly into a sitting position, flexed her fingers. Nothing broken. "Looks worse than it is."

"Scarlett…" Liam said softly. He was squinting at her with one eye, the other now totally closed and bruising rapidly. She turned her face away.

"Tell me… it's not true," was all she could manage.

"I never wanted this. I never wanted anybody hurt."

She felt her body going strangely numb. Post-adrenal crash? Or the fact that Liam had been lying, quite spectacularly, to her all this time? Liam, the person she'd let in, the person she'd allowed herself to trust.

"It was you," she said, still unwilling to look at him. "The one letting the animals out. The one trying to… destroy the cloister." Then the numb, dead feeling was gone. She raised her eyes to confront him. "Why?" She almost spat the word at him. "How could you… hate us that much? What did we… Was it your father? The sandhogs? Did you blame us and our animals for that?"

Liam's face contorted.

"Yes! I did blame you for that. All of you. But that's not why…" His voice cracked, and he had to pause for several quick, deep breaths. "I didn't blame you later, I don't blame you now. Did you see? I tried to stop Dokes, keep that thing from getting loose. I knew what it could do. I tried to stop him."

"But the other times, that was you?" The anger began to mix with disbelief. "The whalehound, the sloo… Gil's sandhog? You?"

Liam just shook his head, as if that could change the past.

"Novice Zenn," Hamish said, leaning down. "We must see to your wounded-skin fingers. Let me assist you in standing, and we will go request assistance from the director-abbot and our Sister Hild."

"Scarlett, Hamish, no," Liam protested. "Please, you can't tell Otha."

"We can't? Why not?" Zenn said, getting to her feet. "You could've killed somebody! We could lose the cloister. Lose all the animals, see them all put down. You…" She had to stop talking, and only her rage kept her from breaking down in tears.

"Otha will tell Ren," Liam said, moving nearer to her and Hamish. "Ren will turn me in and they'll send me to prison in Tharsis for sure."

"So?"

"They'll put Dokes away too. I'd be in Tharsis with him. And I'll be the reason he's there." Liam's face went a more sickly shade of white. "You don't know him like I do. He'll kill me, Scarlett. Graad Dokes isn't the kind to forget, ever… and he will kill me."

Zenn knew with absolute certainty that what Liam said about Graad was true. She tried to think.

"Well… what? What do you want me to do? Not say anything? Forget this happened? I can't."

"I understand that, Scarlett. But… there's more going on here than you know. I didn't want to do the things I did. You've got to believe me. They forced me."

"They? Who?"

"There's others involved in this. They'll keep trying to shut down the cloister, even if I'm gone."

"Who, Liam? What others?"

"I can expose them, we can stop them. But I need to get the proof. Give me an hour, a couple of hours and I can bring proof."

"Liam, I don't understand. And even if I did, why should I trust you after… after what you've done?"

"I know. You're right. I don't blame you. But if you can just give me time to get back to the ranch, I can get the proof. And we can put an end to it. Scarlett, I promise you."

He reached out then and took both Zenn's bleeding hands in his. Pain snaked up her arms, but she didn't pull away. "Zenn," he said, speaking her first name for the first time she could recall. "I promise." He said the word with such intensity, his face suddenly childlike...

"Alright," she said quietly. "I'll wait for you. At the dorm." She could imagine any number of ways this could go very badly, but she couldn't think clearly enough to see an alternative. How could she send Liam into the same prison with Graad? It would be a death sentence.

"And you won't tell Otha?" His one blue eye staring... pleading.

"No. Not until you get there."

"Right. Then we'll *both* tell Otha. And he'll see that I'm trying to help. Deal?"

"Deal," she said.

Then he put both hands on her shoulders, pulled her to him and kissed her, his lips warm on her lips and there was the heat of his face, the press of his arms and the scent of sweet hay. Then it was over. He leaned back to look down at her.

"You won't regret this, Scarlett. See you in an hour. Two hours tops."

He took his hands away from her, turned and ran off into the night.

TWENTY-EIGHT

Later, after she and Hamish had returned to the calefactory hall, Zenn made several foolish mistakes. The first was her decision to wait for Liam's return up in her dorm room. The second was sitting down on her bed, and then lying back, to rest her aching, bleeding, exhausted body, just for a moment.

She woke the next morning to the sound of Hild's voice calling her name from down the hall. She instantly realized her third error: letting Liam Tucker out of her sight.

"Zenn. Are you up, child?" She heard the sister's footsteps rapidly descending the stairs. "Otha is waiting for you at the infirmary. The Kiran emissary will be at the south gate soon. I've sent Hamish to let her in. I'm going now to meet her. Zenn!"

"I'm awake," Zenn yelled, her voice hoarse. She sat up, unleashing a cascade of pain from her lacerated hands. She slid off the bed and reached the top of the landing in time to see the door in the hall below slam shut behind Hild.

She stood in the hall, gathering her thoughts.

Liam. Where are you? How could you...

There was no time to dwell on the fact he'd betrayed her

yet again. And this time, she'd allowed him to do it.

You won't regret this, Scarlett...

She strained to force her gyrating thoughts into some sort of meaningful pattern.

Otha, infirmary, waiting... for what? Kiran emissary...

The sunkiller! This was the morning for the sunkiller's bandages to come off. Otha had made a point of inviting the Kiran emissary to come down from the *Helen of Troy* to witness the procedure. Otha had also stressed that he was trusting Zenn to remove the sutures. She couldn't let him down, not in front of the emissary.

I'll just do my part, get it over with. Soon as it's done, I'll tell him about Liam and Graad.

But it wasn't just the prospect of performing a tricky surgical procedure on the priceless royal sunkiller that made Zenn's stomach twist like a wrung-out rag. This was also the day the town council would vote on the cloister's lease.

Not bothering to change out of the clothes she'd fallen asleep in last night, she bounded down the stairs and grabbed her tool belt from its hook on the wall. Fortunately, she'd prepped the belt yesterday morning, knowing she'd need it today. It now held a maser-scalpel, a mini protein stitchgun and a few assorted hand-tools.

Outside, Zenn strapped the belt around her as she jogged down the rock path. The morning air was fresh and cold, and helped to clear her head as she ran. She licked the dried blood off her knuckles as she went, then wiped them on her pants.

Zenn shuddered at the thought of the bloodcarn freed from his cage. Certainly, she, Hamish and Liam would have all died within the first few seconds. She still couldn't take in the idea... that it was Liam behind all that had happened. And she'd been blind to it. How? How had she closed her mind to what was so painfully, obviously clear? He'd been nearby for every incident. Every single one. And she'd missed it, missed the signs... no. Not true. She'd made herself ignore the signs, willfully shut out any possibility of Liam's involvement. Because, she knew know with bitter certainty, she'd thought she could safely disregard the Rule. And now, she was paying the Price.

Reaching the infirmary, she hurried directly into the huge main room, telling herself to put Liam Tucker out of her mind. Permanently, if possible. She looked up at the tethered sunkiller and stopped dead in her tracks, thoughts of Liam and his multiple betrayals no longer a priority.

She couldn't believe her eyes. But there they were. Towners! A teeming mass of them. At least ten or eleven men and women, arranged around the catwalk.

"Ah." Otha turned to her from where he stood in the center of the room. "Here's our novice now." Ten or eleven pairs of eyes turned to stare down at her. The majority of the towners wore white, surgical masks over their lower faces. "Zenn, I think you know most of the folks on the town council."

Her mouth was hanging open. She shut it.

"Yes... um... hello." She could feel her face glowing red.

"The novice will be handling the dressing removal and post-op exam of our Kiran sunkiller," Otha said. As he spoke, he went to the rusting old scissor-lift that squatted on the floor beneath the wide canopy of the sunkiller's wings. Zenn would ride up on this until she was in position. From there, she could reach the bandages swathing the repaired methane plexus at the point where the tail joined the animal's back. Despite the activity in the room, for now the sunkiller appeared to be sleeping soundly, the two huge heads tucked up under its wings.

Otha opened the gate bar on the lift and gestured for Zenn to step onto the lift's small platform.

"I can also now reveal to you and the novice," Otha said loudly, holding the bar open for her, "that this procedure constitutes the third and final phase in Zenn's end of term testing."

This is it? The mystery test? Zenn's initial shock quickly shifted to bewilderment, then gratitude.

"Otha," she said, keeping her voice low. "I knew this was coming up. I was able to study for it... you weren't supposed to tell."

He bent down to speak in her ear.

"I just told you it was on the schedule," he said. "I never told you it would be the third test. Entirely by the book."

"Otha," Vic LeClerc called down to them. She was one of the few who'd opted not to put on a mask. "Are you telling us this girl has never done this before? Is that prudent?"

"She'll be under my direct supervision the entire time, Vic. There's nothing to worry about."

Vic didn't look satisfied, but said nothing else.

"Why are they here?" Zenn whispered as she went by him and climbed onto the lift platform. He ignored her. "Otha," she said insistently. "We need to talk."

He bent close, pretending to help her secure the gate bar.

"Can it wait?" His tone said he thought it should wait.

"It's about the animals, getting out, everything that's happened. It was Graad. Graad and Liam, they..."

"Zenn, not this again." His whisper was razor-edged, but he kept his smile visible for those on the catwalk.

"Otha, they were..."

"Not. Now. We'll talk later, novice."

He stepped back from her, and raised his voice:

"I'd like to thank you all once more for coming out to the cloister this morning. As I'm sure you understand, all of us here at the clinic are passionate about the work we do. But we know this work can be something of an enigma for those of you unfamiliar with exoveterinarian practices. Well, we're very excited to be able to share our enthusiasm with you today. It's our hope that this demonstration will be the first of many. And that it will open a new chapter of greater understanding between the Ciscan cloister and the people of Arsia City."

He gave Zenn a piercing look, as if to say "That's why they're here. Now do your job." She had no choice. She would just have to bear down, and, somehow, get through this.

The councilors gave Otha a polite smattering of applause as Vic stepped away from the crowd and put her hands on the catwalk railing.

"Well now, Otha, most of us know all we need to know about you and your creatures. But, I'm sure everyone…" she gestured at the others, "…is eager to see for themselves exactly how you're utilizing the land out here." She smiled a cold smile down at Zenn and Otha. "And all of us are keenly aware that it's our responsibility, our duty, to decide if that use… is the best use. Best for everyone. That's what our vote today will determine."

Zenn saw that Ren was also among the faces on the catwalk, his left wrist encased in a bright, white plaster cast. He had also opted not to wear a mask.

"Well, I hope your visit today will help you arrive at the right decision," Otha said.

"I'm sure it will," Vic told him, still smiling, sounding very certain.

"So," Otha gestured at the sunkiller, "I've explained the

surgical procedure we employed to correct the defect in the sunkiller's gas-mixing organ, the methane plexus. As soon as our Kiran envoy from the starship arrives, we'll be able to…" The sound of a door opening came from the opposite wall, and everyone in the room turned toward it. "This must be her now."

Sister Hild stepped into the infirmary and held the door open. A second later a very tall figure entered, bowing low in order to pass through. The Kiran was cloaked from head to foot in long, flowing robes of mustard-yellow and vermillion. The face was hidden behind the customary layers of veils, revealing only a small patch of gray-brown spotted facial fur and a pair of slanting, wolfish eyes blue as polished turquoise.

Just behind the emissary came a human in a tunic and boots, hair worn long on one side. It was Fane Fanesson.

"Welcome to the Ciscan cloister, Emissary Luruk," Otha said, raising one hand to the Kiran. "Ladies and gentleman, this is Consan Luruk, aid to the Kire's princeling Sool. And I believe this is the ship's under-sacrist with her." The Kiran inclined her head to the crowd on the catwalk. Fane just crossed his arms and, Zenn thought, tried to look disinterested in the proceedings. "The emissary will be taking the sunkiller back up to the Helen of Troy when we're finished here. Emissary Luruk," he raised his other hand up to indicate the crowd on the catwalk, "May I present the members of our Arsia City town council?"

The emissary and Fane followed Hild up onto the catwalk, where the Kiran towered a good two feet over the head of the tallest human there.

"Now then," Otha said. "Before we begin, are there any questions?"

"Yeah. I got one." It was the quarry owner Pelik Shandin,

one of the council members Zenn knew by name. He was a tall, burly, bear of a man in patched, goat-leather overalls. His sleeveless shirt exposed massive, densely tattooed arms. Tufts of his black beard protruded here and there from the surgical mask he wore. He pointed up at the sunkiller. "What's that thing hangin' underneath the beast?"

"It's the gondola," Otha said. "A training device the Kirans use to acclimate their sunkillers to having structures attached to them. It's the first of many that will be added as they become full-grown adults."

"So, you really trust these behemoths?" Pelik leaned forward on the catwalk railing to address the emissary. "You really live on top of them?"

"In times past, the surface of our world was a perilous place." The Kiran spoke without a Transvox, her voice a breathy, lilting growl. "Over time, the sunkillers became our allies, and our sanctuaries. To this day we are pleased to live in union with them, in the safety of the skies."

"Really?" Pelik said, eyeing the sunkiller. "Well that just sounds a tad risky, wouldn't you say, Ren?"

"Not my idea of prime real estate," Ren said, craning his head up at the sunkiller, then down at Otha. "Just don't make me sorry for talking these folks into coming out here, alright, Scarlett?"

"You won't be sorry. You have my word."

"You are fearful?" The Kiran emissary addressed them all, sounding almost hurt. "I assume that is why you wear the coverings." She lifted a hand-like paw to indicate her own mouth. Zenn assumed Otha had handed out the surgical masks to sooth the anxiety of those towners who'd never been this close to an alien animal before. Apparently, Ren and Vic had been inside the walls frequently enough to know they didn't need the protection.

"This fear arises because you are unfamiliar," the emissary continued. "You know little of our sunkillers. Of our longstanding and beneficial relationship with them. There is no danger, I assure you. Here, I will demonstrate."

She went down the stairs. Fane followed her, and they approached the gondola. Reaching up, she pulled a strap, releasing a rope ladder that unrolled down the gondola's side. A moment later, she and Fane were standing on the woven-reed deck.

"As you see," she gestured at the animal above her, which had taken no notice. "We are in no danger. This young sunkiller is well accustomed to the gondola and to our presence. Come, join me and see this for yourselves. She can easily bear all of you without difficulty. You are curious, surely. Come." A nervous murmur rose from the council. No one moved. "Unless," the Kiran continued, "your human fear overmasters your curiosity." Fane allowed himself a grin at this.

It was too much for Pelik. He pushed his way past the others and stomped down the stairs. Zenn heard him mutter under his breath as he brushed by her: "No talking-dog off-wa calls Pel Shandin yellow."

Zenn tugged at her uncle's sleeve as the rest of council began to descend the stairs, following Pelik. "Otha," she whispered. "Is this a good idea? To let them do this? Now?"

He bent down to speak quietly to her. "This is perfect. They'll see a sunkiller up close, see it's no threat. Wish I'd thought of it myself." Then, in a louder voice, he said, "Novice, why don't you go on up there and help everyone get aboard?"

A minute later, the council members and Ren had all joined Zenn in the gondola – all except Vic LeClerc, who remained on the catwalk.

"Vic?" Otha said, looking up at her. "You don't get a chance like this every day."

"I should hope not," she said. "Really, Otha, it doesn't look safe."

"You afraid to be a few feet off the ground?"

"It's not the ground that concerns me," she said, looking at the sunkiller. "Are you certain it's alright?"

"Seriously," Otha turned to reassure the councilors, "I've worked hands-on with this animal for days now. There's absolutely nothing to worry about."

Vic stayed put.

"I'll just watch. From here," she said.

In the gondola, most of the council members stood gripping the side rails apprehensively as the structure swung gently beneath the sunkiller. The animal had come awake now, the two necks waving gracefully in front of it, heads bobbing to and fro in the air.

Fane came over to where Zenn stood at one of the deck railings.

"Greetings, novice," he said, then turned to the group of councilors. "I hope your people understand what an honor this is, to be allowed so near the royals' beast."

"I'm sure they appreciate it," Zenn told him. "But frankly, I just want to get on with the procedure."

"The procedure?"

"I'm going to be removing the sutures." She patted her tool belt.

"You?" He gave her a crooked, white-toothed smile, and leaned closer. "We must hope sunkillers are unlike yotes. Two heads would be worse than one, vomiting."

"Very funny," she said. She'd expected something like this from the boy, and he didn't disappoint her.

"Alright then," Otha said from his place below them on

the infirmary floor, "Now that you've all had a good, close-up look, I think we'll have you disembark so our novice can get to work. Time to take the bandages off and see if this little beauty is air-worthy again."

This, Zenn knew, was a bit of showmanship. Otha would have already run a deep scan to make sure the tissues had fully healed before they removed the bandages and cut the sutures. It wouldn't do for the royal emissary, or the town council, to see anything less than a successful result.

"Wait!" The harsh shout came from below. Zenn leaned over the gondola railing to see Liam rushing in through the infirmary door. When he saw Zenn and the council members, he sprinted toward the gondola, waving his hands. "No! You shouldn't be up there!"

"What is it, boy?" Otha said, going to Liam, resting a hand on his shoulder.

"They need to get down." He ducked away from Otha's hand, ran to the gondola and pulled himself up the rope ladder, then bounded onto the deck, pushing past Fane.

"Zenn, get off, now!" Liam took hold of her arm and shoved her toward the ladder. "All of you, you have to get down."

"Liam," Vic shouted at her nephew. "Liam, you need to…"

A loud "crack" cut through the infirmary then and the gondola pitched violently, throwing everyone to one side. Something long and thin whipped past Zenn's head as she held onto the railing to keep from falling. Amid the shouts of the crowd, another loud crack, and then another. Zenn realized what it was – the restraining cables had snapped. She looked over the edge of the railing, and saw the ground receding as the entire sixty-foot expanse of lighter-than-air sunkiller floated up, taking the gondola with it. They rose slowly at first, then faster, heading toward the infirmary ceiling. The sunkiller was fully alert now, the twin heads darting about on their lithe necks.

"Otha," she yelled down. "Otha, what do I do?"

"Hold on," he yelled back. "Everyone stay calm. I'll get a line up to you."

Something jolted the gondola hard, and there was the horrific sound of synthwood rafters splitting. The basket swung wildly back and forth, throwing several of the councilors, screaming, to their hands and knees. Now red clay roof tiles cascaded down to smash on the floor fifty feet below, and she saw Otha, Hild and Vic running to avoid the barrage. The sunkiller's double cry filled the air with deafening screeches.

Then the light abruptly brightened. A fresh wind blew in Zenn's face. They were outside, in the open air. They'd gone through the infirmary roof. They were floating up into the sky!

TWENTY-NINE

As the sunkiller rose through the air, its two heads called out again, the sounds echoing off the red cliff walls on either side of the compound. Below them, the buildings of the cloister shrank as the ground dropped away. The wind was blowing hard above the cloister, and it blew harder the higher they went.

The council members had drawn into a frightened knot in the very center of the cane-and-bone gondola, retreating as far from the outer edges as possible. The emissary stood near the bow. Ren detached himself from the huddled councilors and staggered to the stern, where Zenn, Fane and Liam clung to the hand railing.

"Scarlett!" the constable yelled to make himself heard above the wind. "We gotta get these people down, before somebody gets killed."

"I can't," she told him.

"Whaddya mean you can't?"

"I can't control it." she shouted at him, her throat tight, ready to cry, refusing to cry. This was the end of the cloister. Even if they somehow got back down to the ground, the council wouldn't just vote against them. They would tear the place down with their bare hands.

"Listen, girl," Ren put his face close to hers, jaw set, words squeezing out from between clenched teeth. "You get this damn thing to set us back down on the ground and you do it now."

"I told you I can't." She pointed at Liam. "And it's because of him!" She couldn't keep the words from coming. She didn't even try. "It was you! All of it. Everything that's happened."

Liam held up his hands, as if to ward off a blow.

"Scarlett, I didn't do this."

"Then why didn't you come back? Last night?"

"It was Dokes. He was waiting for me at Vic's. He jumped me. When I came to I was locked in the milking barn. It took me till this morning to get out."

"What the...?" Ren yelled, cutting Liam off. "What the Nine Hells are you talking about?"

"Graad Dokes. He cut the cables," Liam shouted.

"Right..." Ren muttered, looking from Liam to Zenn. "You two have obviously lost your damn minds." He looked toward the bow. "You!" He shouted at the emissary, then staggered forward to talk to the Kiran.

"I'm telling the truth, Scarlett," Liam said, gripping the railing next to her. "Graad said he was going to do something to the creature. Something the council would never forget. I came to warn you."

"What?" Fane yelled, joining them. "This was done on purpose? Someone severed the sunkiller's anchors?" He shouted into Liam's face: "And you allowed this?"

"I'm not talking to you, off-wa," Liam yelled at Fane, who showed no sign of backing off. "It was just to scare the council, when the sunkiller got loose," Liam said to Zenn. "You weren't all s'posed to get on this thing. I told her I wouldn't do it." He slammed his fists down on the rail. "I told her."

"Told who?" Zenn said.

"Vic. She said we had to show the council. Show them the cloister had to go."

"Vic? Why?"

He looked into her face, eyes anguished, and the words spilled out of him in a torrent.

"Vic said the valley was settled by her kin. Said the cloister land was hers by rights. She said the land was being wasted, that it shouldn't be used to keep monsters alive. It was her idea that I make friends with Hamish, get him to trust me, so I could do the things I did..."

"And what about me? Getting me to trust you?" she shouted, thinking of Liam's lips on hers, feeling something tearing loose inside her. "That was Vic's idea too?"

"No, Scarlett... well, at first. But not later. Not after Zeus. You nearly made yourself sick to save him. I saw it then. All your animals matter as much to you as Zeus does to me. They deserve their chance, just like him. I know I was stupid not to see that. I see now."

Zenn looked at Liam's battered face, his matted hair, smelled his stupid alfalfa smell and... she'd had enough. She couldn't take any more. She turned away, bit down hard to keep from crying, to keep from screaming, to keep from grabbing the towner boy by the neck and throwing him over the railing.

"Zenn. I know now Vic was wrong about you. About the cloister. About everything. But I waited too long to..."

"Scarlett." Ren was yelling at her as he came toward them, pulling himself back along the railing with one hand. "That off-wa's no damn help." He slapped the pistol on his hip. "What if I kill the thing?"

"What? No!" Zenn shouted.

"Lives are at stake here."

"It won't help. It's the gas in the wings. It'll just keep floating up even if it's dead."

"What if I shoot the wings?"

"There are hundreds of gas bladders. Even if you could shoot them all, there isn't time."

One of the female council members pushed herself away from the group to speak.

"Why won't this thing just... fly us down to the ground?" she said, her thin face pinched and pale with fear.

"It can't fly down," Zenn told her. "That's what the operation was for, to help it control its flight."

"But if it can't go down, what'll happen to us?" Pelik Shandin spoke from the center of the frightened group.

"Look." The thin-faced woman was pointing out at the canyon wall. "We're almost up to the pressure gradient." She was right. They'd come up nearly level with the closest bary-gen. Just above it, Zenn could see the translucent layer of ionized air that stretched its protective barrier over the valley.

"We... we're gonna go through the gradient," Pelik shouted. "We're all dead!"

Zenn wanted to yell at him to be quiet, to tell him he was just going to panic everyone. But he was right. Once the sunkiller penetrated the layer of pressurized air created by the bary-gens, they'd float up into the almost nonexistent Martian atmosphere.

"Kiran," Ren yelled at the emissary, who'd made her way astern to stand near them. "If I killed it, would that work?"

"No." Her turquoise eyes flashed angrily. "You must not. And it would not aid us if you did. The sunkiller would bring us down of her own will... if the healers have done as promised." The emissary turned to Zenn. "Have you?"

"What's she mean?" Ren shouted at her.

Of course. The answer was right there in front of them – or right above them. They still had a chance. A long shot, but a chance, if they acted in time. If she acted.

"The sutures," Zenn shouted at Ren. "They're still holding the plexus valve shut. If we cut the stitches, it'll open the plexus and the sunkiller can control her buoyancy."

"Alright, how do we make that happen?" Ren said.

"I'll have to go up. I have to try and cut the sutures."

"Nine Hells." Ren craned his head up at the sunkiller's underside, then looked down at the distant valley floor.

"You can't. It's too dangerous," Liam said. "I'll go. Tell me what to do."

"You?" Fane growled at him. "Our plight is your fault. Have you not done enough already? I am familiar with the animal. I should do this."

Liam squared off in front of Fane. "Look, off-wa, I don't know who you are, but…"

"Neither of you can do it," Zenn shouted at them. "It has to be me."

"Alright then, do it," Ren said to her, stepping between Liam and Fane. "What can we do? To help?"

"I'll have to climb up at the back, near the tail," she said. She turned and started to work her way along the handrail to the rear of the swaying gondola. "I might need help getting started."

At the stern, the wind produced an eerie moan as it streamed through the web of rigging that held the basket suspended beneath the sunkiller's body.

"If you two can boost me up," she said to Liam and Fane, "I can reach that next row of rigging, get a hold of the tail vertebrae and climb up on her back." The two boys regarded each other for a tense moment.

"Very well," Fane said, gesturing at Liam. "Take her feet. I will lift at her legs."

"I'm taller than you," Liam said. "You take her feet."

"Taller?" Fane leaned into the towner's face. "You are no more than…"

"Liam," Ren cut them off. "Take her damn feet and get her up there."

Liam obeyed, and the two of them managed to raise her high enough that she was just able to get her hands on the rigging.

"Alright. I have it," she shouted back.

"You sure?" Liam yelled.

"Yes. Let go."

Liam and Fane released their hold. Zenn's legs swung out into the empty air so quickly she almost lost her grip on the rigging. Buffeted by the wind, she looked down in terror. Hundreds of feet beneath her flailing legs, a hair-thin streamed writhed through the blood-red sand.

THIRTY

The next second, she'd thrown one foot up toward the tail and locked her knee over a protruding knob of vertebrae. One hand followed, then the other, then her other leg and with one final effort she was astride the base of the animal's tail, looking up at the buff-colored hillock of its huge back. The wind was much fiercer beyond the relative shelter of the gondola, and her loose hair whipped across her face and eyes. She had to grip the sandpaper skin of the tail with all her strength to keep from being blown off. The scabs on her knuckles had now been mostly torn open, and blood had run down into her palms, making it even harder to maintain her grip.

Barely ten feet away, the white mound of surgical dressings covering the methane plexus rippled and snapped in the airstream. She laid her body low along the backbone and, moving hand over hand from one vertebrae to the next, worked her way forward.

At the plexus, she sat up just enough to see better, and unhooked the maser-scalpel from her tool belt. Anchoring herself by gripping a fold of skin with her free hand, she started slicing away at the layers of heavy bandages.

She pulled and hacked away at the dressings until it all came free at once and, caught by the wind, flew off into the air.

A voice sounded, faintly, rising up from below.

"Scarlett!" It was Ren. "We're almost through the gradient." Zenn looked up just in time to see the sunkiller's two heads lift together and penetrate the barrier. They reacted in unison, swooping back down into the valley's air with a keening shriek. The heads dipped out of her sight then, moving as far from the gradient as they could, even as the body continued its ascent.

Bending back to the plexus, eyes watering from the scouring wind, Zenn cut away at the first suture, then cut through three more. The sunkiller's tough outer layer of skin had almost no nerve cells running through it in this area, so she wouldn't hurt it if she missed a suture and cut the flesh. But the valve, hidden beneath the surface layer of skin, wouldn't be able to open until she'd cut the last stitch.

Two more sutures severed. Only three left. The next moment, the wind died, and the air went still and deathly silent. She was at the barrier. She took a last quick breath, bent down against the sunkiller's skin, and then felt herself carried up through the invisible dividing line, thrust into the freezing, airless atmosphere of Mars.

How long did she have? How much air did a human's lungs hold? And how long until the gondola and those in it also rose into the killing zone?

She sat up again, face stinging from cold, eyelashes icing up fast – but at least there was no wind. And at this level, the air pressure had only dropped a little. But once they'd ascended another hundred feet, the air pressure would lessen dramatically. She didn't want to think what would happen to her body then – any organ within an enclosed interior space would depressurize catastrophically. She thought of her eyeballs exploding... and started cutting.

Her bloody hands were already half-frozen. She sawed clumsily at one suture, managed to cut through it. Just two more. Her lungs were bursting, collapsing. All she wanted was to breathe. Even though she knew there was no air around her, even though it would surely be the last thing she ever did, all she wanted was to open her mouth and fill her lungs with something, anything.

Another suture sliced through. One more, just one to go. But her vision was starting to fade, blackness creeping in. She was passing out. She had to breathe, had to. She swiped the scalpel again, but her eyes had nearly frozen shut. Then she felt something on her stiffened, bloody hand – something warm, warm air, blowing outward from the skin. She forced one ice-crusted eye open. There was a slit, in one of the tubules radiating out from the plexus. She must've nicked it. The wound was leaking warmth onto her hand, visibly clouding the air. She fought to think. The tubules... carried gas to the plexus... One of the gases... was oxygen. She had no time, no options, no choice. She cut at the tubule again, enlarged the small cut to almost a foot across, and with a desperate lunge, buried her face in the wound.

She sucked in with all her might, filling her lungs and... she could breathe. Yes! It was an oxygen tubule. She breathed in again, lungs expanding with hot, smelly, glorious air. A few more lungs-full and she felt the ice melt from her eyes. She could see again. She took one more full breath, then risked sitting up. She quickly aimed the scalpel at the last remaining suture and cut it free.

Instantly, the plexus expanded, filling like an oblong, fleshy dome running along the center of the sunkiller's back. The tubules branching out from it filled with gas next, inflating all along the surface of the great wings, routing gases to and from the bladders on the wings' undersides. She thrust her head back into the warmth and air of the tubule. The next moment, the sunkiller cried out, a joyful, wild, soaring double cry – and she felt them dropping through the motionless, icy air, descending toward the pressure gradient.

Zenn breathed deep, the warm, rank air in her lungs radiating out to bring her chilled body back to life.

She felt the sunkiller going back through the barrier, felt the valley's air washing over her – thick, luscious, breathable air. She'd done it. She'd actually done it. She sat up. She shouldn't have.

The violent gusting wind below the gradient struck Zenn's chest with the force of a sledgehammer. A millisecond later, she was no longer on the sunkiller's back, but was tumbling backwards, head over heels. Her cheek slammed into something, skin ripped from her face. She clutched frantically at the tail, got a grip, lost it, blood-slick fingers sliding. Then she sailed free – and fell.

Zenn plummeted through empty, rushing air, her body tumbling, spinning, every sickening turn bringing her eyes back around to the impossible, heart-stopping sight: the sunkiller and its gondola racing up and away into the pink-blue sky.

THIRTY-ONE

Zenn had shut her eyes against the horrifying sight of the sunkiller receding above her. Now, she opened her eyes, saw the Martian surface speeding by far below and shut her eyes again. Her face burned as if branded, her chin and neck wet from blood oozing down her cheek, the metallic taste strong on her lips.

I'm alive. I shouldn't be alive.

There was a painful pinching, like two vices, cutting into her armpits.

I should've hit the ground by now.

"Novice Zenn?" the voice came at her out of the darkness. "Is your brain conscious?"

Reluctantly, she eased one eye open, then the other. Yes. There was the ground, hundreds of feet below her. But it was no longer rushing up to meet her. It was moving… she was moving… sideways.

"I thought for myself." The voice said. "You suggested I think in this way. And I did. And here we are."

She realized then what gripped underneath her arms. Coleopt claws. Hamish. Hamish, holding onto her, flying, wings thrumming.

"Hamish." She felt as if she could cry, but she laughed, despite the pain. She spit blood. "Hamish, it's you."

"It is me. I had no one to ask approval of, do you see? No one to ask if your situation was both dire and urgent. So I thought of the answer myself. And I myself approved the action of coming to see if you required assistance. As I flew upward, you were all at once coming downward. I flew in such a way that I encountered you falling. I was accurate. And here we are, safe and ship-shape."

"Yes, Hamish," Zenn said, crying and laughing and tasting her own blood at the same time. "Safe. Safe and ship-shape."

By the time Hamish circled around to carry her over the cloister's south wall, the sunkiller was already inside the compound. The immense wings arched over the chapel ruins, where the animal had anchored itself to a fragment of stone arch with its long tail hook.

As Hamish slowed down to land, Zenn could see Liam was helping the council members clamber out of the gondola and onto the ground, where Otha and Hild waited. Fane and the Kiran emissary were securing the gondola with heavy lines attached to large pieces of rubble. The sunkiller had brought its two heads down low to watch the activity. But when its four sharp eyes caught sight of Hamish descending, both heads raised up and cried out a double honking alert.

She saw Liam raise his arm to point at them.

Hamish touched down lightly and released Zenn from his grip. The next thing she knew, Otha was there, gathering her up in his arms.

"Zenn, we thought you'd... we thought..." He didn't finish, but held her away from him, up in the air, seemingly unable to speak at all. That was a first.

"Otha. Could you please…?" Still aloft in his grip, Zenn nodded her head at the ground.

He set her down.

"Sexton Hamish." Otha clapped both his hands onto the coleopt's upper carapace. "Well done. Well done, sexton." Hamish seemed unsure of how to respond to this unusual outburst from his director-abbot.

"Child!" Hild rushed up and began to fuss over Zenn, smoothing her hair, pulling out a handkerchief to daub at her bloody face. "Are you alright? Look at you. Ren says you got up on that animal's back. You didn't. Tell me you didn't."

"She did, though," Hamish said. "And then she fell off into the air."

"Oh!" Hild's hands flew to her mouth.

"And I thought for myself!" Hamish exclaimed.

"Scarlett!" Liam called as he ran to where she sat. "You're alive – how in Nine Hells…?"

"I flew without any approval other than my own," Hamish went on proudly. "And I encountered novice Zenn at an altitude well above ground-level and…"

"You? Caught her? In midair?" Fane said, coming to stand behind the others, shaking his head in wonder. "By the Shepherds!"

But Zenn could no longer hear any of them, because Hild had wrapped her in her thin, strong arms, pulling her in close, rocking and crying and tsking and scolding. Which, for once, Zenn didn't mind at all.

After an overwhelming amount of confusion and far too many people speaking at once, Zenn found herself sitting, dazed, on a chair-sized sandstone block that had once been part of the chapel's foundation. Hild made her promise to stay put, then hurried off to fetch the first aid kit. Zenn was happy to just sit, to do nothing, say nothing. Her body ached, her scraped face hurt, her thoughts skittered and slid this way and that.

Close by, the councilors stood in a milling group, their voices a din of excited babble, some of them gesturing toward the sunkiller floating serenely above them.

"Otha Scarlett," Vic's voice cut through the general murmuring. The woman was shouting as she picked her way toward them through the rubble field of the chapel ruins. "What did I tell you?" She whipped her cowboy hat off, flailed it in the air at the sunkiller. "I said this thing was dangerous. And what did you say? You assured me, assured us all it was safe. Is this your idea of safe? Nearly killing these good people?"

"Vic," Otha raised one hand as if to ward off her anger, "This kind of thing, equipment failure like this, no one could have foreseen that it..."

"No. You never should have allowed these people to put themselves at risk to begin with." She turned her flushed face to the group of councilors, her anger now coming under control, turning to a calm, controlled fury. "Well, your little demonstration today has been very educational. Very educational, indeed. And I think I can speak for everyone on the council when I tell you that it would be irresponsible, yes, it would be a dereliction of our duty if we allowed the cloister's lease to be renewed. I'm sorry to say it. I've known you a long time, Otha. But after all the other accidents with your creatures, all the other misjudgments on your behalf, and now this – well, it simply leaves us no choice but to terminate your tenure on this property." She caught sight of Zenn then, and pointed at her. "Your own niece, Otha. Look at her. Think about what might have happened."

"She's lying!" Zenn yelled, jumping to her feet as if waking from a dream. "Graad Dokes cut the cables. To make us look bad. To scare the council and make them vote against us."

"Zenn," Otha turned to her, scowling, eyes flashing. "Don't."

"Otha, my heavens," Vic gave Zenn a pitying look. "Zenn, you've had a frightening experience, a terrible ordeal. You're confused." She turned to the crowd. "But we mustn't blame her. It's not her..."

"It's true. Graad Dokes did it," Liam yelled, his voice brittle with emotion. He'd climbed up on a mound of rubble behind the crowd, and they all turned as one to stare. "He made me do the other things, the whalehound, the sloo."

"He... he doesn't know what he's saying," Vic said, half-laughing, walking toward him.

Liam pointed down at Vic, who shook her head, to show how sad he was making her.

"We did all those things. Me and Dokes. And it was all her idea."

"Me? Liam, that's... how ridiculous." She laughed again, to show them all this was simply too outrageous to believe. "How could I ever make you do such things?"

"You told Dokes. And Dokes told me. Told me if I didn't do it, he'd make me sorry. That he'd hurt me. That he'd... hurt Zenn."

"Graad Dokes said that?" Otha took a step toward Liam. "You heard Graad threaten Zenn?"

"Vic." It was Ren. The constable had been listening from behind the group. Now, he came forward. "You know what in the Nine Hells any of this is about?"

"I assure you I have no idea. It's... I have no idea."

"Uh huh..." Ren looked from Vic to Liam.

"Why would I be involved with anything like this? This boy... Liam here has no proof. Not a whit. It's all in his mind. What with his mother taking off, being left on his own. You all know what a hard time he's had, the trouble he's gotten himself into. It's no wonder he's got things all mixed up in his head. And really, now, what reason could I possibly have to..."

"This kind of reason," Liam said. He pulled an old file folder filled with yellowing paper out of his shirt. He brandished it in the air.

"What is that, boy?" Ren said, going to him.

"It's proof. The original cloister lease," Liam shouted out so everyone could hear.

"Where'd you get that?" Ren asked.

"From Vic's file cabinet, at the ranch."

"Liam Tucker," Vic said, going toward him. "You had no right to go pawing through my... Ren, these are private documents. He has no right."

"Give those to me, boy." Ren walked over and took the folder from Liam.

"Those are private, Ren." Vic came at Ren and tried to snatch the papers out of his hand. He pulled away from her. "Ren Jakstra, give me those."

"Vic, I asked you about the lease documents two months ago, when this whole thing about the vote came up. You said you didn't have the papers, had no idea where they could be."

Vic said nothing to this, but just reached again for the file. Ren held her off with the cast on his arm.

"I can tell you what it says," Liam shouted. "It says if the cloister lease is ever revoked, the land goes back to the original lease holder. That's the LeClercs."

"Vic?" It was Pelik Shandin. "You never mentioned you had a stake in this vote." Pelik came to peer over Ren's shoulder at the papers. "You gettin' the cloister land? That would be a conflict of interest, Vic. Clear conflict. You shoulda told us."

Several voices in the crowd agreed.

"Now listen, Pelik Shandin. Listen all of you," Vic said, confronting the group. "You know my family's been in this valley since day one. You know the very land we're standing on right here used to belong to the LeClercs. And the LeClercs took care of it. We've been the lifeblood of this valley since the first settlers got here. We supplied you and your families with food. Food when there was nothing else. Now, you want to let the fruits of this land go to keeping these monsters alive? Instead of feeding you? Feeding and clothing your children? If that's what you want, then you go right ahead. But I'm here to fight for you. I'm here to fight for the human beings in this valley."

She stood then, her angry gaze raking the crowd, going face to face, her body rigid, her entire being daring someone to speak, daring anyone to tell her she was wrong.

"So, Vic," Ren said. He squinted at her over the rims of his dark glasses. "Is it true? You put Liam up to it? And Graad? You have them interfere with the animals out here, to make the council vote your way?"

Vic said nothing, but just stared hard ahead, looking out at the ruins of the chapel.

"Huh… well," Ren tucked the folder under his cast arm and took Vic gently by one elbow. She jerked away from him. He took her arm again, more firmly this time. "I think you better come into the station with me. We'll get Graad to come in, too. Have a little talk. Liam…?" Ren turned, but Liam was gone. "Damn. Anybody see where that boy went?"

No one had seen.

"Alright. No matter. I'll round him up later." Ren addressed the crowd. "I'll need statements from you folks about the whole council thing. Pelik, why don't you come by this afternoon and we'll arrange a time when we can get everybody together."

Hild arrived with the first aid kit, and began daubing antiseptic on Zenn's torn cheek. The Kiran emissary was at Zenn's shoulder then, leaning down close enough for Zenn to smell the sweet, musky scent of incense that clung to the red and gold robes.

"Please allow me to extend my thanks to you, novice. Your efforts to save our sunkiller, to in fact save us all, were nothing less than extraordinary." The Kiran straightened, addressed Otha. "I can assure you my report to his highness Sool will mention this. I will not stint in praising the quality of the healers in training at your cloister."

"Well, we appreciate that," Otha told her. Then, in a louder voice, he said, "And, everybody." The crowd stopped its muttering. "I just want to say, in front of Zenn and all of you here: I was wrong. When things started going bad at the cloister... I blamed Zenn. I should've known better. Looking back now I can see it. In every case, she put her animals' welfare ahead of her own. And as you all know, she just risked her life to save your lives. And the life of her patient." He looked down at where Zenn sat. "You did us proud." His big hand rested softly on her shoulder as he grinned down at her. "And I think it's safe to say your performance today evens the score for you."

"What?" Zenn said, her dazed mind unable to keep up.

"Your third test. Perfect score. Congratulations, Novice, First Order."

The rush of relief that rose up inside Zenn was almost

enough to bring tears. But she was too exhausted even for that. With what remained of her strength, she stood and hugged her uncle tight.

"Alright, Vic," Ren said, nodding at the woman. "Come on now."

"No." She braced her feet, refusing to move. "Not till we vote." Her voice was shaking, her eyes wide. "Not till I see this land returned to its rightful owners."

Ren was about to push her on ahead of him when Pelik stepped out in front of the crowd.

"Wait a second, Ren. If that's what she wants, might as well get this outta the way." He turned to the others. "Lookit, I know we've all got our issues with the cloister. I know Otha here prob'ly owes most of us for unpaid bills. But I think we also know without a doubt that we owe our lives to this girl here. Am I right? Show of hands. All in favor of extending the land lease to the Ciscan cloister for the next five-year period?" Every councilor's hand went into the air. "All opposed?" He turned to Vic. "Looks like you're outvoted, Vic."

"You think this is the end of it?" Vic hissed, her face a twisted mask. "Well it's not. There's more going on here than you little people and your little minds can even comprehend." She thrust one hand into the air, pointing at the sky. "Earth has not forgotten about Mars. There are changes coming to this world." She brought her arm down, pointed out at the land around them, at the crowd of people standing, open-mouthed, watching her. "Changes. Changes are coming. And you people... will either be part of them, or be swept away. All of you. Swept away!"

"Alright, Vic," Ren said, nudging her to walk ahead of him. "Let's go, before you make this worse than it needs to be."

With a last, wild-eyed glare, Vic spun away from the crowd.

Zenn watched Ren escort her away toward the main gate and all at once she was simply unable to stand on her feet any longer. She sat down hard on the stone block, all her unfelt aches and pains flooding back, along with a surge of fatigue so powerful it was difficult to hold her head up.

"You are truly blessed, Healer," Fane said to her. As he walked off to join the emissary, he looked back to give her a final, bright smile. "Surely, the Ghost Shepherds guide your path."

Zenn couldn't muster the strength for a reply to this, and just rolled her eyes at him.

"To think, Liam Tucker," Hild said, steadying Zenn's face with one hand so she could apply a layer of derma-plast to her wound. "Why, I've known that boy since he was a baby."

Zenn couldn't make herself think about any of it anymore, not Liam or Graad or Vic or what had just happened.

"Liam should've come to me," Otha said, his face dark. "He should've come to somebody, said something."

"Well, this should do till later," Hild said, inspecting her handiwork on Zenn's cheek. "I'll take a closer look back at the infirmary. See if you need stitches. Now then, can you walk?"

THIRTY-TWO

As it turned out, Zenn could walk, if she leaned on Hild, and she didn't need stitches. She did, however, feel as if she needed to lie down and shut her eyes and not move a single muscle for a very long time. Half an hour later, she was in her own bed at the dormitory, with Hild fussing over her.

"I still cannot believe you did such a thing, climbing on that animal's back, that high up." Hild looked down at where Zenn lay. "But I suppose you are your mother's child. And this is exactly the sort of thing Mai would have done. Just to see the looks on our faces."

"It's not like I thought it through, you know," Zenn said stiffly, the act of speaking making her cheek smart. "I just... did it."

"Well, thinking it through or not, it was you who kept our little cloister from being bulldozed down for goat pasture. Your uncle has lost a lot of sleep the past few weeks, I can tell you. Worried himself sick over the lease, and over you, child."

"I know," Zenn said. "And Sister, do me a favor, please." Hild regarded her. "Tell Otha I've decided I'll be doing my acolyte year here at the cloister, will you?"

"Did he think otherwise? Whatever gave him that idea?"

"I..." Zenn felt a momentary pang of guilt. "I can't imagine."

"Well, I'm sure he'll be relieved to hear it. Relieved that everything is finally settled, the cloister safe."

"It is safe then? For another five years?"

"As far as the council is concerned, yes..." Zenn could tell there was more to it than that.

"But...?"

"There's still the mortgage to deal with, of course."

Of course, Zenn thought. The bank in Zubrin wouldn't wait forever. If only her father was here to help. If only the Indra problem... wasn't a problem. If only Liam Tucker hadn't lied to her over and over. If only, if only....

"Sister, what will happen? To them... for doing what they did?"

"I can't say, child. Vic's in custody. Ren will have to track down Graad and the boy. Then we'll see what everyone has to say."

"I guess I owe Ren an apology, huh? For even imaging it was him." Zenn balked at the thought, but she'd been wrong and had to own up to it. "I suppose I should've known he wasn't the kind who'd do bad things to our animals. I should've seen what Vic was up to."

"Yes, well, I've known Vic LeClerc since forever. And I didn't see it."

"What do you think she meant? About Earth not forgetting about Mars? About everything getting swept away?"

"Who can tell, child? Vic isn't quite right just now, if you ask me." She gave Zenn a long, appraising look. "And you, Zenn. These... spells you've been having around the animals."

Zenn started to speak. But Hild raised a hand to her. "Otha told me. He's been worried about you. I'm sure it's just been the strain. All the disruptions. I know you blamed yourself. But now we know who was behind all of this."

"No." She tried to sit up. Hild rested a hand on her shoulder, eased her back down. "It's not the strain. I'm sure it's something else. I can't really explain it."

"And on top of it all, you've gotten yourself into a state over your father." Hild said, seeming not to hear what Zenn was trying to tell her. "Warra will get in touch any day now, and tell us he's fine, I'm sure. You need to stop worrying."

"Hild…"

"Hush now, hush." She patted Zenn's shoulder, smiling down at her. "No more talk." She went to the door and switched off the light. "You get your rest. You've earned it. Good night, novice."

Hild went out and closed the door. The room was dark and, after all the commotion, deeply, wonderfully quiet.

Zenn decided Hild was right about one thing. She desperately needed to sleep. She'd just gotten comfortable when she heard Katie emerging from her hiding place behind the desk.

"Katie-kate," Zenn whispered. Leaning over on her side, she signed: "Katie come up. I missed you."

The rikkaset padded over to the bed, sprang lightly up and moved to sit at Zenn's side, her big eyes fixing on the derma-plast coating Zenn's cheek.

"Friend-Zenn bad there, bad on the face? Hurts?"

"Doesn't hurt," Zenn signed back. "Not much. But I'm tired. Very sleepy. Katie sleepy?"

"Yes. Katie and Friend-Zenn sleep right now."

The rikkaset moved to the head of the bed, paced a few quick circles to knead the pillow to her satisfaction, plopped down and wrapped her tail around her body. Zenn nestled her head next to the rikkaset's warm, soft fur, reached up to scruff one of her velvety ears and closed her eyes.

Zenn couldn't identify the sound that woke her. She lay still for a few seconds, sat up and peered into the darkness. The night breeze on her face was sharp with the sweet-and-sour scent of blooming gensoy. Hadn't Hild closed that window before helping her into bed?

Then, she sensed movement in the darkened room and, like the touch of ghostly fingertips, something brushed against her neck. There was a quick prickle of heat on her skin and instantly, as if smothered by some great weight, she fell back onto the bed. She tried to move, but her body simply failed to respond. She was paralyzed!

She lay awkwardly, just as she'd fallen. She could see, but her vision was beginning to blur and she couldn't blink her eyes. She could hear, but the only sound was her own breath, heaving in her chest.

She saw something going past her head. It was Katie. The rikkaset jumped from the bed to Zenn's desk, where she crouched low. Then, the animal's form grew faint, and she blended, disappearing from view.

Zenn was facing in the direction Katie had been looking. In a nauseating flash of dread, she saw it: someone, something, in the room, motionless, in black shadow below the window. Her mind told her to cry out, but no sound came. She felt herself growing groggy, weak, like she'd been drugged... Sedative? Neuro-toxin?

She fought to maintain control, to keep from panicking. The figure by the window came toward her, moving with a strange, shuffling gate. It looked like – no, that couldn't be right – it seemed to be walking on three legs. No known life form had three legs; even in her fear and increasing mental haze she knew that to be true.

A pencil-thin thread of blue-green light leapt from the head of the figure. The beam swept across the room, turned to a blue dot as it hit the wall, slid down to shine into her fixed, open eyes. The light blinked off then, as if it had taken all it needed from her. The black shape hobbled closer. Zenn strained to make herself stand, to push herself away, to hide, to escape, but it was no use.

The dark figure clutched a small object in one hand. It passed the device near her head. A sensation of heat caressed her forehead and swept down across her face. Some kind of scan?

"Yes. It is there!" The figure's voice was a grating, guttural whisper. The voice wasn't human, but Zenn couldn't tell more than that, other than a vague, nagging hint of familiarity, as if she'd heard it, or something like it, before. The creature put the device away and went to her desk, pulled out the file box that held her computer shards. It turned, looked around the room, saw what it wanted and grabbed up her leather field kit. Opening the pack, it dumped the shards into it and slung it up onto its back.

Shambling to where Zenn lay, the intruder reached underneath her with both arms and lifted her easily from the bed. It gave off a strong scent, a pungent, herbal smell, like sage, or tumeric. It turned and moved back toward the window, carrying her limp body.

But before they'd gone halfway across the room, there was a high, shrill and very angry shriek. It could only come from one source: an enraged rikkaset. The thing carrying her barked out a low grunt of surprised pain – and then the familiar-yet-foreign sensation was there again, the molten surge of heat and dizziness, the vortex whirling somewhere deep inside, her mind somehow opening, receiving. She felt pain – this time, on her forehead, hot blades cutting her flesh. And then there was more. Images again, like with Liam's injured cat. Colors and shapes cascading over her, flooding her mind. She was seeing... through other eyes. Whose eyes?

Scenes rushed at her, a hallway, a corridor, the images shifting, moving too fast to comprehend. Voices, garbled words, some she could almost understand, but none that quite made sense. And, again like with Zeus, she knew with absolute certainty she was experiencing the past, not the present. Whose past?

Next, the view of a door opening, an office, more garbled words. A person in the office, behind a desk. A human face... copper hair, a beard – her father! Yes, her father's face. She was seeing through the eyes of someone, something, that was looking, had once looked, at her father.

Warra Scarlett shouted at whoever had entered the room; he was mad, rising from the desk. An arm rose into Zenn-not-Zenn's line of sight. There was a bulge at the end of the arm, on the wrist, something alive, like a shell of some sort. The shell opened, a long, fleshy tendril shot out from it and touched her father on his neck. He collapsed at once, knocking papers and computer shards from the desk as he toppled to the floor.

A voice croaked, harsh, inhuman. It was the voice of the being whose eyes she was looking out of. It was the voice of the creature that had come into her room.

"Get him up," the voice said. Gloved hands reached in to take hold of her father, dragging him. The same voice again, "Take the shards. Take them all. Then seal this room. We are done here."

A momentary flashing like static interrupted, and then: a

different room, her father's body, stretched out on a low table or hospital gurney. He was breathing, but unconscious. Around him, devices, machinery – medical equipment, biosensors, cabinets, medicines. Like a hospital room, but smaller. Different. What was this place?

And then a totally new sensation engulfed her. No, not a sensation – a rapid cascade of emotions: stunned disbelief, then shock, then anger. It was the mind of the creature who held her, in the present again, at this very instant. Her abductor was sensing Zenn as she sensed its thoughts, its memories. It was realizing for the first time that they were linked, that it was not alone inside its own head. Like a whisper, distant but distinct, a single word rose up in the creature's mind: *Nexus*.

A new sound cut through her, snapped the link, threw her back into her own body. The sound of growling, hissing. Katie. Zenn was back in her darkened room, where only a second seemed to have passed.

Still held in the intruder's arms, Zenn could tell from the sound that Katie was close, just above her – on the creature? The intruder reeled backwards, turned and tossed Zenn roughly down on her bed. From where she lay, Zenn saw a mass of red-purple fur covering the top of the creature – Katie had attached herself to the head of the shadowy figure, clawing, biting as the intruder flailed with his arms, trying to knock the furious animal from him. That's what she'd felt when she entered the creature's mind – Katie's claws tearing at the creature's face.

The intruder managed to grab Katie by the neck. Pulling her off, it threw the rikkaset hard, out of Zenn's line of sight. Something crashed loudly to the floor. Bookshelf? Zenn couldn't see where Katie landed. Was she injured? Dead?

The intruder snorted in anger, came to the bed, hefted

Zenn's body up across his shoulder. He went to the window and climbed through it, lowering itself down the wall. A moment later, they were out in the dark of the cloister yard, running across the ground, Zenn bumping up and down painfully on the creature's shoulder as it ran.

They were almost to the north wall when Zenn caught sight of a bulbous shape on the ground to one side of the path. As the creature carried her past, she saw what it was: Hamish. Dead? No – his antennae twitched lightly as they hurried by. Paralyzed, like her? Again, she willed her body to act, to do something, anything. But it was as if she had no body at all. And now, as the creature made its way onto a barrel top, and from there up and over the wall, she could tell the substance that flowed through her veins was about to make her lose consciousness. And then... darkness.

THIRTY-THREE

Zenn came to with her cheek pressed to a cold, packed clay floor. There was a corrugated metal wall several feet from her face. Her hands and legs were bound tightly, tape sealed her mouth. Her body ached as if it was one big, girl-sized bruise. The skin on her neck burned fiercely; she assumed from whatever had been used to paralyze her last night. Was it last night? She had no idea how much time had passed. She was about to attempt sitting up when she heard someone speaking. She froze.

"...no, no. I was forced to act. I told you, the plan to use the goat-woman failed." It was the guttural croak of the creature that had taken her. She forced herself to breathe carefully, slowly, so it wouldn't notice she was awake.

The creature's voice paused now, and Zenn could hear the tinny, electronic sound of another voice, too faint to make out any of the words. Her abductor was talking to someone on a communicator of some kind.

"Yes," the creature croaked. "The Ciscan healers will now keep their lands. And the human girl would be kept from us behind their walls. The presence of the girl's bug-guard prevented my taking her at the goat-woman's residence. If we were to seize her, this was our only chance. You said the bug-guard within the Ciscan grounds could not be evaded. And I say the whip-whelk dealt with him as it did the girl. I have succeeded, where your overcaution has failed."

The other voice spoke again, a little louder. Zenn could tell it was angry.

"Yes, failed, that is the word I use," her abductor said. "I have the girl, and I will have the credit."

The other voice, the tone even more upset.

Then, the creature's voice. "Yes, yes, yes, I will conceal her in a place I know of and smuggle her onto the Helen. But I ask as I have asked before: will she do as we wish, when the time comes?" A pause as the other spoke. "Yes, I understand the value of having her father, I am not a fool. My question remains: is that enough? Sufficient to make her comply?" A longer pause. "Then the outcome rests upon you. Any failure will not fall on Pokt or my kind.... I will contact you when I have her aboard."

At the sound of steps approaching, Zenn shut her eyes and held very still, her heart pounding so hard she was sure the creature could hear it thump. The binding on her hands was grabbed roughly and shaken. Then the bindings on her feet. It was testing to see if they were tight. Apparently satisfied, the creature's footsteps retreated. There was the sound of a chain rattling, the metallic sound of a lock being secured, more footsteps, a more distant door opening and slamming, then silence.

After a few seconds more, she rolled and, gasping from the pain it caused, forced herself into a sitting position.

Her father! Had she really heard that? That they had him? She had to get out. She had to get free. They had her father, he was being held captive. She had to help him.

She surveyed her surroundings. She was in a storage area,

behind a woven wire fence that reached from wall to wall,
floor to ceiling, in some larger metal building. Beyond the
fence that confined her was a small, outer space with shelves
filled with boxes reaching to the ceiling and a single door.
On pegs next to the door hung several battered hard-hats
and three or four pairs of dingy workmen's coveralls. There
were no windows, just a few skylights in the roof.

She saw the creature had left her field kit backpack on
one of the shelves outside the fence. As she was looking at
it, trying to think what she could possibly do next, the
backpack moved, and the flap lifted up as if by an invisible
string. A blurred swirl of purple-and-cream appeared, and
then the face of a rikkaset materialized, gold-amber eyes
blinking at her.

Katie! Katie is here. My Katie.

She must have hidden in the pack back in her dorm room.

Katie scampered up to the chain link fence, sat, and
signed: "Friend-Zenn. Come out now. Katie hungry. Katie
eat right now?"

Zenn tried to speak, but the tape over her mouth was
firmly adhered. Pushing clumsily with her bound legs, she
maneuvered her body over to the fence, turned and pushed
herself back-first against the wire barrier.

Her tied hands had just enough leeway to sign.

"Katie, Friend-Zenn needs help. Katie help?"

She craned her head around to see the rikkaset's reply.

"Katie hungry. Hungry. Hungry Katie. Katie eat?"

Zenn breathed deeply, trying not to panic. Her abductor
could return any second. And her only hope was a food-
obsessed rikkaset.

Zenn signed again. "Katie eats soon. But first, help Friend-
Zenn. Help now."

"But Katie hungry, and very."

In desperation, Zenn pulled hard with her arms, sawing the bindings into her wrists, feeling friction burn of the rope. The rope. If it was same material that bound her feet, the binding on her hands was hemp-weave rope. Hemp was edible.

"Katie, bite the rope," she signed. "Eat. Eat the rope on Friend-Zenn's hands."

"Rope good for hungry Katie?"

"Delicious rope, yes. Good for hungry Katie."

A second later, there was the tickle of a furry head next to her hands, and then tiny, sharp teeth gnawing at the binding on her wrists. The rope, it turned out, was in fact good for a hungry Katie.

Once her hands were free, she ripped the tape from her mouth and untied her feet. She went to the fence, shook it, and found it quite solid, the gate secured with a thick chain held in place by a large, metal padlock.

"Friend-Zenn come out now?" Katie signed.

"I'm trying!" Zenn cried.

She pulled on the chain. It was much too heavy to break. She reared back and kicked at the door with all her strength. No visible effect. She rattled the fence again, making her wounded knuckles bleed, not caring. She looked around the cage that held her, searching frantically for another way out, any way out. There was none.

"Katie wants home," the little rikkaset signed. "Go home now and eats?"

The sound of shattering glass came from the roof, and Zenn saw a pair of legs descend from the broken skylight. The legs thrashed briefly in the air, then a body lowered into sight, then a face, one eye in the face puffy and ringed by a halo of black and blue.

"Liam?" Zenn was afraid she might be hallucinating, still

under the influence of the paralyzing drug.

"Who else?" he said, hanging by his fingertips from the edge of the skylight. He let go, dropped the eight or nine feet onto the top of the shelf below him, and jumped down to the floor. "Come on, we gotta get you outta here before that skirni comes back."

Zenn watched, too amazed to say anything further, as he pulled with both hands at the door between them. It didn't budge, and he ran back to the shelves, searching.

"I need something to pry with…" he said, but he found nothing. He saw Zenn's vet kit, tore it open and rummaged inside. "Anything in here we can use?"

Zenn's mind was blank. Then it was filled with all the reasons Liam shouldn't be here.

Why isn't he running, hiding someplace? Why is he pretending to care what happens to me?

"Scarlett," he said. "Is there anything in here?"

She stared dully at him.

After a few seconds, she seemed to finally come fully awake. "Yes. The kit, bring it here."

He brought the pack, and held it up so she could reach into it through the fencing.

After a few moments she pulled out the items she wanted: a small spray vial and a pair of heavy metal forceps.

"Stand back."

Liam gathered Katie in his arms and moved back.

"What's that stuff?"

"Super-cooled nitrogen, for freezing dermal growths."

"What good will that do?"

She didn't answer, but sprayed the freezing nitrogen onto the lock securing the chain, shielded her eyes with one hand, and swung the forceps. The lock shattered like a china plate. She stepped through the door, free.

"Whoa," Liam said. "Nice work."

She picked up her vet kit and signed to Katie. The rikkaset hopped out of Liam's grasp and into the pack.

It was at this point Zenn noticed her teeth were chattering. She was freezing. Looking down at herself, she realized the reason: she was barefoot, and dressed in the faded, yellow cotton pajamas she'd had on when the intruder took her.

She went to the wall where the workmen's coveralls hung, grabbed what appeared to be the smallest pair, and pulled them on over her pajamas.

"Liam, what are you doing here?" she said, as she rolled up the coverall pant legs.

"Uh... it isn't obvious?" He gestured at the broken skylight. "Rescuing?"

"No," she said, slinging one of the vet pack straps over her shoulder. "How did you find me?"

"I was watching your room last night, alright?" he said sheepishly. "I needed to talk to you. Anyway, I saw the skirni go in through the window, then he came out, carrying you. I followed him here."

"The skirni? The same one who was out at Vic's?"

"Yeah, same one. Listen, Scarlett, can we have this talk later?"

A skirni. Of course. In her room, the intruder's shuffling gait, but not moving on three legs; walking with two legs and a tail.

"We'll never reach the skylight," Liam said, looking at the ceiling. He went to the door in the far wall. "We'll have to leave this way."

Slowly, carefully, he eased the door open and peeked out, then signaled for Zenn to follow.

Was Liam telling the truth? Was this a trick of some kind?

Should she trust him? It really didn't matter. There were no other options.

The room beyond was cavernous and filled with shipping containers, barrels and boxes, all piled one on top of the other. There was a door at the far end of the building, and they started for it.

As they passed one of the biggest shipping containers, something alive roared loudly and threw its body against the container's inner wall.

"What *is* that?" Liam said.

"Sandhog…" Zenn said, peering at the container. A bright yellow label read CAUTION. LIVE ANIMAL.

"It's Gil Bodine's," she said, reading the label. "He said he was going to ship it back to the seller on Sigmund's Parch. That means we're in a warehouse at the launch port in Pavonis."

"I coulda told you that," Liam said.

With Liam's hand poised to open the door to the outside, they heard the sound of shuffling footsteps approaching.

"Damn." Liam whispered. "He's coming back. He's wearing a weapon, and it's alive – some kinda shell thing on his wrist. I saw him take down Hamish with it. We can't let him spot us."

Zenn whirled around, took a few steps back into the room, eyes darting. They had to hide. Now. Where? Where?

Zenn's gaze settled on the sandhog's shipping container. She dashed to the dumpster-sized crate, tossed her vet kit up onto its flat topside. A muffled squeak came from her pack.

"Sorry, Katie," she said softly, then pulled herself onto the crate. A second later, Liam was next to her. They both lay flat on the cold metal, and waited. The sandhog snorted and rumbled beneath them.

The sound of the building's door creaking open was

followed by shuffling footsteps going quickly to the room where she'd been kept. She heard the inner door being opened, followed immediately by an inhuman howl of rage.

"No! Gone? No. No no no. The nexus. The nexus, gone. How? Devilry. Sorcery."

The skirni's anguished wailing continued, first from nearby, then farther off, as the sound of his footsteps retreated and advanced from one part of the building to another. At last, he was silent, and she heard only the footsteps running, then slowing to a walk and, finally, the sound of something electronic being switched on. The skirni began to talk, using the com device again.

"...it is not Pokt's fault," he barked. "I was outside for seconds, mere seconds. When I returned, the human was gone. I searched the building. The gate-lock was broken. And there is a hole in the roof-glass, as if the girl flew away. As if by witchery." A pause, the other, unintelligible voice, then the skirni again. "Oh? A superstitious savage? I am not. I told you before. The nexus is awake, inside the human. I know this."

Liam turned his face to her. He mouthed the word: "Nexus?" Zenn just shrugged.

The other voice said something, then the skirni, "I know because I... felt the nexus, felt it reach into my mind. It reached into my thoughts in her room at the Ciscan stronghold. And it permitted me to see, see into this human. She is unaware. I saw this in her. She has no idea what is happening, that the fate of worlds lives within her. How could I know all of this, unless the nexus is waking?"

A pause, the skirni pacing. "No. I cannot risk remaining on this planet. The goat-woman has been apprehended. The man Dokes attempted to escape. I am told the local enforcer Jakstra confronted him. This Dokes failed to comply and was shot in his leg with a gunpowder weapon. They will both be imprisoned, I am sure. They have been told of the consequences if they speak of me, but I cannot trust in their silence. I must leave."

Another pause, then the skirni: "No, this does not matter. If the boy is found, he knows nothing... Yes, he told me of the girl and her communing with the animals, but he knows nothing of the nexus. He is of no importance." It was Zenn's turn to give Liam a questioning look. He didn't meet her gaze.

The skirni went on: "I will return to the *Helen*. We will decide then what to do." A short burst from the other voice. The skirni stopped his pacing, shouted, "I am not to be blamed for her vanishing. It is not Pokt's error."

No further words were spoken. The skirni's footsteps receded, the door opened and shut.

"Any idea what that was all about?" Liam said as he helped lower Zenn down from the crate. "Something... inside of you?"

Zenn shrugged. "It's... nothing I can really explain."

"Yeah, fine by me. Less talking, more leaving." He was at the door again. He opened it, scanned the area outside. "He's gone. Come on."

"No," Zenn said. He turned back to her.

"What do you mean, no?"

"I mean... I'm staying."

"Staying? Here?" Liam said, incredulous. "You can't stay here!"

Zenn walked back to stand next to the sandhog's shipping crate.

"Gil's hog is being shipped back to Sigmund's Parch on the *Helen of Troy*."

"So?"

"Liam, before you got here, I heard the skirni say they… have my father."

"Warra? Why would they have Warra?"

"They took him. Kidnapped him. On Enchara."

Liam gave her an indulgent smile. "Yeah… um… Why would anyone kidnap your father?"

"I don't know. But they've got him. And my only chance of helping him is to follow that skirni."

"Alright. Let's say you're not as looney as you sound, and that these guys have your dad. How are you gonna…" Zenn turned to the hog's container. "No. Scarlett, you aren't serious. You are not gonna…"

"The skirni said he's going back to the *Helen*. This crate is going up there. I'm going with it."

"This is crazy, Scarlett. Wait, what about Otha? We'll go to him. I'll go with you. He could help."

"My uncle wouldn't believe me."

"Sure he would."

"Liam, I told you about what's been going on with me lately, the… mental thing with the animals at the cloister. Otha thinks I'm… Wait a second." She reached out and took the boy's arm, turning him to face her. "What the skirni said just now. About you telling him about me and the animals. What did he mean?"

Liam turned his face away, then back to her, his expression pained.

"Scarlett… Pokt, the skirni…"

"So you know his name?"

"Yes. He…was asking lots of questions, right? About all kinds of stuff. Some of the questions…"

"Were about me? About my linking with the animals? Is that it? You told him about that?" He nodded, and she dropped her hand from his arm, fury rising inside her. Fury and regret. "Then that's how he knew I had it inside me. This... nexus thing. I can't believe you did that."

"Scarlett... Zenn, I didn't know! I told you. He was asking everybody at the ranch about all kinds of stuff."

"It doesn't matter now. It's done," she said, staring hard at him, then turning to look up at the crate. "And I don't have time for this. Once the *Helen* leaves orbit, that's it."

Zenn hoisted herself back atop the hog's crate. A moment later Liam had joined her. She told herself she didn't care if he followed her, she didn't care if he left to save his own skin. She knew what she had to do and she was going to do it. Liam Tucker was no longer part of the equation.

She knelt next to a square, metal plate at one corner of the container's roof.

"What's that?" he asked.

"Feeding chute hatch. All crates like this have them." She tugged at it. "It's jammed. Help me open it up." He stood looking at her, swiped the hair out of his face.

"You're insane. That hog'll rip you to shreds."

"You going to help or not?"

With both of them pulling on it, the door finally flipped open. As soon as the hog spotted them, he launched himself to crash against the ceiling of the crate, shaking the container so violently they both fell to their knees.

"There. Now he's really mad," Liam said, getting to his feet. "Convinced? Can we get outta here now?"

Zenn said nothing, but went to her vet kit. Katie had buried herself inside, and she gave Zenn a small *yip* of annoyance when Zenn nudged her to one side. She pulled out the portable seda-field unit. Not bothering to extend the dish's tripod, she held it in one hand, aimed it down through the open feed hatch, dialed it up to seven and switched it on.

The sedation took effect, and the sandhog's body drooped

backwards on its tail, the enormous digging claws folding inward on its belly. Finally, it sagged to the floor of the crate, and fell over on one side. It lay there in a slowly heaving heap, emitting a gurgling snore.

"I shoulda known you'd have something like this up your sleeve," Liam said. "Damn you, Scarlett. Guess now I got no excuse *not* to go with you, huh?"

Zenn wasn't sure what she'd expected of Liam. But she realized this wasn't it... This was more than she could ask, even if she didn't care.

"Liam. You don't have to do that. I never meant you had to do that."

"Who cares what you meant?" He was smirking his familiar, annoying smirk. "What?" he said, "I don't get a vote? Look, Graad is pinched. He'll do time at Tharsis. I stick around here and... well, we already hashed that out. Nope. Mars isn't a safe place to hang around. A free trip to Sigmund's Parch?" He walked over to the hatch. "That's just what the doctor ordered. Doctor."

Zenn almost smiled at this, but didn't.

"Liam, I..."

"Yeah yeah, save it. Let's go before I lose my nerve. Or Tiny down there wakes up."

"Alright." There wasn't time to discuss it. "Go ahead."

"Oh sure. Send the dumb towner in. He's expendable."

"I need to keep the seda-field focused. Go on. He's asleep."

"Easy for you to say..."

Liam sat down, scooted his legs over the edge of the hatch and with an apprehensive glance back at her, disappeared from sight.

"I'm fine," he said from the darkness. "Thanks for asking."

"Here." She handed down her vet pack. Then, trying to hold the seda-dish steady, she sat down at the hatch and angled her legs into the feed chute opening. Gripping the inside hatch handle with her free hand, she slid down into the darkness, pulling the hatch door shut as she fell.

She landed in something soft – the hog's most recent ration of sandy soil.

They both retreated to the corner of the crate farthest from the hog. Zenn kept the dish aimed at the slumbering animal while Liam gathered bedding straw for them to sit on.

"Whew." Liam complained as they settled into their respective mounds of straw. "That's one rank animal."

"You'll get used to it," she said dryly.

"Damn, I hope we're not in here that long."

Any further conversation was cut short by the clanking sound of the building's large, metal loading door being rolled open. This was followed by the putter of an engine. The engine noise got very close, and there was the grating of metal beneath the crate, the sensation of being lifted into the air and moving. Some kind of forklift? After a series of bounces, sharp bangs and more screeching of metal, the crate came to rest.

"We must be inside a ferry's cargo bay," Liam whispered. Zenn shushed him.

She wasn't sure how much later it was that the ferry's engines ignited, but the noise made Katie spring awake and scurry up out of the pack into her arms.

"Whoa," Liam muttered as the ferry's engines powered up. "Here we go..."

THIRTY-FOUR

At first, the launch wasn't as loud as Zenn had feared, but the sound quickly built to a frightful roar, making crate vibrate alarmingly. She felt the ferry lift from the ground, and quickly an invisible force began to press on her body.

"Scarlett?" Liam had to shout to be heard over the thundering engines. "You sure this was really a good idea?"

She wasn't remotely sure, but didn't say so.

Katie was too frightened to sign now, and simply buried her head in Zenn's lap, blended and vanished from sight. The engine's noise at last overwhelmed their ability to shout, and she and Liam could only give each other encouraging looks... and wait.

Zenn struggled to keep the seda-unit aimed at the hog. But it really didn't matter – nothing could move under this kind of acceleration. The pressure continued to build, until Zenn was forced down flat in the straw, with the invisible Katie pinned in position on her stomach. It occurred to her maybe she'd made yet another bad judgment. Maybe it was not, in fact, possible for something as fragile as a human, or a rikkaset, to survive a ferry launch in an unprotected cargo-crate.

But, of course, it was too late to reconsider. They must be miles above Mars by now. Miles beyond the familiar world of the cloister walls and her animals, beyond Otha and Hild and Hamish. And despite what she felt, or didn't feel, about him, at least Liam was with her, at least she had the company of another person. She wouldn't let it mean anything beyond that. After all, Liam had his own reasons for leaving Mars.

As the ferry hurtled skyward, Zenn told herself she also had still another unspoken, but crucial reason to follow her abductor. She had no clue what the skirni meant by the term "nexus." But it had to be connected with her sudden capacity for linking her mind to the minds of others. It meant she hadn't imagined it all, dreamed it up, that she wasn't losing her grip on reality. There was a logical, real-world explanation for what was going on inside her. And the skirni knew what it was. If nothing else, she would make him tell. If she survived.

A knot of doubt materialized and tightened within her. Would she survive? Would any of them? Maybe she should've gotten herself and Katie out the crate when she had the chance. Maybe she should've listened to Liam.

Too late now. She tried to lift her hands, to comfort the rikkaset, to stroke her and make the sign that it would be alright. No, that would be a lie. But she could sign she was sorry. Her hands weighed too much to raise them more than an inch or two. She gave up.

Her helplessness spawned a fresh wave of fear, and the fear grew quickly, like a dark blossom opening. She saw her younger self, terrified beneath a flapping canvas tarp, breathing in dust and fumes in the back of Otha's speeding truck, saw herself boarding the ferry that would bear her aloft to witness the inconceivable wonder of a living Indra, to witness her mother's final moments within the creature's impossible body.

As the rapidly mounting g-forces of the ferry's violent ascent threatened to tip her into unconsciousness, an unbidden memory rose up through Zenn's fear and doubt: the honeyed scent of apricot blossoms, laced with just a whiff of antiseptic. She heard her mother's voice, the words spoken years ago, ages ago, in another lifetime:

...sometimes Zenn, doing the right thing... is the scariest thing of all.

Something brushed her fingertips: Liam's hand, fighting gravity to edge its way slowly onto hers. With her entire world reduced to shuddering chaos and noise, it came as a sudden, almost refreshing shock: the touch of another, at this moment, in this place, was something, maybe the one thing, she needed to feel more than anything else. Liam's fingers closed around hers. She allowed her fingers to tighten in reply.

Then, the rushing, black oblivion pressing in on her faltering awareness pushed its way beyond her final measure of will power. She had no choice. She let it in. And in her last instant of knowing, one last thought:

Never... leave... the cloister.

ACKNOWLEDGMENTS

Thanks to:

...my mother Betty and sister Sue, the former an English teacher who simply expected all her children to love books, so we did; the latter a sibling who helped me appreciate the power and magic in language and art.

...every teacher or professor I've ever had. Teachers. They rock.

...Dr Jenni Doll, DVM, who let me look over her shoulder and ask many, many questions as she ministered to our farm-full of animals or worked on her own menagerie of domestic and exotic beasts. The same goes for her husband Torben, whose extensive herpetological knowledge I also mined. Any mistakes or questionable extrapolations in this book are, however, mine alone.

...Adam Schear of DeFiore & Co, the genre-savvy agent who rescued the book's manuscript from oblivion while cleaning out his Kindle files, and then dove into the story to help me polish the novel until it was ready to be exposed to the light of day.

...Amanda Rutter, my editor at Strange Chemistry Books, who thought the book might be worth publishing and, following its acquisition, immersed herself in Zenn's world, then applied her formidable expertise to ensure that world was prepared for visitors.

...my wise and patient wife, shield-maiden and best friend Kathleen, whose encouragement, willingness to listen and deep affection for all creatures great and small made her both an inspiration and the ideal companion as I wrote *Zenn Scarlett*.

....and all the dozens of animals who have ever shared, brightened, saddened and/or complicated my life.